Hidden Chains

A Marti Wells Thriller

Mike Donohue

ALSO BY MIKE DONOHUE

MAX STRONG SERIES
Sleeping Dogs (prequel)
The Devil's Angel (prequel)
Shaking the Tree
Bottom of the World
Hollow City
Trouble Will Find Me
Burn the Night
Crooked Prayers
The Salt House

MARTI WELLS SERIES
Hidden Twists (novella)
Hidden Chain
Hidden Sins

SHORT STORIES
October Days

For my daughters—

The strongest chains are not those that bind us,
but those that connect our hearts.

"And one's enemies will be
those of his own household."

Biblical proverb

HIDDEN CHAINS

Chapter One

Martha 'Marti' Wells didn't look up from the columns of numbers on her laptop screen, she was so close she could taste it; she wasn't going to get distracted now, but she could hear them whispering on the other side of the closed office door. She couldn't make out the actual words, just two female voices talking in low tones. Ironic, she thought, before fully focusing back on the spreadsheet. The steel-reinforced door could hold its own against a hail of bullets, but words slipped right past.

Her little office was in the basement of the apartment building and shared space with the tenant laundry room. Most of the time, the washers and dryers provided gentle white noise and the pleasant smell of perfumed dryer sheets. As officemates went, the old Whirlpools weren't bad. They didn't gossip or eat tuna fish for lunch in the break room. But they also didn't provide a steady stream of walk-in clients. Martha was okay with the trade-off.

The rent was dirt cheap, practically free, thanks to some cash slipped to Pedro, the live-in super, and presumably the lack of knowledge over the arrangement by the building's owner. Pedro might be under the impression that she had more contacts and pull with the Jersey City police than she did, but she kept an eye on the place, more out of self-preservation than any allegiance to her fellow tenants, but she told herself she hadn't outright lied. They both seemed satisfied with the situation, and she couldn't afford anything else.

Nor could she justify pricier office digs. Most of her work now came via email or phone calls. On more than half of her jobs, she never saw her clients face-to-face. If she did need an in-person meeting, she had a table on an informal retainer at Cafe Grand down the street. She couldn't recall the last time someone other than Pedro or Gwen had been inside the office. She glanced up at the stack of papers, books, mail, and assorted gym clothes that sat on the pair of mismatched chairs across from her secondhand desk. It had been a while since she had visitors.

There was a tentative knock at the door. Dammit. She could feel the small thread she'd been following through the columns of numbers slip from her fingers. She pushed back from the desk and rubbed her eyes. They were dry and itchy. She rummaged in the top drawer until she found some saline drops. She'd been up most of the night. The red wine hadn't put her to sleep, and she'd tossed and turned for three hours before giving up and coming downstairs to poke at the Figueroa case. And to her surprise, she'd made progress. Was perhaps on the verge of a real breakthrough until ...

She assumed one of the temperamental machines had eaten the women's six quarters and they were looking for a refund. Marti knew people would go to extreme lengths to recoup a couple of bucks. They'd piss away six bucks on a designer coffee but would scratch tooth and nail for two bits. It had happened before. She'd once witnessed two gray-haired women dive on the floor and knock heads chasing after a stray quarter. It turned out both had cataracts and had risked a concussion over some stray dryer lint.

Marti's door was the only one in the laundry room other than the exit. People sometimes assumed it was for the manager. There was nothing on the door to give that impression. It was unmarked save for dents and chips in the faded green paint and a small strip of paper scotch-taped to the door at eye level with the neatly printed words: 'Small mysteries served. The kind you can't solve yourself.' Her friend Gwen had put it there when she'd discovered where Marti's office mail was delivered. Gwen thought it was a joke. Some days, Marti agreed. Other days, Marti liked to think that even the tiniest mystery wasn't inconsequential to the person looking for answers. On those days, Marti liked to think that providing even small answers brought a little balance to the world. It was true those thoughts usually occurred after some wine, but it was still good to have a little purpose in your life. However small.

***

She glanced at the clock and was surprised to see it was past nine. The tiny casement window above her head was coated in decades of grime that acted as a very effective shade. It was perpetually five minutes to midnight in her office.

She pinched a few drops of saline in each eye and tossed the bottle back in the drawer. She stood up and crossed to the door in three long steps. She pulled it open quickly and startled the two women. The one on the right, slightly taller with dark shoulder-length hair, had her fist raised in the air. The one on the left, with lighter hair that fell below her shoulders and striking blue-green eyes, actually took a half step back. Marti was about to snap a quip about not having any change but took a moment when she saw the skittish look in the woman's eyes. Maybe this wasn't about laundry. The woman looked scared. Scared of her? Maybe. Probably. Marti was five-foot-ten in her sneakers and had a good six inches on these women. She'd been up all night, grinding through financial data on a cheap laptop. Her clothes were wrinkled. She was sure her hair, unruly in the best of times, was a hive of tangles. She likely bore more than a passing resemblance to a demented Medusa.

She absently brushed at her hair with one hand. "Yes?"

Her voice was dry and cracked. As if she hadn't spoken to anyone other than Rita Mae and the Chinese delivery guy in the past three days.

The women glanced at each other before the one on the right recovered and said, "Ms. Wells?"

Not about the laundry then. She was curious despite the poor timing of the interruption. "That's me."

"Miles Rothchild sent us."

Chapter Two

M arti gestured them in, her office a study in what she would call 'organized chaos,' and closed the door. The taller woman entered first, her gaze flicking over the mismatched furniture, the scribbled notes on the whiteboard, and the haphazard stacks of case files and discarded workout clothes. The younger woman trailed behind, her eyes still wide, taking in the details of Marti's world.

"Have a seat," Marti said, grabbing the gym clothes and an empty pizza box and tossing them behind the whiteboard before indicating the pair of worn-out but comfortable chairs that faced her desk. , the old leather creaking pleasantly in protest. She did love that sound.

She studied her guests more closely. Despite being similar in age, they made a mismatched pair. Both women appeared to be in their mid-to-late twenties. The one with the dark hair, the one that had knocked, appeared to be a few years older. She wore a simple but classic gray suit with a white blouse. She might have stepped out of the nearby PATH train station on her way to work. She spoke first. "Thank you, Ms. Wells. I'm Angela Blythe. This is ..." she paused, casting a glance at the girl, "Cassidy Calderone."

It took a beat to register what she'd just said and then Marti raised an eyebrow. "Calderone, as in Calderone Innovations?"

"Yes, that's correct," Angela said. "Cassidy here," she motioned toward the woman seated beside her, "recently found out through a DNA test that she is the biological daughter of Alex Calderone, the recently deceased CEO."

Cassidy Calderone was not dressed for a business meeting, at least not on Wall Street. She wore ripped black jeans with a baggy peach-colored sweatshirt that hung off one shoulder. Marti could see the start of a sleeve of tattoos on the exposed shoulder. She was thin and her clavicle looked like a wire coat hanger trying to hold onto the sweatshirt. The bones and her delicate facial features framed by her feathery, light hair made Marti think of an injured bird.

The sudden and mysterious passing of Alexander Calderone, the quietly dynamic leader behind the black box firm, triggered a seismic shift in the global business landscape. It wasn't just a ripple, it was a tsunami, reverberating through the financial district's glass towers, spilling over into the mainstream news, and causing a media frenzy on a global scale.

Calderone Innovations was shrouded in layers of tantalizing secrecy, but there was no doubt that it was one of the world's most valuable companies with a market capitalization that Marti had trouble even visualizing. Its enigmatic nature was a magnet for intrigue, and conspiracies. Its operations were guarded with a fervor that bordered on fanaticism.

Calderone's death had left a power vacuum at the helm of Calderone Innovations, igniting a scramble for succession that was more akin to a bar brawl than a corporate power struggle. He had died young and a succession plan or comprehensive will had not been put in place.

From what Marti recalled from the news stories, the Calderone boardroom was no stranger to infighting. Alexander had designed it that way to force the company to never settle or get comfortable. Publicly, the man was quiet and reserved, but privately there were numerous anecdotes of how Alex relished a combative argument. The battle for the Calderone throne was only just beginning, and it promised to be a brutal, no-holds-barred affair with the ultimate winner wielding vast wealth and power.

Every news story noted the lack of surviving family and the end of the Calderone bloodline. A biological daughter had never been mentioned. But, if true, that would make the inheritance and control of the company, depending on the will and the voting shares, more straightforward.

"And you're trying to stake your claim?" Marti asked Cassidy, pushing her a little. Marti tried to get a read on the woman sitting across from her. She looked up at the question and finally met Marti's eyes for the first time. Marti appreciated the spark she saw. Whatever she was doing, she hadn't done it without thinking it through.

Cassidy nodded, her lips a thin line. "I reached out to my ... uncle, I guess, it still feels strange to say out loud, the current interim CEO, but he hasn't responded."

Alexander Calderone's brother-in-law, Victor Rathbone, also an executive at Calderone, was the acting CEO.

Marti frowned. It certainly wasn't uncommon for extended families to get tangled in battles of wills and inheritance, but something seemed off about that response. "How long ago did you reach out?"

"Two weeks."

"And no response? No lawyers? No cease-and-desist order?"

"No, nothing," Cassidy said.

"That's not quite right," Angela interrupted. "Since then, strange things have started happening. Threatening calls, shadowy figures following her, a near-miss car accident."

"And you think these incidents are related to your claim?" she asked Cassidy. Marti worked to keep the skepticism out of her voice, but the girl heard it.

Cassidy swallowed hard; her blue-green eyes now filled with uncertainty if not fear. "I don't know." She suddenly put her hands in her hair and rubbed vigorously. "This has all been so crazy. But Angela is right, the timing is strange, and I don't know who else would want to hurt me. I work at a used bookstore and a coffee shop. I only moved here six months ago."

"Have you told anyone else about the paternity finding besides Angela? A roommate? A coworker?"

"No. No one. I don't ... have a lot of close friends."

There was something left unsaid there, but Marti let it go for now. "How about you Angela?"

"No, not specifically about Cassidy. I reached out to a few colleagues for more information about Calderone Innovations and the board fight, but I never mentioned why or her specifically."

"What about Miles?" Marti asked. "How did he find out?"

"Yes, I did tell Miles and eventually he met with Cassidy. I trust him."

"You work with him?" Marti made an educated guess based on how the woman was dressed.

"Yes, I work for him."

Okay, Marti thought, still reeling from the firehouse of information. The Rothchild family owned one of the largest private wealth banks in the country and Miles Rothchild was some type of executive. What he did, like much about Miles, was mostly a mystery to Marti. She knew one thing. She trusted Miles Rothchild about as much as a coiled cobra in the corner of the room. She put that aside for now.

"You verified Cassidy's results?"

"Of course. With two different labs."

"So there're people there that might know."

"No, that's not quite right. It's a little more complicated than that. The original sample from Cassidy went through BlueprintBiology and didn't trigger any hits. At the time she was using her mother's maiden name. Bergman. But Blueprint is one of the public companies that provides its findings to GEDMatch, the public database. You might have heard of them recently because of how many cold cases have been solved using the available profiles. Or those of a close family member."

"The Golden State Killer."

"Exactly."

"And Alexander Calderone's DNA is on that public website?" Marti frowned.

"I know. It seems like an odd choice given how private he was in the rest of his personal and professional life, but do you know anything about Calderone's parents?"

Marti shook her head. "No, I don't think so." Most of the profiles she'd seen started when Calderone was at Stanford and starting his company.

"They were killed in a home invasion while he was in high school. Both parents were killed but he and his sister, Isabella, survived. She later died of breast cancer. But the murder case was never solved. He doesn't talk about it in the media but behind the scenes, he was very passionate about the recent advances in DNA to potentially solve his parents' case. Along with investing some of his private wealth, he also put genetic samples online for his immediate family."

"And there is a way to run a search on GEDMatch?"

"Yes and no. It's not a push-button thing like you'd upload a sample and press a button to search for matches. That's sort of the first step, but it doesn't get you all the way there because humans already share 99% of the same DNA. You get near matches and then you need a professional analyst to compare the matched samples in multiple places to verify a potential relationship."

"What made you submit a sample in the first place?" Marti asked.

"I didn't," Cassidy said, and Marti felt a pang of sympathy at how thoroughly her life must have been turned upside down in the last two weeks. "That's the irony in all of this. I did nothing to bring this on. It was a birthday present from my friend. She comes from a big family and always felt badly that I had no extended family, even though I was fine with it personally. It was just my mother and me, and now she's gone. The friend submitted my DNA. It was supposed to be a surprise but when it still came back with so little, she went the extra step."

"And got the surprise of a lifetime."

"Something like that," Cassidy responded without enthusiasm. She was now slumped in her chair and the small spark that had been in her eyes before was gone.

"So that's a few more people that might know about this or might have told someone. Hard to keep something like this a secret for long," Marti said. "Why not just drop it?"

"I might have if these ... incidents hadn't started. I'm not sure dropping it is an option now."

"Okay, that's a good reason. If true."

"It's true," Angela said with some heat.

Marti held up her hands. "Okay. We'll get to that. I'm not calling you guys liars. Just wrapping my head around all of this." Marti leaned back in her chair, studying them. "What exactly do you want me to do?"

"Two things," Angela said. "First, we need help filing the paternity claim and, more importantly, we need someone to keep Cassidy safe."

There was a moment of silence as Marti chewed over the information. This was no small task they were asking of her. Money, power, and secrets were always dangerous.

"Why me?"

"Miles said we could trust you to do the right thing," Angela responded. "And he said you owed him a debt."

Chapter Three

After Angela and Cassidy left, Marti sat back down in her lumpy chair and cast a wary eye at the columns of numbers on the laptop screen. She could feel Figueroa slipping through the net again. The thought of resetting her traps and starting over made the sleepless night crash down on her like a physical weight.

"Dammit," she muttered under her breath, rubbing her forehead with her fingertips. Her brain felt like it was full of sand, the grains grinding against each other in a way that made her want to just close her eyes and slip into oblivion. But she had a new case now, a case that promised to be as complex as it was intriguing. "Later," she told herself, "I'll deal with this later."

Without another thought, she pushed herself up from the chair and made her way through the empty laundry room to the narrow staircase leading up to the third floor and her living quarters. The apartment was small, with just three rooms, a bedroom and a bathroom, and a living room with a tiny kitchenette but large windows.

The bathroom was surprisingly spacious; in addition to a shower stall, it boasted an antique claw-foot tub, a vestige from a bygone era that she cherished and used every chance she got. It was her sanctuary, where she could wash away the grime of the city and the stress of her job in warm, sudsy comfort. Preferably with a glass of red wine.

The living area was an exercise in strategic space utilization, making the most of what she had. A compact galley kitchen stretched along one wall, its narrow confines providing everything she needed within arm's reach—a stovetop, a sink, a fridge, and cupboards though those were usually bare because, while she liked to eat food, she didn't like to shop for it.

The apartment's charm, as any real estate agent would say, was in its aged details. The row of towering windows, their glass old and wavy, sat above rusting radiators that groaned and hissed in the winter. The windows framed shifting vistas of Jersey City, views that changed with the sun's arc and the city's fickle moods. The original hardwood floors, scarred and worn from decades of foot traffic, bore the marks of countless previous tenants, a tapestry of lives lived and moved on. Exposed brickwork along one bedroom wall, raw and weathered with the patina of time, was an additional testament to the building's history. And, if she stood at the correct angle and squinted just right, she could catch a sliver of the Hudson River, a glittering ribbon of water that played hide-and-seek with the distant New York City skyline.

But Marti wasn't interested in the view right now. Peeling off her clothes as she went, she dropped onto her bed, the old mattress creaking under her weight. She didn't bother with a blanket or a pillow, just let her body sink into the springs, her mind already drifting toward sleep.

***

Four hours later, she awoke to the sensation of tiny needles tapping her face. She tried to swat it away, but the tapping returned, more insistent this time. Marti's eyes fluttered open to find her tabby cat, Rita Mae, staring at her with those laser-sharp green eyes that seemed to say, 'You forgot my breakfast, human.'

"Mmmph," she groaned, pushing herself up on her elbows. Rita Mae was not a patient cat. If the gentle pawing didn't work, she would resort to meowing loudly, knocking items off the bedside table, or chewing and pulling Marti's hair.

With a sigh, Marti swung her legs over the side of the bed and stood, stretching the sleep out of her muscles. She found a pair of sweatpants on the floor and pulled on a St. Peter's sweatshirt then padded over to the kitchenette, where she poured some cat food into Rita Mae's dish. The cat dove in with a purr that sounded suspiciously like a satisfied chuckle.

As Rita Mae ate, Marti grabbed a glass of water and leaned against the kitchen counter, as her mind churned over the information Angela and Cassidy had shared that morning. There was a lot to unpack, and she'd probably need more than four hours of sleep to do it justice, but she would head downstairs and get started.

"First things first, though" she murmured to herself, finishing her water and setting the glass aside. She needed a shower, some fresh clothes, and a trip to Cafe Grand for an IV drip of caffeine. If they were out of IVs, she'd settle for an Americano.

***

A half hour later, Marti sat with a slumped posture, her lanky frame crumpled in a corner booth at Cafe Grand, her favorite coffee haunt that was dangerously close to her apartment building. The afternoon sunlight, diffused by the cafe's plate-glass windows, cast a lazy glow over her table. The hustle and bustle of the cafe hummed around her, an orchestra of clinking china, the frothy hiss of the espresso machine, and the low murmur of patrons' conversations. The smell of roasting coffee beans was thick in the air, punctuated by the lingering, sweet aroma of that morning's freshly baked pastries.

She could hear Sophie, the cafe's ever-cheerful barista, chattering away with the regulars. She recognized the cadence of the conversations, the familiar ebb and flow of the local gossip, but the words themselves washed over her.

The sleepless night chasing Figueroa followed by Angela and Cassidy then the midday crash had left her feeling disoriented and wrung out. But it wasn't just the exhaustion. The name Miles Rothchild had unsettled her, yanking her back to a past she'd packed neatly away into a corner of her mind.

She remembered Miles Rothchild. How could she not? There was a time when he had consumed her thoughts and been an uninvited guest in her dreams. Time had blurred those memories, dulling their edges, but they were still there, laying dormant in that box, ready to burst out at the slightest nudge. And she had to admit, she did owe him.

Marti took a slow sip of her rich and dark Americano. As she stared into the swirling depths of her cup, she found herself pulled back nearly two decades, to a time when she was a fresh-faced grad from the police academy, a bundle of nerves and raw ambition. Her career had been a blank canvas then, waiting for her to leave a mark. Little did she know how complicated and twisted the lines of her life would become.

Chapter Four

S he had joined the Jersey City police department after a recruiting effort in the late nineties. It had not been her first career choice. She'd tried teaching, and it hadn't stuck. She learned quickly that kids, especially those she was teaching, were a challenge. She kicked around doing odd jobs for a few years until she looked up one day and realized she was closing in on thirty with a poetry degree, a divorce, and no discernible career prospects. She saw the poster in ShopRite of all places and something just clicked. She was in the academy within a month and out on the streets in a uniform by Christmas.

An armchair psychologist, or cynic, would say she was still chasing after Daddy's approval. That might have been partly true even if her old man was retired by that point, but she did truly love it. She loved the kinetic energy. She loved trying to make her community safer. She liked the face-to-face interactions and getting to know the streets at an almost microscopic level. If that finally gave her something to talk about with her dad during their weekly phone calls, and maybe put a little spark in his eyes, so be it.

She loved it, but she was also good at it. Some of the guys in the squad room started calling her Smartie Martie for always having an answer and her knack of being in the thick of it. But it wasn't a knack, or a fluke, or luck. It went beyond instincts. Marti paid attention.

She listened. And people talked to her. Even after the initial buzz of putting on the uniform had worn off, she still cared. She still had pride. She still loved it.

It all combined to end her career just as fast as it had started.

***

The trouble began with her partner. Joel Rincon. He was the senior officer in the car but still a couple of years younger than Marti. But that wasn't unique. Everyone on patrol was younger than Marti. She was Smartie Martie but they also called her Mom. Most of the time they said it with a smile.

Joel was an ex-Marine and it was clear to Marti, after just two hours into their first patrol together, that he'd joined up to try to reproduce whatever feeling of belonging he'd found with the Marines. She wondered why he ever mustered out; she asked him about it once but he never really answered the question and she didn't pry. Everyone had secrets.

Joel was affable and outgoing for the most part, and she didn't mind sharing a squad car with him. He didn't treat her any differently than any other fellow officer. Maybe that was also something he learned in the Marines. Manners and gender equity were not Joel's problems. Joel was eager and impatient and lacked almost all self-awareness. He was always on the make, always looking for a shot at moving up and getting out of uniform. He still wanted something that kept him on the streets, just not on patrol. And he was convinced the next bust or next bit of intel he brought in would be the thing that punched his ticket.

Rincon wasn't particular. He didn't crave being a detective like Marti. He would take Vice or Narcotics or OC but what he talked most about was the Vig, the VGT, officially known as the Violent Gang Task Force. It was a special unit commissioned by the upper brass with the broad, and purposefully vague, objective of rooting out street violence in Jersey City. The unit had exceeded all expectations in the two years it'd been in existence. They were the department's golden boys. Almost untouchable. And coveted among a certain type of officer like Rincon. Marti couldn't deny their results, but it wasn't the type of policing that she wanted to do. She knew it was necessary at times, but she preferred a different approach.

Marti didn't fault him for his ambition, either. He was hardly unique among her fellow officers. Her issue was how it affected their job. That go-for-broke attitude often put them in dangerous situations because Rincon wanted to be the hero. She often told him dead cops were heroes too, but they didn't work the Vig. He always laughed it off. In his mind, it was just how policing worked.

***

She could recall more than one instance, after the morning briefing, where she'd watched Rincon try to start up a conversation with Herschel or Traymon, two of the detectives that effectively ran the Vig. Just thinking about it made her cheeks color in embarrassment for him. It was like the star seniors on the high school football team patting the equipment manager on the head. Even worse, Rincon always thought it had gone well. He would analyze the brief conversations backward and forward in the car for the next two hours. Maybe he was right, maybe any publicity was good publicity. But she had her doubts.

"Why do you want a spot in the Vig so much?" She'd asked one day.

He looked at her like she was a talking fish. Sort of like how Herschel and Traymon had looked at him earlier in the squad room. "Are you kidding? You don't?"

"No. I'm good."

"You get a spot in the Vig and you can write your ticket. It's a career-maker."

"Maybe."

"Maybe? You think if the chief knows your name, or maybe the mayor too, that you're ever going to end up in traffic?"

She shrugged. "Careful, Rincon. It's a double-edged sword. What goes up, must come down. You can't fly that high for that long. Your buddy Herschel might end up in TD yet."

Rincon laughed. She just shook her head. It was like she was speaking Greek. "Herschel will never end up sorting traffic data."

She knew she couldn't push too much. She had to keep the peace in the car. "You're probably right."

"You ever see that guy's hands? Like giant catcher mitts."

"They'd at least be easy to spot if he ever did pull a detail at the mall during Christmas. Giant traffic signals to get people safely onto Route 7."

"Visible for miles," Rincon said, laughing.

"But they probably don't make those nice white gloves in the right size," Marti responded.

It was July and sweltering in the city that year. The cold of Christmas felt very far away. If nothing else had happened, she thought that is what she would have remembered the most. The unrelenting heat from the first weekend after the Fourth of July holiday straight through to Labor Day. The dark polyester uniforms provided no relief. It felt like working inside a trash bag while living in an oven.

She started taking salt tabs with her multivitamin in the morning, and she and Joel both carried gallon water jugs in the patrol car. She'd sometimes lose five pounds or more during a single shift. She stopped three or four days a week at Abbott's on her way home for a milkshake just to maintain her weight. Which sounded, and tasted, great the first week, but soon the smell of dairy started to turn her stomach.

Joel had continued to try to sidle up to Herschel at the station and continued to get rebuffed. No one wanted a pet Labrador nipping at their heels. It only made the man try harder. He kept going back for more. Marti had given up trying to talk any sense into him.

It was in late July when things started to change. It was a Thursday night before she had four days off. She was planning on heading down to the shore where she'd rented a cheap room and she'd read, eat crappy boardwalk food, and not wear any polyester. It was still hot, but the temperatures had fallen back into the mid-80s by sunset and in comparison to the near triple digits they'd been dealing with lately, it felt twenty degrees cooler. The brief respite from the heat had brought people out onto their stoops and sidewalks. It was like a fever had broken. As they cruised down Lenox Avenue, knots of people mingled on the sidewalk. There was almost a block party atmosphere.

Joel was driving. They were rolling slowly, with an hour to go in what had been a quiet shift. After three weeks of near-constant heat, all the small jealousies and penny ante beefs had burned themselves out. Everyone was too hot and tired to do much except mingle, chat, or try to find some air conditioning.

She had her arm resting on the door with the window rolled down and realized she'd missed what he'd said. "What?"

"Look at those guys up there on the corner. I bet there's something there."

They were coming up on the intersection of Grand and Lenox and she could see a group of young people hanging out on the corner outside the Korean bodega. It was mostly young men, but she spotted the long braids and colorful tops of a few women. As far as Marti could tell, the group was just chilling on the corner. A few were drinking sodas or eating ice-cream novelties from the store. Someone had set up an old-school boombox nearby and Marti could hear Nelly's "Hot in Here." It was omnipresent that summer as every radio station couldn't resist the obvious.

She didn't see any reason to bother the kids but maybe she'd missed something. "You spot something?" she asked Joel.

"No, but that doesn't mean shit isn't happening. I'm going to short stop them and see what shakes out."

"Short stop? What are you talking about?"

But he didn't answer, only said, "Get ready."

She didn't have time to ask anything else as Joel gunned the engine and the souped-up Ford Taurus shot forward. They were aimed directly at the knot of kids.

She placed a hand on the dash. "Joel! What the hell!"

Just as quickly as he accelerated, he slammed on the brakes and stopped at the curb near the kids. She heard shouts of "Five-O. Five-O." Some of the group stayed put and looked as confused as Marti but a few took off running. Joel jumped out of the car and gave chase.

"Shit," Marti said and struggled to unlatch her seatbelt. She jumped out and looked at the remaining kids. She thought she recognized a few of them. Part of her wanted to stop and apologize and try to smooth things over, but she also felt like she couldn't leave her partner alone. Joel was already half a block away. "Goddammit, Joel," she said as she took off after him.

She was in better shape from her morning river runs than the more muscle-bound Joel and she quickly started to close the gap. She grabbed her shoulder mic to ask for backup and then paused. What was she going to say? Who were they pursuing? A better question: Why were they pursuing? How were they going to explain this in the report? She needed to catch up to Joel and keep things from escalating. She re-clipped the mic and concentrated on pumping her arms faster.

She was ten feet behind Joel and maybe twenty from the pair of kids when they hit another intersection and the kids split in different directions.

"Which way?" Marti asked as she pulled alongside Joel. She could see he was laboring. Maybe this whole thing would burn itself out with no damage done.

"Right," Joel huffed.

They hit the intersection and skidded around a building into an alley lined with dumpsters, dented garbage cans, graffiti, and rusted fire escapes. Marti could see a chain-link fence fifty yards ahead dividing one property from another and stopping the alley from being used as a cut-through. Just before the fence, she watched the kid reach into his pocket and toss something away. He hit the fence a moment later and scrambled up and over the twelve-foot barricade almost without slowing down. It was not his first time pulling that maneuver.

Marti reached the fence and stopped. She was not going to attempt to climb it. The kid turned as he reached the mouth of the alley on the opposite side. He slowed to a stop when he saw they were no longer in pursuit. He flashed her a smile and then his middle finger before he disappeared around the corner.

He'd probably wait fifteen minutes then rejoin his friends on the corner. What a waste of time, Marti thought, as she turned around to find Joel searching the edge of the alley.

"What the hell, Joel?" Marti said. "What was the point of that? You need some exercise?"

"This," Joel responded. He had a big smile on his face as he held up a small baggie. She snatched it. Three joints, half a dozen pills, probably Molly, and some gummies, probably with THC.

"Great, so you ruined their night, but I don't think you won the war on drugs."

He saw she didn't share his enthusiasm and dropped the smile. "Every little bit helps. Isn't that what you always preach to me?"

She shook her head. It was something they argued about occasionally when it felt like their day-to-day had little impact on the stream of crime and suffering they often encountered.

"You know that is not what I mean. There was no reason to do that. It only put us both in danger. We had no backup and no real cause for going after them. What would we have put in the report?" She tossed the baggie into an open trash can and started walking back to the car.

"Hey," she heard Joel yell, but she didn't turn around.

Chapter Five

J oel turned in the baggie of drugs and wrote up the report and nothing came of it. Not right away. Two days later, as the morning briefing was breaking up, she watched Herschel approach Joel and give him a fist bump. Herschel's V-neck T-shirt was tight across his chest and biceps. She could see the top of a tattoo at the base of his throat—a thin blue line flag. She was too far away to hear what was said between the pair, but she could read their faces. Herschel then repeated a fist bump and walked out of the room. She watched as Joel turned, unable to hide the big smile on his face. Burns, standing nearby, slapped him on the back and said something. Joel nodded. She could see he was doing his best to play off the interaction but the false modesty wasn't working. Whatever the fist bumps had been about, it had been positive and other officers had noticed. She grabbed the morning's info sheets and headed for the locker room to grab her bag and try to figure out why she was annoyed.

As they pulled out of the lot, Marti sensed that Joel was on the brink of spilling the beans, though he attempted to downplay it. His composure was faltering. His agitation was nearly palpable. He practically vibrated. She let it go for five minutes and silently read through the warrant sheets from the briefing one more time. Eventually, she recognized her own pettiness and decided to let it go. She folded the sheets up and stuck them in the passenger door's pocket.

"Saw Herschel talking to you as the meeting was breaking up," she said.

"Yeah."

"What did he want?" Herschel had presented two of the three warrant sheets they'd reviewed in the briefing. "Something on the warrants?"

"Nah, it was about the bust the other night."

"Bust?" She was honestly confused at first. They'd had a string of drunk and disorderlies as people drank themselves into a stupor just to forget the heat, plus the regular domestic calls and open warrants, mostly on petty charges, but she couldn't think of a reason for Herschel or the Vig to take any notice. It was run-of-the-mill stuff. "Was one of our drunks more interesting than we thought?" Occasionally they'd pull over a politician or a politician's relative and have to quietly and quickly figure out how to handle it but that hadn't happened in a while.

"Nah, the drug thing." He looked over at her. "The one you gave me shit about for chasing the kid."

That caught her off guard. Now she was curious. "I was right to give you shit about that. I still maintain it was bullshit."

"Herschel disagreed."

"Really?"

"Told me it was solid work. The type of bust that helps us keep control on the streets."

Marti shook her head. "Herschel thinks that terrorizing a bunch of kids hanging out on the corner is the best way to police these neighborhoods?"

Joel shrugged, not finding any part of it confusing or unexpected. "That's what he said and let me remind you that they weren't all just kids hanging out. Two of them ran and we know for a fact," he punctuated the word by tapping a fist on the steering wheel, "that at least one of them was holding."

Marti ground her molars together. She knew that a strong argument could be made that arresting anyone for the small amount of drugs they'd found in that baggie was only contributing to the problem, but she also knew that opinion was a very, very small minority among her fellow officers. She bit back the additional commentary that she knew would only make the next seven hours tense between the two of them, but then something else occurred to her as well. "That move with the car. Driving up on them fast, hitting the brakes, and jumping out? That's something Vig does, right?"

She watched his cheeks color and knew she was right.

"That's right. So what? It works. It flushes out the guilty people. You got a problem with that, Marti?"

She did have a problem with it. She thought it was close to entrapment and didn't like the implied threats and intimidation that came with the technique. She couldn't see how it helped make the city safer or their job easier. It only put more strain on the already fraught situation between the department and the citizens they were supposed to protect. Again, she knew the type of proactive policing that Joel and Vig believed in was a popular plan of action within the department. The arrests and spectacles often played well with the politicians and bureaucrats, too. All the people who didn't actually have to live in those neighborhoods. She kept quiet and backed off.

"I have no problem with arresting the guilty. You know that."

"We both get to the same place in the end."

She knew he was trying to make peace. She let him think he was right. She grabbed the warrant sheets from the door. This was a safer topic. "Let's just work the warrants today and try not to freestyle." He gave a half grunt that she took as his tacit assent, if not outright agreement.

She studied the rough photocopy at the top of the first sheet. The details of the mug shot were rough given the quality of the photocopy but it didn't need to be sharp.

"Jesus Christ, criminals are stupid. Can you believe this guy's tat?"

Randall 'Popeye' Jones had a large and detailed spider web covering the left side of his face, running down from his hairline, over his eye, and continuing down his neck. It included a black widow spider creeping up and over his jawline.

Joel glanced over. "Solid ink work."

"True. Must have hurt like hell but if you're going to make breaking and entering your career, you might want to think through the conspicuous nature of your face."

"Thinking things through and a career choice of breaking and entering are sort of mutually exclusive."

"Good point," Marti responded.

They made it through their shift.

Joel wouldn't die for two more days.

Chapter Six

The evening sun wouldn't give up. It beat down relentlessly along this stretch of Delgado Avenue. Shadows spread across the asphalt like pools of tar. Marti was behind the wheel and fiddled with the air-conditioning vents as she tried in vain to find an angle that would make the car's tepid air feel cooler on her hot skin. She knew it was a lost cause but couldn't keep from trying. Joel was slumped in the passenger seat.

She glanced at the time on the laptop bolted between the seats. They'd been swapped over to the second shift for the next two weeks and she was still adjusting. She felt sluggish and out of sorts. It wasn't even eight yet. They hadn't even been on shift for two hours but the heat made everything feel sludgy. She wanted to close her eyes and dream of cooler places.

She refocused on the road. She drove slowly. She was hot and listless. They had no active calls and no plan coming out of the briefing other than to patrol and be seen. She watched pedestrians, clad in light summer attire, hurry along the cracked sidewalks, seeking refuge in pockets of shade or stepping into air-conditioned shops. She would never wish for a call that would indicate someone in distress, but she yearned for something to distract her from the heat.

"How about Lin's?" Joel suggested, his voice pulling her out of her thoughts. She glanced at him, sweat droplets beading at his hairline and trickling down his neck onto his uniform.

"Sure," she replied, though she didn't particularly feel like Chinese food, she lacked the energy to argue.

Joel pulled out his phone. "What do you want?"

"Cold and spicy sesame noodles," she replied.

After a quick check of his phone, Joel stashed it away. "Ten minutes."

She drove for another mile down Delgado and then turned left on Escalar and parked in a red zone three doors down from Han-Lin's Garden.

"Is that Neely?" she asked as Joel opened the door to climb out.

He looked up the street to where a skinny Black man in a sequined jacket was turning in a circle and occasionally talking to himself. The few people that were out on the street gave him a wide berth.

"Looks like it. Who else would be wearing that outfit?"

Marti climbed out. "I'm going to check on him."

"You want me to come?"

"Nah," she waved him off. "Grab the food. He knows me. Just stay on the radio."

Joel didn't fight her. "You got it." She knew he didn't like psych calls. He turned in the other direction and went inside the restaurant to collect their food.

Jordan Neely was a well-known homeless man in Jersey City, often seen impersonating Michael Jackson. He usually stayed near the PATH and ferry docks where there was more foot traffic. Today, seeing him so far from his usual location was unusual, a sign that something might be wrong. As she approached, she noticed two young women crossing the street to avoid him.

"Jordan?" She stopped ten feet away, giving the man space to react but she received no response. "Jordan? It's me Marti? Officer Wells?" Still nothing. He kept his head down, shuffling his feet and muttering something too low for Marti to catch. It appeared like he hadn't hit any shelter in a while. She could smell his body odor even from this distance. He was in his costume, but the black pants were stained and his sequined jacket was torn at one elbow.

Her approach in these situations was to meet people where they were, treating them with dignity. She knew how much that small act of kindness could mean to someone struggling. Marti also remembered her father's words: 'High or low. Everyone has value. Everyone is equal.'

She looked over her shoulder. Joel had just emerged from the restaurant carrying a brown paper bag. She noticed he looked excited. She knew one of his main hobbies other than weightlifting and following the Giants was to eat, but this look was different. This wasn't his hungry look. This was his puppy look. He started in her direction. She knew he'd have no patience for Neely. She tried a different tact.

"Michael? Mr. Jackson?"

This time he responded and looked up. She watched him study her and then his eyes cleared as he came back from wherever he was and recognized her.

"Officer Marti, how are you doing? Still looking fine, I see."

She smiled. "Thank you, but I'm more concerned with you. What are you doing over here? Those tourists need you down at the docks."

"They sure do," he agreed, but then he paused and looked around in confusion.

Marti took a step closer, trying to catch his eye again before he spiraled back into his own world. "Are you hungry?"

He considered the question. "I could eat."

"You like noodles?"

"Depends. Sometimes they remind me too much of my Jheri curl days, but they're all right."

She turned to Joel. "Gimme the bag."

He handed it over. "He can have yours," he whispered.

She took the container of noodles and a pair of chopsticks and handed them to Neely.

"Thank you," he said.

"No problem. Get back to the water, Michael. The people need you. Waiting for the ferry is too dull without a little song and dance."

He smiled as he opened the container and pulled a noodle out with his grimy fingers. "You got it, Officer Marti."

His eyes were clearer, and he appeared calmer. As they walked back to the car, Marti made a mental note to call Mary Higgins, a clinician who worked with the homeless community. The food was a temporary relief, but Neely needed more substantial help.

Joel put the bag of remaining food in the back seat.

"Lose your appetite?" she asked.

"No, we got a call."

They got in the front, Joel behind the wheel now, before she asked, "What? When? I didn't hear anything on the radio."

"Didn't come in over the radio. Got a text on my cell phone."

He pulled out hard, no lights or sirens, but drove fast toward the river.

"You taking requests now?"

"It's from Herschel. He needs some extra hands. Or eyes. Some help, basically."

"Lieutenant Herschel?"

"That's right."

"He texted you?"

"That's right."

She could tell he was enjoying stringing this out. She was not. "Cut the shit, Joel. What's going on?"

"Herschel requested some help watching an address over in Paulus Hook. Asked for us. Said he cleared it with Command."

She was tempted to get on the radio to confirm but knew that wouldn't sit well with Rincon, especially if it all checked out. Communicating via cell phone was a little unusual but not unheard of, especially for street units where radio traffic was often monitored. She dropped it and focused on the task. "What do we know?"

"Just an address. Told me not to sit on it but to stay close and stay alert. I assume he'll let us know more when we need to know."

Joel didn't seem bothered, maybe his past Marine training dampened down the instinct that had the hairs on the back of Marti's neck standing up. She didn't push it, maybe she should have, but she didn't. She let Joel concentrate on driving.

Chapter Seven

Paulus Hook was a desirable and upscale Jersey City neighborhood known for its historic charm, architecture, and waterfront location along the Hudson with an unobstructed view of the Manhattan skyline. It started life as a 17th-century trading post for the Dutch West India Company. Over time, it had evolved and gentrified into a thriving and tony residential area of cobblestone streets and brownstone townhouses. It was not a location that the Jersey City police typically received calls about.

Joel steered off Columbus and turned south on Hudson. Marti could see the Colgate Clock four blocks down along the water. The factory was long gone but the almost 100-year-old timepiece still remained. Joel hooked a left on Essex, went a block, and then turned right on Greene then left on Grand. He coasted through the intersection with the four pocket parks. Besides the pricy real estate, Paulus Hook also boasted several preserved green spaces. The most prominent was Paulus Hook Park, which offered a waterfront promenade, playgrounds, sports courts, and a dog run. Marti glanced out the window as they drove past. There was plenty of activity despite the heat. There was a desultory game of pickup basketball on one corner court. People were slowly strolling various paths, maybe hoping to catch a fleeting breeze off the river or anticipating the sunset. A few families picnicked in the shade near the climbing structure.

Joel idled in the street and checked his phone. "We're looking for 126 York." He looked around. He wasn't a native of Jersey City and despite his years on patrol still struggled with the geography at times.

"It's a block north toward Columbus," Marti responded. "But it's one way. Let's go down to Marin and then cruise the length of it. Get the lay of the land. I don't know where exactly 126 is on York."

He'd long ago ceased being annoyed with taking driving directions from her. He was capable of admitting what he didn't know. One of his more admirable qualities. He drove four more blocks south to Marin then turned right past The Golden Cicada bar and then took the next right on York.

The target address was a classic townhouse with a well-preserved brick facade. The term townhouse somehow seemed inadequate, however, as the structure took up three-quarters of the block. The exterior included ornate scrolling at the cornices and large windows framed by decorative moldings. A small wrought-iron fence surrounded the property, separating it from the sidewalk and the tall, mature shade trees.

Joel drove past the house twice and then found a street spot near the corner of Warren that provided a clear view of the entrance walk and front door.

"Herschel say anything about staying out of sight?" Marti asked. They weren't parked directly across the street, but they weren't exactly hiding either.

Joel picked up his phone, glanced at it, and then dropped it again. "No."

They settled in and watched. As the sun set and the light faded, the foot traffic also dissipated. The street became an almost static tableau.

Occasionally a car would pass. Or a pedestrian or dog would walk by in one direction. But this was not a cut-through. It was a quiet street. Joel ate his food. With the car off, they kept both windows down. It helped with the smell of Joel's garlic and bean curd. Marti picked at the container of white rice and ate both fortune cookies. She read the slips of paper: A person of words and not deeds is like a garden full of weeds. And: A short pencil is usually better than a long memory any day. She didn't know what to make of either of them. She dropped the fortunes in the bag with the empty containers. The automatic streetlights turned off at eleven.

Marti had to fight to keep her eyes open. The shift switch was messing with her. She glanced over at Joel. Not just her. His head was leaning against the window and a small trickle of drool ran from the corner of his mouth. The empty carbs of the Chinese food had been a mistake. She nudged him.

"Huh, what?" He came awake with a start.

"You were asleep."

"Was not."

She didn't bother to answer that, just wiped away a bead of sweat as it ran through her eyebrow and into her eye.

The radio had been quiet. They'd received no calls or requests for assistance since they parked so perhaps Herschel had been on the level. Still, she had always been suspicious of the quiet. When she was growing up, the quiet times were right before or right after her parents had been fighting. She always found the sudden quiet unsettling. She had a thought now as she stewed in the late-night heat that Jersey City was either sleeping like Joel or was gathering itself before unleashing a torrent of hell.

"We can't sit here all night," she said.

"Why not? If Herschel cleared it, that's what we'll do."

She knew he was right, but she felt sticky and clammy in her uniform which made her irritable and eager to pick a fight just to take her mind off the heat. "You always follow orders?"

Joel looked over and raised an eyebrow. It must have come out more sharply than she intended. "You might want to rethink your current career choice if that's how you feel about the chain of command."

She softened but wasn't yet ready to throw in the towel. "You don't find any of this unusual? Herschel just taps us out of the blue to be his eyes and ears?"

"No, not really. And it's not totally out of the blue. You've seen me talking to him. I had that bust. Look, you're still pretty raw." He reached out and tugged the arm pleat on her shirt. "Still fresh. We've got ranks and chain of command and procedure but it's mostly window dressing, Wells. You move up by being noticed. You gotta work the system. You're naive if you don't think politics or favorites don't come into this."

"Just like the Army?" It was her peace offering. She knew full well that ex-Marine Joel would disparage any other branch of the Armed Forces if given the chance.

"Fuck that. I wouldn't know but I assume they need all those rules and regulations just to take a shit each day. There's a reason the Army is only trusted with land ops."

"Oorah."

"Goddam right."

At eleven thirty, a man walked down the street from the opposite direction. His face flitted in and out of the shadows. Marti sat up straighter. She couldn't make out distinct features and was left with just an impression. He was slim with a loose gait. He gave off a different vibe even at this distance. This was not a man on the way home from the park or the bar. He was not out walking his dog.

As he approached, she could make out more details. He wore a dark suit that looked well-tailored, maybe even bespoke. He walked with familiarity and confidence. Halfway down the block, he glanced around and then cut across the empty street. She felt Joel straighten and stiffen beside her. Both of them were wide awake now. The man nimbly hopped up the front steps of 126 and paused at the top. He was in profile and the lamps outside the entrance showed a white male in his late twenties or early thirties with a well-defined jawline and an aquiline nose. His hair was light brown or blond, it was difficult to tell from the passenger seat of the patrol car, and cut short. After a pause, the door swung open and he disappeared inside.

"Key?" Joel asked.

"Must be. Can't imagine he picked the lock. Look at that place. You think they skimp on the locks?" She swung the mobile computer over to face her. "Should have done this before. This goddam heat is melting my brain."

She keyed in the address and waited for the database to spit back the owner's information.

"The owner is listed as Phoenix LLC."

"What state?"

"Doesn't say but probably doesn't matter. Regulations vary by state. Most states don't restrict LLC ownership. An LLC can be designated to a single individual, several members, corporations, other LLCs, or even a foreign entity."

"A lot of words to say it's a dead end then?"

"Or something we won't get at quickly but the fact that the owner is an LLC tells us something."

"Dollar signs."

"Yup. Did Herschel tell you anything else about this address?"

"No, you know as much as I do. Address, watch, wait."

"You going to text him about the guy?"

"Not sure. Maybe. Let's wait a few minutes and see if he does anything worth reporting."

She focused back on the long front facade. A light on the first floor turned on but it was a room in the back. They could see the glow extending toward the front showing indistinct lumpy shadows of furniture through the windows but nothing else. After fifteen minutes, another light came on, on the second floor.

"There must be a back staircase," Joel said.

Marti made a grunt of agreement and then watched the man come to a window and look out at the street. He'd lost his suit jacket and tie but still wore the white dress shirt. She could almost feel his eyes sweep over their car, but they didn't pause or stop. After a moment, he pulled the shade. Then a second shade in the next window was pulled.

"Probably getting ready for bed," Joel said.

She was about to reply when she caught movement on the first floor. This time, it wasn't the man they had seen. It was someone else entirely, dressed in black, including a black ski mask that covered his head. The figure moved outside the window frame, but he was followed by another figure who appeared in almost identical black garb. It was clear from their posture that they were moving slowly and carefully.

"You see that?" she asked.

"Roger that," Joel replied. His voice now tight.

"What the fuck is going on, Joel?"

He picked up his phone. "No idea and before you ask, no updates from Herschel."

He tapped out a quick message and hit send. The whoosh of the sent message sounded loud in the car. Joel's eyes ping-ponged back and forth between the phone and the house. The men reappeared in the next window and then disappeared from sight again.

Then all the lights in the house went out.

"Shit."

"That's not good," Marti said. Her heart pounded as the adrenaline kicked in.

"Nope."

"Call it in?"

He glanced down at his phone again. Nothing. "Yeah."

He keyed his mic but before he could say anything they both heard two distinct pops and saw a flash of light from the house and then they were out of the car and moving. She could hear Joel shouting into his mic, calling it in, as they ran across the street. They hit the stairs and took them two at a time. Joel didn't pause. He carried the momentum and hit the door with his shoulder and immediately fell back with a grunt. That might work on housing project doors that were bid out to the cheapest contractor but not on a century-old building with a solid oak door.

Marti tried the knob. Locked.

Chapter Eight

"**A**round the back," she said.

They reversed back down the stairs and ran to the corner and down the next street until they reached a wooden fence that guarded the alley that ran between the blocks. A padlock hung open on a hasp. Marti pushed through. It was dark and narrow, with just enough room for a single car or garbage collection that must exit from the other end. A few low-wattage security bulbs along the divider fence provided meager light. Black and rusting fire escapes hung off the walls of the opposite building. The York house side was all dark windows and clean lines. Marti took this all in with a sweep of her eyes. She didn't hesitate but kept running. She could hear Joel a few paces behind her. Halfway down the alley, she skidded to a stop by a plain unadorned door that looked just as strong as the one that hadn't budged for Joel in front. In addition to a deadbolt, a security keypad was set into the wall to the left. She tried the knob anyway. Locked. How had the men gotten inside? A key? The code? She glanced around. A flutter of movement caught her eye. She backed up. The windows on the first floor were set up high above her head, but one was also open a crack.

"There," she whispered to Joel and pointed. "Boost me up."

"I don't know."

"Joel, those were shots. That guy is going to be harmed or killed if we don't intervene. That is the definition of probable cause."

"Wasn't worried about that."

"Don't find your chauvinism now. Either we pull back and wait for backup or you boost me up and I let you inside."

Later she would wonder if she was goading him into action. If he had been right to hesitate even if it was for the wrong reasons. But she was caught up in the action and after a moment she saw him let go and join her.

"Okay."

He moved into position and intertwined his hands. Marti put her foot into the makeshift stirrup and Joel lifted her with only a mild grunt. She grabbed the edge of the window and chinned herself up. She listened but didn't hear anything. Using one hand, she pushed up the window, which mercifully slid up easily and without any noise, then gracelessly bellied her way through the opening and dropped inside.

She found herself in a spacious living room that appeared tastefully decorated with midcentury modern furniture that was in contrast to the outside historical appearance of the building. The room featured a fireplace framed by custom-built bookshelves along the far wall. She moved quickly but carefully through the room, making sure she didn't trip or knock anything over. She exited into a hallway. She turned right into an open-plan kitchen that appeared to be a chef's dream. She found the back door and let Joel in.

Together they retraced their steps to the hallway, went past a formal dining room, and found an entry foyer with high ceilings, polished hardwood floors, and a modern glass chandelier. She paused to glance out the window but saw and heard nothing. It felt like at least an hour, but in reality it had been less than two minutes since they'd heard the shots. She unlocked the front door and left it open a crack, but they were on their own for the time being.

As she put a foot on the first step, she heard a voice from somewhere above.

"Where's the cash?"

Then the sound of flesh on flesh followed by a crash. She put a hand to her gun. She had yet to pull it from its holster since she became a cop. Not on duty. She'd shot at the range to qualify, and they had training classes at the academy but much of it was paper-based tests and theoretical classroom discussion. This felt very different.

Another bang. This time it sounded like a hand slapping a table. "Last chance." The stress and frustration in the tone were not difficult to hear. The situation was on the edge of going sideways in a bad way. She could feel it. She pulled the gun and clamped her left hand down on the baton and pepper spray on her belt to mute the sound as they climbed. She glanced back once at Joel and saw he was mimicking her. His eyes were pinpricks, and she could see his pulse racing through the vein in his neck. She wondered if he realized he was smiling.

At the top of the stairs, she turned left down the hallway. A door was open at the far end. She waved Joel over to the other side. The hallway was narrow, but she didn't want to make both of them easy targets by stacking up one behind the other. They passed other open doors. Two bedrooms, a home office that would likely provide a nice view of the park during a more tranquil time, and a well-appointed bathroom.

They reached the end of the hallway. Marti could hear movement and more muffled voices. She felt Joel move up on her shoulder. They framed the edge of the door. He made a motion with his hand. She nodded. He put up three fingers and counted down. As she watched his fingers, she realized two things. First, one of them should have grabbed the Benelli shotgun from the rack in their patrol car, and second, in their rush to respond to the shots, they hadn't put on their body armor. She pushed both thoughts away. They weren't helpful. She focused all her attention back on the room. She couldn't get distracted if she wanted to survive this. When he reached zero, she didn't hesitate. She spun into the darkness and went left. In her peripheral vision, she saw Joel mirror the movement to the right.

She let her gaze sweep the room. The bedroom was huge with large windows and high ceilings. She caught a glimpse of an en suite bathroom dead ahead that might have been larger than her apartment just a few miles away. To the left, a walk-in closet completed the suite. She could see a rack of suits just inside the door. She was sure the closet would have accommodated the entire contents of her wardrobe and she would still have room to sublet the rest of the space.

All of that might have made her jealous, but it wouldn't kill her.

The two men in black certainly could.

She took a cautious step farther into the room. One man stood across the room next to the man they'd seen enter from the street earlier. He sat now in a cushioned chair near the bedroom's tall window. His hands were zip-tied in front of him. Marti could see two bullet holes puncturing the upholstery near his head. She could smell the cordite in the air.

The second man was closer, just inside the door, turned away from Joel and Marti, and focused on his partner and the bound man. Still, he must have sensed the movement at his back. He started to turn and Rincon put his gun at the nape of his neck. The man froze. For an instant, nothing moved. Marti could feel the situation balanced on a knife's edge.

Then the second man's tongue darted out over his lips and he spoke in a dry voice.

"Got a problem here, Boss," he said.

The other man turned but kept his gun pointed at the man in the chair. Marti watched him assess the situation. The whites of his eyes stood out in stark contrast to the black ski mask. He took a step back and to the side. His gun hand shifted slightly to open up his angle and give him options. Cold beads of sweat gathered on Marti's wrist and made her service weapon slick in her grasp. A tingling sensation prickled across her scalp, a silent alarm of danger. She forced her eyes to stay open, knowing that in this room, a blink would be an eternity. She kept her gaze locked on the man's chest, watching it rise and fall with each measured breath he took.

One. Two. An eternity.

Then his lips parted, "Do it."

The quiet tension in the room was shattered in a cacophony of gunshots, cries, and the heavy impact of bodies colliding. The walk-in closet door flew wide open and revealed a third man. His arm was up and he let loose a volley of gunfire. The muzzle flashes cast bright, intermittent bursts of light across the room. Marti's instincts took over. Fight or flight. She dropped to one knee and returned fire, her gun echoed sharply. She didn't know if she hit him, but the man fell backward and out of sight.

More chaos ensued. She heard Joel yell. She looked over but Joel and the other man were a pile of jostling arms and legs. Marti turned her attention back to the other man, but he was already charging her, gun raised. She felt something hot buzz past her ear. She fired, but he was too close, his momentum carrying him into her. They crashed into the wall. The impact sent her gun skittering away.

In the dark, the fight took on a brutal, primal quality. Marti, her senses heightened with adrenaline, punched and kicked against the man's bigger bulk. She felt her fist connect with the man's jaw, the impact jarring up her arm. But the man was simply bigger, relentless, and unyielding.

He smothered her attack, his movements just as swift and ruthless. She heard his ragged breathing and felt the heat of his body as they grappled. She tried to keep her footing, but he was everywhere, a whirlwind of violence. She felt something pop in her side, maybe a rib, and she gasped with surprise and dropped her guard, and with a speed that took her by surprise, he landed a blow to her head. Pain exploded behind her eyes, white-hot and blinding. She staggered, her knees buckling under her. She fought to stay conscious, to keep fighting, but the darkness charged in.

Her last thought before everything went black was of her partner, of the bound man, of the fight that was far from over. And then, there was nothing but silence and darkness.

When she came to, the room was eerily quiet. It was still dark. She didn't think that she'd been unconscious for long. Bodies were splayed on the floor. She smelled copper and cordite. She crawled over to Joel and placed a hand on his chest. Her partner was unconscious but alive. The three men in black also lay on the ground. Dead or unconscious. How? She tried to get to her feet, but a hot poker of pain made her gasp and go back down. She heard the sound of sirens somewhere outside, then she heard another sound. This one was closer. The sound of water running. Then the sound of footsteps. With effort, she turned on her side and looked up. The bound man stood over her, his face a cold, emotionless mask.

"There's an envelope on the bed. Use it."

"What?" she managed.

He leaned down and looked at Joel's gunshot wound and touched around it. Joel groaned but didn't open his eyes. He stood back up, took out a handkerchief, and wiped his hands. "Stay out of my way," he said, before disappearing into the night.

Chapter Nine

M arti roused herself from the warm cocoon of the booth and exited Cafe Grand. She decided to take the scenic route home, strolling a few blocks down to River Street Drive. The towering Lefrak Lighthouse, a beloved local landmark, greeted her with its red and white Dr. Suess-like stripes, as she reached the path along the waterfront. The lighthouse, though no longer functional, was a beacon of the neighborhood's history, standing tall against the backdrop of the Hudson River.

The breeze off the water was refreshing, bringing with it the salty tang of the sea mixing with the river. As the caffeine kicked in, she began to feel more like herself again. Her focus sharpened and she felt ready to tackle the Calderone research.

She walked briskly back to her apartment and ran into Pedro, the building super, bent over a broken radiator pipe in the lobby. Pedro was in his late forties, with a friendly smile and a tireless work ethic. He took immense pride in keeping the old building ticking, always tinkering, fixing, and improving something around the premises.

"Hey, Pedro," Marti greeted him.

Pedro looked up, the lines on his forehead deepening as he smiled. "Hola, Marti. Just fixing this old pipe. Mrs. Consuelo swears she can hear it whistling "The Girl from Impanema" at night. You know that song?"

"I know it."

They shared a quick laugh, but Marti knew Mrs. Consuelo might be right given the quirks and eccentricities of the old building that they all called home. The various pipes that snaked throughout their building did sometimes appear to rattle and hum in a way that often sounded like its own language. She left Pedro to his work and headed down to the basement.

Marti nodded at Mrs. Sanchez, a second-floor resident folding her laundry. Isabel Sanchez was a petite woman in her late sixties with an ever-present headscarf. Having lived in the building longer than anyone else, she exuded an air of sage insight. Marti always appreciated the snippets of wisdom Maria offered during their basement encounters, the echoes of the washing machines providing a halo of privacy for their chats.

"Good afternoon, Isabel," Marti said. "How are you today? How is your hip feeling?"

Isabel looked up from her laundry, her dark eyes twinkling. "Ah, Marti, dear. I'm doing well. There is always something to complain about at my age. I won't bore you with my doctor's notes. What about yourself?" she asked, her voice carrying a lilt that suggested a life lived in different corners of the world before finding her way to this building in Jersey City.

"Just the usual, working on a new case," Marti responded. "Could be interesting."

"Ah, the life of a detective," Isabel chuckled, neatly folding a colorful blouse. "Exotic locales, shaken martinis, fancy technology. Always something new, eh?"

Marti laughed. It was an old joke between them. Isabel had heard Marti complain many times about the mind-numbing boredom of many aspects that came with being a PI. "Coffee later this week?" Marti asked. "I'm six months behind on the book club but would love to catch up."

Isabel nodded in agreement. "I'd love to. Maybe we could include some chocolate croissants?"

"That's always included, Isabel."

Marti left Isabel to her laundry and retreated to her small annex office. The hum of the fluorescent lights and the click of her keyboard were the only sounds to accompany her as she began her deep dive into the life and mysterious death of Alexander Calderone, the former driving force behind Calderone Innovations. She started with the mainstream media reports, some of which she'd read before, but this time she read more slowly and carefully.

Alexander Calderone had been born on September 30, 1965, and passed away just over two weeks previously at the age of 57. Not that much older than Marti herself. He had been the founder and creative force behind the company renowned for both its technological innovations and its intense secrecy.

As of 2021, the most recent numbers quoted in the stories, the company was valued at more than $500 billion. Its primary areas of business included the development of proprietary software systems, AI technology, and cybersecurity solutions. The company's headquarters were located in Silicon Valley, California, with significant operations in Europe and Asia. Their client list remained confidential but was rumored to include both the Pentagon and large defense contractors along with many Fortune 100 companies in the pharmaceutical, automotive, aerospace, and manufacturing sectors. In short,

Calderone had a piece, sometimes a very large piece, of the global economy.

After his death, Calderone was succeeded, at least temporarily, by his brother-in-law, Victor Rathbone, as the firm's managing director while Calderone's will and succession plan were finalized.

There were endless search pages of links and stories about Calderone, but they almost exclusively focused on the business and after reading a handful of stories, those details and the canned PR biography began to get repetitive. The details of Alexander Calderone's death, however, remained stubbornly elusive. He had died during an overseas business trip to Asia and the exact circumstances of his death were not publicly reported.

In the absence of details, there was a flurry of speculation and confusion. Despite the media frenzy, the company remained tight-lipped. Victor Rathbone held a press conference where he read a brief statement acknowledging Calderone's passing and promised to continue his legacy. He took no questions.

The secrecy only added to his enigmatic persona. The man who had always been a step ahead in life had left behind a puzzle in death.

***

After hours of searching and sorting through the intricacies of Calderone's business empire and hitting a dead end about his death, Marti turned her attention to his personal life. She felt like she was attempting to find a reflection in a fogged mirror, an image that was there, yet persistently just out of focus.

His digital footprint was practically nonexistent. Social media platforms, the modern playground of public personas, held no trace of him. There were no candid photographs or impromptu tweets, no LinkedIn endorsements or Instagram posts. To the world outside his business, Alexander Calderone had been a ghost.

He appeared to have lived a life devoid of romantic entanglements, at least publicly. Marti found no evidence of dalliances, let alone a significant other. He hadn't been married, and there was no record of him fathering any children, at least none that he openly recognized. The paparazzi, always hungry for a juicy story, had little to offer. The few times his face graced their lenses were at charity galas, where he was always impeccably dressed and professionally bored.

If Cassidy was telling the truth, she would be a stark outlier in Alexander's otherwise sterile personal life. How did she fit into his world? What was the nature of their relationship? And why was there no official acknowledgment of her from Calderone himself or his company?

Marti enlarged a close-up photo of Alexander Calderone on her laptop screen, studying the sharp angles of his face, the intense gaze of his eyes. She tried to superimpose the image of the young woman who had sat across from her that morning onto the man in the picture. Was there a shared curve of the eyebrow, a similar set to the jaw? She couldn't be sure.

Marti shook her head, her brow creasing in thought. Was this all a fabricated story? A lie? A con? She couldn't dismiss those theories just because Cassidy was her client. Not with this much money on the line.

She checked the time. The evening was settling in. That morning, before they left the office, the three women had arranged to meet at Angela's apartment later that night to plan their next move. She had a little over an hour to make the trip across the river. Shutting down her laptop, Marti locked up her office and climbed the stairs to her apartment. Rita Mae, ever the unfazed feline, barely glanced at her as she came in. She combed her hair and added fresh deodorant in the bathroom and filled Rita Mae's water bowl before grabbing a light jacket and heading out again.

Chapter Ten

She walked briskly in the cool evening air to the PATH station and boarded the subway to 33rd Street. From there, she transferred to the NYC subway and rode the 4 train uptown along Lexington Avenue before she disembarked a few blocks short of the address Angela had given her.

Angela's apartment building presented a striking contrast to Marti's modest brownstone. Nestled in the heart of the Upper East Side, even from the sidewalk, it was a beacon of luxury and exclusivity. The building stood tall and grand, its facades of polished stone and glass reflecting the fading hues of the sunset. A uniformed doorman tipped his hat as Marti entered the opulent lobby, its walls adorned with expensive art and tasteful decor.

A call was made and Marti was buzzed upstairs. She stepped out of the elevator and into a wide, hushed corridor lined with plush carpet. She felt underdressed just standing alone in the hallway. She found the apartment number Angela had provided and knocked.

The door swung open to reveal Angela's residence, again a world away from Marti's own home.

"Come on in," Angela said. She was dressed in a casually elegant outfit that seemed to mirror the sophistication of her apartment. A tailored, dove-gray blouse was tucked into a pair of slim, black trousers. "Make yourself at home," she continued and indicated a cream-colored sectional.

"Thanks." The smell of warm spices and pad thai hit Marti's nose as she entered. Her stomach grumbled. She hoped not loudly enough for Angela to hear.

Inside, the apartment was sleek and modern. The open-concept layout gave way to a sunlit living room adorned with plush, contemporary furniture and an array of abstract art on the walls. The kitchen, with its gleaming stainless-steel appliances and glossy marble countertops, was separated from the living room by an island bar, where a variety of fresh fruits were neatly arranged in a modern chrome bowl.

Adjacent to the living room was a tidy office space, its glass desk surface immaculately clear save for a slim laptop and a few neatly stacked papers. A large floor-to-ceiling bookshelf filled with an assortment of books and decorative knick-knacks lined one wall of the office. Beyond the office, a hallway led off toward what Marti assumed were the bedrooms.

It was a reminder of the different worlds they inhabited and the vast gulf that separated the life of a private investigator from that of a ... whatever it was Angela did for the Rothchilds.

***

Cassidy was perched on a taupe leather armchair, as she flipped through a magazine. Marti watched her leg bounce up and down and her fingers tap out a rhythm on the chair's arm. She looked up as Marti entered and offered a small, tentative smile.

Angela moved to the kitchen, retrieved the takeout pad thai from its bag, and placed it on the coffee table. She then settled herself on the edge of the sectional couch. The three women formed a small circle around the low table and spent a few minutes eating.

Once Marti had quieted the direst of her hunger pangs, she leaned forward in her chair and said, "Cassidy, aside from the DNA results, do you have anything else that could help legitimize your claim?"

"DNA's not enough anymore, huh?" Cassidy said.

"I didn't mean that," Marti responded.

Cassidy waved her off. "I know what you meant." Her eyes unfocused a bit as she drifted into her memories. "After my mother passed, I had her things boxed up and put in storage. I mostly used a service. I ... wasn't in any shape to do it myself. After getting the DNA results, I went and looked through them more thoroughly. I found a snapshot and a single earring. I don't recognize the person in the snapshot and never saw her wear the earrings, but I found them together in a small box. My mother and I had a good relationship. Great, even. We only had each other for family. But I'd never seen any of that before. The box, earring, or photo."

"You think the photo is of Alexander?"

She shrugged. "It's not the best photo. It's a silly snapshot in bad lighting. You only get a sort of side profile, but you do get a feeling from it. These two people liked each other. There's also a date on the photo. It's roughly nine months before my birthday," she revealed, her voice steady. "Angela also had the earring tested for DNA. It matches ... my father."

"Okay, that could help build credibility."

Cassidy sighed, "I'm not on trial here."

Marti raised a hand to interject, "I know, but let's not be naive. You will be tried in the court of public opinion. These things will help buttress what you're saying."

"It won't make me look like *only* a gold digger. Is that what you mean?"

"Exactly. It will at least make you look like a tragic gold digger."

Cassidy stared at Marti for a moment before cracking a smile. "Better than being thought of as a fame digger or an energy vampire."

"Now you're getting it," Marti nodded, then ventured her next question to get them back on track. "So, your mother never talked about your father?"

Cassidy shook her head. "She died of liver disease and morphine was the only thing that helped manage the symptoms at the end. She said a lot of things on those meds, mostly nonsense that might have meant something to her, but she never mentioned my father."

"Did she know who he was?" Marti asked, her brow furrowed.

Cassidy shrugged, her expression pained. "I don't know. If she did, she never let on and I never asked. I felt like I didn't need to know. I was happy with the family I had."

"I wonder if Calderone himself ever knew?"

***

Marti decided to shift the conversation to lighter fare, giving Cassidy some time to recover. She turned to Angela, her gaze thoughtful. "How did you two meet?" she asked, her eyes flicking between Cassidy and Angela.

Angela let out a small laugh, her eyes brightening at the memory. "That's quite the tale. What would you say if I told you I used to be a pretty good bassist in a pretty good punk band?"

Marti raised an eyebrow in surprise. "You? Punk?" She asked incredulously, looking at the impeccably dressed woman. "I'd say you were full of shit."

"You'd be wrong," Angela confirmed, her smile wide. She stood and walked over to the bookshelf and plucked a CD from a small rack. "The Riot Lillies."

She came back and handed the disc to Marti. The CD cover for 'Punk Petals' was a gritty, high-contrast black-and-white image of the four band members. They were huddled together in an alley, backlit by a solitary light. Angela had traded her ripped jeans and band tees for sleek designer suits but the sharp, intelligent look in her eyes had not faded. She was front and center in the photo, her arm slung casually around the shoulders of a girl with a shaved head.

"Before I started working for Rothchild and living this polished life, I was in an all-girl punk band. We were pretty decent, even managed to land a small European tour with our debut album."

Cassidy perked up. "That's how we met. My mom and I went to their show in Oslo. I was absolutely enamored with them. The music, the look, the attitude."

Angela nodded as she looked at Cassidy and smiled. "We were loud and chaotic and full of energy. After the show, we got to talking with Cassidy and her mom. They were kind enough to offer us a place to crash for the night. The band was flat broke and a free place to stay was a godsend.

"The band didn't last much longer. The usual band issues, ego clashes, creative differences, the works," Angela continued, her voice a little wistful. "But Cassidy and I stayed in touch."

"She's the one who convinced me to move to New York after Mom passed."

"And I'm glad I did. I'm glad you're not dealing with this alone in a different country."

***

They spent some time talking about music and favorite bands and the best live shows before Marti pushed the mostly empty pad thai container away and steered the conversation back to the reason she was there. "Cassidy, tell me more about the unusual incidents that have been happening since you tried to contact Victor Rathbone about the DNA results."

Cassidy took a deep breath, her hands wrapped around a cooling mug of tea. "The first incident was the phone calls," she began, her voice steady but her eyes reflecting her unease. "Or a series of calls. The whole thing was strange, really," Cassidy began. "The calls never mentioned Victor or Calderone, or even hinted at the DNA stuff. I still don't know if they are connected. They were just ... unsettling. Odd questions and comments that didn't make sense. One time, a voice just repeated the phrase, *'Deep waters run still'* before hanging up. Another time, someone whispered, *'The fox knows many things, but the hedgehog knows one big thing'* and then nothing else. It was like they were speaking in riddles or codes. It was unnerving, to say the least."

"How long did that go on?"

"A week or so. Always random times. Day. Night. I'd block the number or not answer but they'd just keep calling or leaving messages or switch to new numbers."

"This was to your cell phone?"

"Yes." Cassidy reached into her pocket and pulled out her phone, swiftly navigating to a saved voicemail. "Here," she said, her tone sober as she hit play, "this is one of them."

'The crow flies at midnight.'

The cryptic, distorted voice echoed faintly in the quiet apartment, sending a chill down Marti's spine. Cassidy was right. It was strange and unsettling, but did it have to do with Calderone or just some strange prank? Marti made a note to have Neon see if he could track it down. It was likely a burner, but any information might help.

"You're right. Very weird. I'm going to want to get a list of the numbers or a phone bill."

Cassidy nodded. "Sure."

"Tell me about being followed."

"I started noticing them a week or so after the calls began. It was always out of the corner of my eye, a figure just out of place. But when I turned to look, they were gone. It happened everywhere—the grocery store, while I was jogging, even outside my apartment."

She shivered, pulling her cardigan tighter around her. The room felt colder, the jovial atmosphere from before dissipating as the seriousness of her story sank in.

"I was never sure, you know. Was I imagining the whole thing? But then one evening after work," Cassidy continued, "I had just locked up the bookstore and was heading to the subway station when I saw a figure in the shadows of the alleyway across the street. It was dark and the streetlights were sparse down there, but I caught a glint of something metallic, I swear, metallic and sharp. I froze. I didn't know what to do. My heart felt like it would burst out of my chest. But then an ambulance passed by and when I looked again, the alley was empty. The guy was gone."

She shook her head. "I know what I saw," she said even though neither Angela nor Marti had said anything. Angela reached out and placed a hand on Cassidy's shoulder.

"The most dangerous moment," Cassidy said, her voice barely above a whisper now, "happened last week. I was walking to work, near a construction site, it was early. I was opening the coffee shop, and suddenly, there was this loud noise and a large piece of metal came hurtling down toward me. I only had a second to react. I jumped back just in time, but the metal crashed onto the sidewalk where I had been standing a second before." She paused, her eyes wide with the remembered fear. "No one appeared to even be working. It was too early. The place was empty." She shivered. "The whole thing was too close. That's when I called Angela."

***

They left Cassidy sitting in the living room, her face pale from the retelling of her experiences. Angela led Marti toward the front door, her bare feet padding softly on the polished hardwood floor. As they reached the entrance, Marti turned to Angela, "She's staying here?"

"Yes. For the time being."

"You believe her?"

Angela paused. "I don't not believe her. If that makes sense. I'd rather have her here than in her crappy apartment way up in Inwood."

That made some sense to Marti. The doorman and fancy lobby wouldn't deter anyone who wanted to get in, but it might give them pause and slow them down. "The incidents have stopped since she moved in?"

"Yes, that's a new phone and new number, though I had them transfer over the saved voicemails in case we needed them. She hasn't mentioned anything else recently. She's mostly stayed inside. But you can see," she glanced over her shoulder, "it's all taking a toll."

"And they're probably still looking."

"Yes, I agree. I don't think she'll be invisible here for much longer."

"Okay, I can help with that. Give me a day to set it up." Marti thought of something else. "Why not go to the media? Get the story out there. Insulate her through being in the public eye. I have some local contacts if you need them," Marti said.

"We tried that," Angela responded. "It lasted all of six hours before a shitstorm of cease-and-desist orders rained down. It took only three hours for word to get back to Calderone Innovations. Now, no one in the legitimate media who could make a difference will touch it. Calderone maintains its secrecy with a heavy legal presence. Now, it appears, with Rathbone in charge, the trigger finger is even twitchier. They have the lawyers and the money to grind even the most formidable paper or media outlet to dust."

Marti turned to leave but then turned back. More questions and thoughts tumbled through her mind. "I'm stuck on the why. Why would Calderone Innovations try to silence Cassidy? I'm sure any company spokesperson worth their salt could spin this story into gold."

Angela smiled but there was little humor in it. "Money. If I had to guess. A whole lotta money. All those zeros can warp a person's mind. I might wear the trappings now and I'm not ashamed of it, I work hard, but I grew up in Newark. One thing I learned? Rich people have a way of making things complicated. Cassidy is a nice story but it's also potentially an expensive story for those currently in charge at Calderone Innovations."

Chapter Eleven

A s she exited Angela's building and walked toward the subway with Cassidy's stories in her head, she couldn't shake off a newfound sense of paranoia. She scanned her surroundings with more intensity than usual. But New York was being its usual self—noisy, busy, uninterested. Nothing and no one out of the ordinary caught her attention.

She descended into the subway station just as a train arrived and quickly found a seat for the ride downtown. The rhythmic clatter of the subway car provided a strangely comforting backdrop as she mulled over the evening's revelations.

Marti decided she had two initial things she could take care of. First, she needed to get those phone records examined. She took out her cell and dialed NeonNerd. Not his real name obviously, but his online handle was the only name Marti knew. He was a young, green-haired tech whiz with a penchant for vintage sci-fi and an uncanny ability to dig up information on the internet that was meant to be hidden.

Neon picked up, the sounds of virtual warfare punctuating his casual greeting. Despite the late hour, for Neon, it was early. Marti cut straight to the point. "I've got some phone records I need checked out," she said over the cacophony of digital explosions.

"Probably a burner," Neon replied nonchalantly. "Anything sus these days is done on a burner."

"I know," Marti agreed. "But any scrap of info could lead to something. Can you take a look?"

"Your dime," Neon said, signaling his agreement.

"Thanks, Neon," Marti said. They disconnected and Marti sent a text with the mobile phone login account information Cassidy had provided and added a short note about the specific numbers she needed checked. For the rest of the ride, she thought about the second thing she needed to do.

***

Marti exited the subway at West 4th Street, the sounds of the city's nightlife engulfing her as she ascended the stairs to the street. Greenwich Village was vibrant and alive, even at this late hour. She walked along the sidewalk, her destination only a few blocks away. She passed by the storefronts, quaint cafes, and independent boutiques that were the heart and soul of the Village. The area was a charming blend of bohemian spirit and urban chic, a hub of art, culture, and creativity that always made Marti feel a little more alive and happy putting up with some of the city's more urban annoyances.

Turning a corner, Marti approached Blossoms and Buds, tucked in-between a small Italian deli and a bookstore. The shop was a splash of color amidst the brick and stone of the cityscape. Even in the dim street lighting, the array of flowers in the window display was vividly beautiful, an artful chaos of blooms in every imaginable color. Above the storefront was Gwen's loft, a cozy space Marti had visited often. The light from the shop spilled onto the sidewalk, casting a warm, inviting glow. Although it was late, Marti could see her friend inside, toward the back, busy arranging a bouquet of dahlias.

Marti approached the glass door, rapping her knuckles against it. Her friend looked up, surprise registering on her face before she quickly moved to unlock the door.

"Marti!" Gwen greeted her, pulling her into a brief hug.

Gwen Torres's past was a tangle of contradictions, as complex as the city she called home. Born and raised in Brooklyn, she was a true New Yorker, toughened by the gritty realities of city life. From a young age, she was drawn into the city's darker underbelly, becoming embroiled in its criminal underworld. She quickly learned that survival required a certain set of skills, a certain toughness, and a talent for navigating dangerous situations.

Her grandparents, however, offered an entirely different world. They owned a small farm Upstate, where Gwen spent her summers, learning about nature, developing a love for plants and flowers, and experiencing a tranquility she lacked in her city life.

As she grew older, this dichotomy continued in her life. Her love for nature and the grounding peace it brought led her to open a flower shop in the Village. It was a surprising move for those who knew her past, but Gwen was full of surprises. Still, she was never able to leave her past behind. It haunted her at times, but she enjoyed it too much. It gave her life a spark and vitality that running the flower shop simply couldn't. In the end, she managed to blend her two worlds in a way that worked for her. Marti often wrestled with the guilt of drawing her friend back to her darker side, even if Gwen had long made peace with it. She'd come to believe it was a necessary balance for her. Marti thought that might be bullshit but Gwen just smiled, and Marti hadn't yet come up with a better response. Also, she often still needed Gwen's help.

Gwen and Marti's paths had originally crossed at a self-defense class that Gwen was teaching. Marti, whose work sometimes put her into dangerous situations, was there to brush up on some basic moves. They formed an unlikely friendship, and Gwen's unique skills and deep knowledge of the city often came in handy on Marti's cases.

She stepped back and looked at Marti. "What brings you here this late?"

Marti paused, considering how to start. "I need your help, Gwen," she began and quickly explained Cassidy's situation.

Gwen listened quietly. She didn't interrupt with questions and didn't press for details. That was one of the things Marti appreciated most about her friend—she was always ready to lend a hand, no questions asked.

"Of course, I'll help," Gwen agreed readily. "I have someone who can mind the store for a few days, no problem. Just tell me what you need."

"Thank you."

Marti placed a quick call to Angela, arranging for Gwen to meetup with Cassidy in the morning. She didn't think they were in any immediate danger—Angela's apartment would be safe for tonight but Gwen would add an extra layer of protection tomorrow.

Angela's comments as she was leaving about the rich and powerful had Marti questioning if she might be out of her depth with this job. With Gwen's help, it felt good to know she wouldn't have to face all of it alone. Tomorrow would bring a new set of challenges, but for now, she felt a little more confident, knowing she had a friend by her side.

***

Business done, she spent some time catching up with her friend. An hour later, Marti stepped back out into the night, leaving the warm glow of Gwen's flower shop behind her. The city was still alive with its usual nocturnal hum, the distant sounds of traffic, and the occasional hushed voices of late-night wanderers. She descended into the subway, switched to the PATH, and rode home again with her mind full of thoughts, plans, and questions.

As she stepped into her apartment, she was immediately greeted by Rita Mae. The cat wove between her legs, purring and rubbing her head against Marti's shins. "Hey there, girl," she murmured, bending down to scratch behind Rita Mae's ears. The cat responded with a contented purr, her green eyes half-closed in pleasure. She couldn't figure Rita Mae out. Some days she looked right through Marti. Other times, it was like this.

Marti glanced at her bathroom longingly. The idea of a long, hot soak was tempting, but she still had work to do. Instead, she grabbed her laptop and settled onto the couch.

She typed in Victor Rathbone's name. As the search results started to load, her eyes grew heavy. She blinked, fighting the pull of sleep. It was a losing battle, though. Her head drooped and she was out like a light, her fingers still resting on the keyboard. At some point in the night, she stumbled down the hallway to her bed.

Her dreams were a jumbled mess of images and sounds. A shadowy figure, a whir of machinery, the smell of fresh flowers. The details were elusive, slipping away like smoke whenever she tried to grasp them. When she woke up in the morning, the only thing she could remember was a deep sense of unease that lingered like the echo of a nightmare.

Chapter Twelve

She was back on the subway in the morning. The car was packed with morning commuters, each engrossed in their own world as the train rattled through the labyrinthine tunnels of New York City. Marti stood amongst the press of bodies, rocking gently, her senses tuned to the rhythm of the city, the flow of people around her.

Getting off at 57th Street in midtown, she joined the throng of people spilling onto the streets. The city was coming alive with the morning rush hour—taxis honking, vendors setting up their stalls, the din of conversation filling the air. She was just one among a sea of people, all moving with a purpose, navigating their way through the concrete maze of the city. Ahead, Astral Tower, the skyscraper that held the executive offices of Calderone Innovations, stretched toward the sky, its gleaming glass facade reflecting the hazy morning light.

The building was an impressive display of modern engineering and architecture—a seamless blend of glass and steel that towered over the neighboring buildings. Despite its size and grandeur, it was almost unobtrusive in its elegance, like a silent sentinel watching over the city. Marti joined the stream of people heading toward the building, her gaze analytical, her mind ticking over every detail.

Calderone Innovations didn't dominate the building. In fact, their presence was almost understated. In the sprawling atrium, amidst the variety of businesses listed in the lobby directory, Calderone Innovations was just one single line and three midlevel floors. To the untrained eye, there was nothing that screamed of the vast power and wealth behind that name, nothing that hinted at the company's expansive global reach or the secretive nature of its operations. Marti thought it was an apt testament to the company's ethos—discretion in display, dominance in industry.

The company's main research and development operations were based in Palo Alto, but this building was where the business side of things happened. It was here that the global board meeting would be held in less than two weeks, deciding the fate of Alexander Calderone's business legacy. A meeting that Marti needed to attend.

***

The atrium of the skyscraper was an expansive panorama of immaculate white marble arranged in a design that blended modern aesthetics with functional form. To the left, before reaching the sleek banks of elevators, sat a lively coffee shop open to the public. The aroma of brewing coffee was a pleasant contrast to the otherwise sterile environment. Marti joined the queue.

As she waited, she subtly surveyed her surroundings. Uniformed security personnel were strategically positioned throughout the lobby—some stationed near the entrances, others by the key card-required gates, a few more inconspicuously tucked away in corners, and a couple stationed outside. Her gaze flitted over a handful of visible cameras, but she had no doubt there were more hidden to the untrained eye, along with a host of other concealed sensors to deter unauthorized access.

As a security guard patrolled past her, she scanned the uniform, her eyes landing on the logo stitched onto the chest of their navy blue uniform blazer. A small smile played on her lips. Reynolds Security—a firm with strong links to retired cops.

***

Marti exited the lobby with the hot coffee cup warming her hands and a plan forming in her mind. She threaded her way back through the crowds to the subway station. The journey back to Jersey City was uneventful, the outbound traffic at that time of day was minimal, a blur of tunnel lights and faint chatter that faded into the background as she thought over her next steps.

Marti didn't head back to her apartment, instead she veered around to the back where her trusty old Subaru awaited. As she slid into the worn, comfortable driver's seat, the smell of past road trips and countless journeys filled her nostrils—a blend of stale coffee, takeout food, and dog-eared paperback books. Each scent was a testament to the vehicle's reliability over the years, and perhaps, to her less-than-stellar cleaning habits.

She buckled in, her fingers tracing over the familiar texture of the seatbelt. Giving the dash a ritualistic knuckle tap for good luck, she turned the key in the ignition. The old girl cleared her throat with a grumble, coughed, then turned over and settled into a familiar, chugging rhythm. The sound was like a familiar and favorite song to Marti.

***

A quick internet search had provided the address for the main office of Reynolds Security in Morristown, New Jersey. Just over half an hour later, guided by her GPS, Marti pulled into an unassuming office park.

The office park was a sprawling complex of low-rise buildings, their exteriors done in a uniform shade of dull-beige brick, almost blending into the landscape. It was one of those places designed with functionality over aesthetics in mind, offering little in the way of charm or character. Rows of neatly aligned windows punctuated the monotony, reflecting the gray overcast sky.

Toward the rear of the park, she found the Reynolds building. A solitary blue flag fluttered in the wind, bearing the company's logo, a flash of color in the sea of beige. She parked in a visitor spot close to the entrance and got out, zipping up her light jacket against the bite of the Jersey air.

The inside of the building was modern and clean, with a bland professionalism. It was devoid of any personal touches, almost sterile in its uniformity. Marti thought the look, such as it was, was likely intended to mirror the company's focus on security over decor. Or, just showcased Frank Reynolds' complete lack of imagination.

The reception desk was positioned to allow the man behind it a clear view of the entrance, as well as the rest of the lobby. His eyes, hidden behind a pair of sleek glasses, lifted from the computer screen to meet Marti's as she approached. A practiced smile crossed his face as he greeted her, "Good morning, how may I assist you?"

***

Several years ago, Frank Reynolds had found himself in a bind that threatened not just his second career, but his reputation and potentially his freedom. His younger brother, Danny, had gotten himself entangled with some unsavory characters and ended up on the wrong side of a major drug-trafficking charge. The DA was pushing hard, including some not-so-veiled threats, to look into Frank's past too.

Though Danny was far from innocent, Frank was convinced that he had been framed for the larger operation. Or, at least made to look like the patsy. The evidence was too perfect, too conveniently damning. But the police department was eager to close the high-profile case and Danny was the perfect scapegoat, even if a former officer was tarnished in the process.

Out of options, and desperate to save his brother from a lifetime behind bars, Frank had turned to Marti. She remembered the near-defeated man who had walked into her small, cluttered office. He had laid out Danny's case, asking for her help with a desperation she was sure he hated to admit.

She was also sure that, despite their brief shared history on the force, she was not the first place he'd turned to for help. Even still, Marti had taken the case, throwing herself into it with a dogged determination that Frank would forever be grateful for. She had eventually pieced together a clean trail of evidence that led to the real perpetrator—a midlevel enforcer looking to climb the ranks by any means necessary.

Thanks to Marti's work, Danny had been acquitted of the major charges and Frank had been cleared completely. Danny still faced time for his involvement, but it was a far cry from the life sentence he had been staring down. She'd been paid for her work, but they both knew the debt ran deeper than any invoice.

Today, she was here to collect.

***

"Good morning, I'm here to see Frank," Marti said, maintaining a casual smile.

"I'm sorry, do you have an appointment?" the receptionist asked, his fingers hovering over the keyboard of his computer. His voice held the faint trace of a gentle drawl that told Marti he grew up far from the turnpike or the Atlantic City boardwalk.

"No, I don't. But Frank and I are old friends. I'm sure he'd like to know I stopped by," she replied, trying to keep her tone light and friendly.

"I'm sorry, but without an appointment, I can't let you through," the receptionist replied, his polite smile never wavering. "I can help you schedule a meeting if you'd like."

Marti paused for a moment, her gaze steady. "I understand your position, but do we have to do this? If you would please let Frank know Marti is here, I'm sure he'll want to see me."

The receptionist looked at her skeptically but seemed unwilling to object further. A few silent seconds ticked by before a door on the far side of the lobby swung open and a man's head popped out.

"Marti?" Frank called out, his face breaking into a smile when he spotted her. "Scott, it's okay. Let her through," he instructed, his voice carrying easily across the quiet lobby.

***

Frank guided her toward a corner office, motioning to a chair as they entered. The man himself was a study in late middle age, the years etched on his face in deep lines and weathered skin. His hair, once a vibrant chestnut, was now a muted silver but still cropped close to his head. A cop cut. He carried the solid build of a man who had once been in peak physical condition, though age and the sedentary demands of an office job had added a layer of softness around his midsection. His eyes, sharp and intense, still held the same spark she remembered. He'd been a good cop. One of the ones Marti admired.

"Marti," he grunted in greeting, leaning back in his worn office chair.

"Frank," Marti responded. "How's Danny?"

"Still a pain in the ass but doing better. He works at the Lowe's here in Morristown. A manager if you can believe it. Also engaged."

"Good for him. Glad he was able to find his way. Just takes some people a little longer."

"That's a generous view, but I'm happy it didn't take a stint in Northern State to scare him straight."

"Me, too." They lapsed into a brief silence then Marti got to the point of her visit. "Frank, I need a job. A one-day gig."

Frank's brows knitted together, his eyes narrowing suspiciously. "You? A security guard? You're joking, right?"

She shook her head, her face serious. "Astral Tower. I need to be on the inside for a day, Frank. A specific day in two weeks."

Frank sighed heavily, rubbing his temples, not saying anything. Marti didn't say anything else. She had laid her cards on the table.

"Marti, I owe you, but this ... this is risky," Frank said at last.

"I know, Frank, and I wish I could tell you there won't be any trouble, but I can't. All I can tell you is that I need this and if there is any blowback, I'll stand with you."

Frank stared at her for a long moment, the need to repay his debt to her battling with his better judgment. Finally, he sighed again, somehow even heavier this time, and nodded.

"All right, Marti. I'll get you in."

Chapter Thirteen

M arti stepped out of Reynolds Security with a final wave to Scott. As she fumbled in her pocket for her keys, she saw her phone lit up with a barrage of notifications. She'd silenced it before going inside to meet with Frank. Her stomach dropped as she pulled out the phone and saw the missed calls and messages from Gwen. She quickly scanned the messages as she pieced together what had happened.

She dialed Gwen's number, her heart pounding in her chest. After a few agonizing rings, Gwen picked up.

"Marti," Gwen's voice came over the line, strained but steady. "I guess you've seen the messages."

"What happened?" Marti asked.

"We were leaving Angela's apartment," Gwen began. "I had a bad feeling, so I told Cassidy to stay close. As we were getting into the car, two guys came out of nowhere. They tried to grab Cassidy."

Marti's grip tightened on her phone, her mind racing. "And? Is she all right?"

"I got to them before they could get her inside a waiting car," Gwen said, a hint of steel entering her voice. "I managed to fight them off, but one of them must have sensed how it was going. The finesse plan went out the window and he pulled a gun. Cassidy was hit. She's alive. It was a through-and-through to the shoulder. I think she'll be all right. I'm at the clinic. The doc is working on her now. "

"Did you get a good look at them?" Marti asked, her mind already whirring with the implications of the attack.

"Didn't recognize them," Gwen replied. "But they knew what they were doing. It was a professional crew. This wasn't some random mugging. They just weren't expecting me. Or weren't expecting any resistance. They jumped in the car and took off. I got a picture of the plate."

Marti nodded, despite knowing Gwen couldn't see her. "I'm on my way."

All the confidence and momentum of making progress and a plan drained out of her and was replaced by a feeling of dread. This morning the case had been about a woman reconciling with her past and getting what was her due inheritance. By the afternoon, it was blood and bullets and attempted kidnappings.

***

Marti barreled down Route 78, pushing the Subaru to its limits. The old girl whined in protest as she flirted with speeds she hadn't seen in a decade. Marti was probably breaking more traffic laws than she could count, but the urgency to get to the clinic overrode any concerns about speeding tickets. Her thoughts were focused on one thing—getting back to New York City as fast as possible.

The clock on her dash read just past one as she finally emerged from the Holland Tunnel. New York was in its typical daytime frenzy—a ballet of yellow cabs, pedestrians, and the occasional daredevil bike messenger. But Marti was used to the city's chaos. It was her second home, just across the Hudson, and she navigated it with the deftness of a seasoned native. She weaved her way south through the city's arteries until the familiar streets of the Village came into view.

Nestled on Minetta Lane, a quiet street just south of Bleecker, was the unassuming facade of Dr. Elise Kramer's private medical clinic. She only circled three times before lucking into a street spot. Marti parked and jogged down the block and up the steps of the clinic.

***

Dr. Elise Kramer was once a celebrated surgeon at New York-Presbyterian where her skilled hands and sharp intellect had saved countless lives. But it had come at a cost. Elise had developed a dangerous dependence on painkillers. It was her supervisor who discovered her secret and reported her. But here the red tape of modern health care stepped in to save her. Elise had performed a life-saving surgery on the supervisor's boss's father. Recognizing Elise's talent and indebted for her father's life, the higher-up had reached out to Marti. The resolution was quiet and discreet—a subtle dance to preserve reputations and careers. Elise had lost her prestigious position but had gotten clean and kept her medical license and her dignity.

Marti had helped broker a deal with some private investors who saw potential in Elise's fall from grace. They established a private clinic, a haven for those seeking top-notch medical care and the utmost privacy. Word of mouth spread, and before long, the clinic was a sanctuary for celebrities, politicians, and ... anyone who might require a certain level of discretion around the reporting of various wounds.

As an extra benefit, she was always open to helping Marti and her friends if the need arose.

***

As she stepped through the clinic's doors, Marti was immediately enveloped in the hushed, sterile atmosphere. The clinic was sleek and modern and resembled a hip hotel or spa more than a doctor's surgical suite. There was a sense of calmness that pervaded the space and was something Marti needed given the swirling chaos of her own thoughts.

"Ms. Wells," the receptionist greeted her with a warm smile. "Dr. Kramer is expecting you. She's with Gwen and Cassidy now."

Marti nodded and followed the receptionist through the softly lit corridors. Her heart pounded with anticipation. Gwen had said Cassidy was alive, but Marti wanted to see for herself. She knew it wasn't quite rational, but she felt responsible for putting the girl here. Never mind that if she had been alone, without Gwen, it might have been far worse.

The receptionist led her to a private room and closed the door behind her. The room was softly lit, the walls painted a calming shade of gray, with modern minimalist art hanging in strategic spots. In the middle was an adjustable bed, where Cassidy lay unconscious, her shoulder heavily bandaged. The medical equipment surrounding the bed beeped softly in the otherwise silent room.

Dr. Kramer herself was an impressive figure. Tall, with a shock of silver hair pulled back in a severe bun, she carried an aura of quiet authority. Marti believed she was only a few years older than herself but had never confirmed it. Her eyes were sharp and assessing, hidden behind a pair of wire-rimmed glasses.

She looked at Marti with a hard expression. "I can't believe you put a child in this situation, Marti," she said, her voice low but carrying a note of steel.

"I'm glad that's how you think of me, Elise. She's hardly a child and Cassidy had trouble before she met me. But we can argue about fault later, can you first tell me how she's doing?"

Kramer dropped her eyes to the tablet she held in her hands and composed herself before looking over at Cassidy. "She's a fighter. The bullet, small-caliber as it was, still did some significant damage. It didn't hit any major arteries or nerves, thank goodness, but it partially fragmented upon impact."

She gestured to Cassidy's bandaged shoulder. "The main damage is to the muscles and soft tissue. I had to remove a few pieces of the bullet that had scattered within the wound. Some of the muscle tissue was torn, and I had to suture it back together as best I could. The shoulder joint itself wasn't impacted, but the damage to the surrounding muscle will make movement painful and difficult for a while. We also had to administer a substantial amount of pain medication due to the trauma. Her recovery won't be easy."

"Aren't painkillers pretty standard in this type of operation? I can't imagine you cut on many people these days without it."

"True, but ..." She adjusted her glasses, looking back at Marti. "How much do you know about her?"

"I met her two days ago. I know the roughest outline of her life and what is relevant to the case."

Kramer stepped over to the bed and moved the sheet aside to reveal Cassidy's other arm. Faint but visible marks crisscrossed the skin—a delicate network of pale dots formed a trail reminiscent of miniature roadmaps. Some marks appeared fresher, exhibiting a slight reddish tinge around the entry points, while others had faded to near-invisibility.

"She has a history of drug use," Kramer said. "I also checked other needle sites and saw some scars behind her knee. Any painkillers might need careful oversight. She'll need to go through a detoxification process to prevent withdrawal symptoms once she's off the medication. But," she added, her voice softer, "she's young, healthy, and strong. With proper care, rest, and physiotherapy, she'll recover, at least physically. It will take time and it won't be a walk in the park, but she can get there."

Marti exhaled, the tight knot of fear in her chest loosening slightly. "Thank you, Elise," she said. She hesitated, her gaze flickering back to Cassidy. "How soon can we move her? I ... I'm worried about who did this. If they could track the ambulance ... You don't want that type of trouble on your doorstep."

Dr. Kramer's eyebrows furrowed, concern etching her features. "I understand your concern, Marti. But moving her too soon could complicate her recovery. Right now, she needs rest and continuous monitoring to ensure there are no complications from the surgery."

She pursed her lips, considering. "Under normal circumstances, I'd recommend she stay here for at least a week. But given the circumstances ... we could move her in three days, but it would have to be done carefully and she would need immediate access to medical care at the new location."

Marti nodded, her mind already racing with the logistics. "I can arrange that," she said.

Chapter Fourteen

D r. Kramer excused herself from the room, leaving Marti and Gwen alone with the unconscious Cassidy. Other patients needed her attention and she had done all she could for Cassidy for the moment. Marti watched Cassidy's chest rise and fall in a steady rhythm then she nodded her head toward the door and they both stepped out into the hall.

Gwen pulled out her phone and flipped through her photos until she found the one she was looking for. "This is the car I saw," she said, holding the screen up for Marti to see. "Want me to see if I can track it down?"

Marti hesitated, weighing her options. She wanted to get to the bottom of this, but she also wanted to ensure Cassidy's safety. And Angela's. She glanced back into the room where Cassidy lay. "Not yet," she decided. "Let's make sure Cassidy and Angela are safe first before we go on the offensive. I have a guy I can get started on the intel. If they're pros, it's likely not going to lead anywhere."

Gwen nodded, understanding. "I can stay, keep an eye on things here," she offered. There was an almost eager spark in her eyes. "Things have been slow lately. Could use some excitement. I'll run home and grab some supplies."

Marti nodded her thanks. With Gwen watching over Cassidy, she could focus on gathering more information. Information they now desperately needed as the situation escalated. She exited the clinic and scanned the street from the top of the steps but didn't see anything or anyone that caused her concern. She knew Gwen would make a more thorough recon herself before settling in for the night. She climbed into the Subaru and made slow bumper-to-bumper progress through the tunnel and back to her apartment in Jersey City.

***

She was too drained to even contemplate cooking, so she stopped by DiNardo's, the pizzeria and sub shop on the corner. She ordered a large meaty calzone to go, the kind where the cheese oozed out and the crust was always perfectly crisp. It smelled heavenly and she had to work hard to resist eating it standing on the sidewalk.

Back at her building, she bypassed the chaos of her office. She stopped briefly at her apartment to check on Rita Mae, who played it cool from her couch perch, and grabbed a cold beer from the fridge before she made her way up to the roof. Here, she could find a quiet space away from the world. To one side, the sweeping views of New York City glittered in the fading light, while the other side offered the constant hum and snarl of traffic on I-95. When she didn't have to drive in it, she found the white noise oddly soothing.

She unfolded the lawn chair she kept stashed against the wall, sat, unwrapped her calzone, and took a long pull from the beer. As she ate, she stared out at the city, her mind churning over everything she knew so far. Cassidy had come to her for help with a paternity claim, a simple job that had quickly spiraled into a complex, dangerous mess.

She claimed to be the unknown daughter and heir to Alexander Calderone's vast personal and business fortune, a declaration she had substantiated with DNA test results and potentially some secondary family artifacts. The court documents had been filed, but a rapid gag order had shut down any publicity. Angela had tried to leak the story to friendly journalists, but those efforts had also been quickly stifled.

Victor Rathbone, Alexander's brother-in-law and a key figure in the enigmatic Calderone Innovations, had been contacted by Cassidy about the paternity results but had not responded. But since then, odd occurrences had been plaguing Cassidy—strange phone calls, the unsettling sensation of being watched and followed, and finally, the kidnapping attempt that morning and the gunshot wound she was now recovering from.

Marti sighed, rubbing her temples. Rathbone was the obvious suspect, but they didn't have any concrete proof against him. Yet. In less than two weeks, there was going to be a board meeting in New York City to decide the future of Calderone Innovations. Marti had a hunch that presenting the paternity findings to the board before Victor could seize full control would be the key to resolving the case. She was confident she could get in the room, but would she be able to present Cassidy's evidence? She wasn't sure. They might throw her out on her ear before she got a single word out. She'd likely need some help or support from several board members. Unless. Should they consider the board of directors suspects as well? If Rathbone was convicted or somehow cut out of Calderone's will, who would benefit most then? Greed could be a virus.

When she finished the calzone, she watched the last of the sun's rays disappear behind the city's skyline, replaced by the artificial lights of the city. The day had been long and exhausting, a rollercoaster of emotions, but there was still work to be done. If she went to her apartment, the allure of a tub soak and another beer would be too difficult to pass up, so she dragged herself back down to her office in the basement. She needed to find out more about Victor Rathbone and do some research on the Calderone board. If she managed to get into that board meeting, she needed to know who might be a friend and who might be a foe. With a long sigh, but a full stomach, she fired up her laptop and began to dig.

***

Two hours later, Marti was bleary-eyed and staring at the glow of her laptop screen. Her desk was cluttered with scribbled notes. She was immersed in her research on Victor Rathbone but the man was proving to be as elusive as Alexander Calderone, a silhouette dancing on the edge of the spotlight.

From the sparse information available, Marti could sketch a skeletal outline of Victor's life. He was an MIT graduate with a degree in cybersecurity and his career began at a prominent tech firm that specialized in creating advanced algorithms and encryption systems.

A chance encounter with Gabriella Calderone, Alexander's sister, at a cybernetics symposium in Boston was a turning point. They found common ground in their passion for technology, and within a year, they were married. But Gabriella succumbed to breast cancer before their fifth wedding anniversary. They never had children.

Victor's association with Calderone Innovations began shortly after his marriage to Gabriella in 1990. He was initially in charge of the company's network and data security division, but his role quickly expanded to managing key AI projects.

And that is where the trail ended. Rathbone continued to work at Calderone, his titles and responsibilities changed as he rose through the ranks, but any concrete details were lacking or glossed over in general terms. It was all neatly packaged and sanitized, like many of the stories she'd read about Calderone Innovations or Alexander himself.

She rubbed at her eyes, ready to throw in the towel, at least for tonight. There was one loose end. Just a sentence or two in one single story about a company Victor cofounded before joining Calderone Innovations while he was still at MIT. NeuraLynx Technologies. The details about this venture were also frustratingly scarce, but the writer appeared to insinuate things didn't end well. The story did provide the name of Victor's former business partner from the late 1980s. Marti typed 'Dr. Benjamin Ackerley' into a new search. She was prepared for very little to turn up. Everyone else in this drama was a shadowy figure with little online presence. Why would Ackerley be any different? But she was wrong again. Ackerley was easy to find.

He was currently a tenured professor at Stanford University, where he had been teaching and conducting research for the past few decades in AI ethics. He had many published academic papers on the value of increasing transparency and accountability in AI. As well as the need for a strong ethical framework for the future development of AI. She opened the papers but after the synopses, she quickly lost the thread in the technical details.

One thing Marti did notice was the lack of mention of NeuraLynx. Just a career footnote, not worth a mention so many years later, or something else? She glanced at the clock and was surprised it was past midnight. It would be earlier in California but still too late, she thought, for this type of call. She'd try to contact Ackerley in the morning.

***

Energized by the potential of Ackerley as a source of information, she pushed on with one more task. She grabbed her phone from the piles of paper and scrolled through her texts until she found the photo Gwen had sent earlier from the clinic.

It was a plain black sedan. Ubiquitous and invisible on New York City streets. Probably a Lincoln or a Cadillac. She squinted at the blurry license plate, hoping to make out the numbers. The image wasn't great, but Gwen had managed to capture the plate reasonably well considering the circumstances.

It was too late to call on a tenured Stanford professor, but not too late for her favorite computer hacker. Marti opened a new message to Neon and attached the photo, then typed out a quick message: Hey Neon, need another favor:) Can you try to enhance this and then run the plate and see what you can find on the owner? Let me know asap. Thanks.

She hoped Neon would be able to find something useful. It could be another piece of the puzzle or a dead end. Either way, it was worth exploring. Marti knew she had to turn over every rock in cases like these. Satisfied, she locked up her office, walked through the quiet laundry room, up the stairs, and fell into bed.

Chapter Fifteen

T he knocking was persistent and rhythmic, like a nail gun, and jolted Marti from sleep. Rita Mae darted off the bed and made a beeline for her sanctuary underneath the bathtub. Squinting at the clock, Marti groaned at the ungodly hour. No one knocked like a cop.

Dragging herself from the warmth of her bed, she shuffled down the short hallway, pulling her St. Peter's sweatshirt over her T-shirt and sweats. When she opened the door she wasn't entirely surprised to find Detective Harvey Klein, beaming back at her like a kid on Christmas morning.

"Good morning, sunshine," he greeted, clearly pleased at having been the one to interrupt her sleep.

Klein was the antithesis of Marti. Standing only about five and a half feet tall, he was round, balding, and not exactly in peak physical condition. His cheeks were flushed from the exertion of climbing the stairs to her apartment, and beads of sweat trickled down his dome into the fringe of his remaining hair. Despite his lack of fitness, Klein was no pushover. He was a seasoned cop out of NYC's 19th precinct, sharp, tenacious, and not easily deterred. If he didn't have a long-standing and mysterious agenda against her, Marti might have liked him. He'd been working inside the system for a long time and still cared. Marti had been frustrated by the apathy she often met from the outside for a long time, so she could only imagine being on the inside for decades and still caring. That counted for something. Still, he was a prick.

Ignoring his cheery greeting, Marti left the door open and trudged into the kitchen to get the coffeemaker going. "You're here early, Klein," she called over her shoulder, "What brings you across the river?"

"Shots fired," he replied, following her into the kitchen. "Yesterday. Swanky neighborhood, 74th and 3rd. On the East Side. Ring any bells?"

Marti froze for a moment, then shrugged. "Swanky indeed, but not my kind of neighborhood. Wasn't there."

Klein leaned on her kitchen counter, studying her. "Maybe not yesterday, Marti, but you've been there recently, haven't you?"

She felt a tingle of unease. The guest log at Angela's apartment. Of course. She poured two cups of coffee, black for her. She put a half-gallon of only slightly past due milk on the counter and nudged the sugar canister at Klein before sinking into a kitchen chair. He sniffed the milk and put it down, then added three hefty scoops of sugar to his cup.

"I have a friend who lives in the building," she said, keeping her voice steady. "Met her for dinner."

Klein sipped his coffee, watching her over the rim. "I thought you said it wasn't your kind of neighborhood."

She shrugged and thought about giving him the photo and the plate but didn't want to reveal her involvement, not yet, and said, "Not where I'd choose to live, or could even afford to live, but I have nothing against those who do. It's nice to visit when I'm not dodging gunshots. The chief must have people stepping on his neck to get this cleared up, huh? No street cams or Ring doorbells to help you out?"

She smiled at him then, a challenge in her eyes. He knew she was holding something back, but he also knew she wasn't going to give anything away.

He just grunted and drained his steaming coffee in three swallows. His throat must be made of Teflon, Marti thought. "Be careful, Marti," he warned, his jovial demeanor slipping as he moved toward the door. "I know you have a knack for dealing with the lowlifes and pond scum that usually pay your bills. But a word of warning: Don't mess with the rich. They're much worse, and much more deranged."

***

Klein had succeeded in one part of his plan. Marti was no longer tired. The fatigue had been replaced by a simmering frustration and racing thoughts. It was too early to try to call Rathbone's old business partner, Ackerley, in California, but now that she was awake, she was determined to dig up other leads on Rathbone and Calderone. But first, more coffee. She got up, poured herself another cup, and peered out the living room window at the brake lights starting to pile up on the city streets. She said a silent prayer that Klein had a long commute back.

As she turned away from the window, Rita Mae slunk out of the bathroom, her green eyes wide and expectant. After she verified that the coast was clear, she padded over to her empty food bowl and sat down.

"I hear you, Rita Mae," Marti murmured, setting down her coffee and fetching the cat food from the cupboard. The soft tinkling of the dry food hitting the bowl was followed by the sound of Rita Mae's purring. Marti smiled, scratching behind Rita's ears.

She retrieved her phone from the bedroom and quickly sent a text to Gwen, checking in. The reply came back almost instantly: All quiet. Good, Marti thought. Maybe the bad guys hadn't traced them back to Kramer's clinic. She made a mental note to call Savvy and figure out the best and safest way to move Cassidy.

She opened her email app and saw a new message had come in overnight from Neon. She clicked it open, her eyes quickly scanning the message. Neon had come through for her, tracing the license plate number of the car that the kidnappers had jumped in. As she read on, her pulse quickened. Maybe she wouldn't have to spend the entire day chasing down digital details. This could be the lead they needed.

Damian Russo. But that's all the email included. She tapped Neon's contact info. The phone rang ten times before he picked up.

"Marti," Neon said his voice heavy with sleep. "I thought we had a deal where you don't call before noon. Preferably not before three."

"Neon, you're a genius, but you need to give me a little more context than just this name. How am I supposed to find Damian Russo."

"You're the detective. I thought that would be the easy part."

"Very funny."

"Okay, here's the context. That car was reported stolen yesterday, wait, I guess it's now two days ago right off Second Avenue. Caught the thief on the street camera. Young guy, face hidden in a hoodie. He had a Slim Jim in his hand and was quite handy with it."

Marti smiled. She knew the story didn't end there since they had Damian's name, but she let him tell it. Neon liked to indulge in drama.

"But here's the kicker," Neon continued. "I backtracked Hoodie's approach and caught the car that dropped him off two blocks south. That car isn't stolen. It's registered to Anne Lombardi from Paramus. Her record's clean, just a middle-aged woman from the suburbs, but I found a connection to a guy who's not so clean. Her nephew. A lowlife with a few hits for car theft."

"Damian Russo."

"Bingo."

"I poked around a little on Damian. He might be young and small-time, but there are a couple of notes in his police file that say he's been associated with the Bellini crew in the past. If you're going after this kid, be careful."

The information came rapidly, and Marti found herself scrambling to take notes on a kitchen napkin. "That's more than I had, Neon. Thank you."

He yawned loudly into the receiver. "Sure thing, Marti. Oh, one more thing. I'm still tracking those numbers from the mobile account you sent over." It took Marti a moment, then she remembered. The strange messages that Cassidy had received. "All of the calls come from prepaid mobile phones using a cheap wireless service that mostly contracts out with Verizon for service."

That was about what she expected. If Victor Rathbone was ultimately behind the harassment, he'd likely be well insulated. She doubted any names attached to the phones would lead anywhere. Still, she had to kick the rocks.

"Thanks for trying, send me the invoice."

"I'm not done yet. I'm going to try a few more things. I probably can't get the owner unless I go into the service provider database, but I might be able to get the originating location of the calls. Gimme another day."

With that, he hung up, leaving Marti alone with the name Bellini echoing in her mind.

Chapter Sixteen

S ix hours later, Marti was parked on a side street off the main commercial strip of Ridgewood, New Jersey, about an hour from New York City. She sat in an old cab, borrowed from a former client, as she surveilled three men—Damian Russo and his two older pals—having lunch on a breezy patio of a popular local restaurant. The restaurant was owned by the Bellini brothers. The Bellinis ran a successful construction and real estate development company, Bellini Development and Construction, with offices in Ridgewood, that served as a front for their illicit activities.

Marti slumped down in the driver's seat, her eyes fixed on Damian Russo and his cohorts. They were laughing, completely oblivious to her watchful gaze. Her back ached from hours of sitting, a testament to the dilapidated state of the cab's seat. She was hungry, too. Watching the trio devour their sandwiches was a cruel form of self-torture. She shifted and grimaced as a particularly pungent waft of musty odor filled the cab, reminding her of the many fares who'd occupied the cab before her. But the cab was a necessary evil—it was the perfect cover. Untraceable, unassuming, invisible in the city's hustle.

Damian Russo was young, a court jester in the company of seasoned criminals. As she'd suspected, he wasn't the brains of the operation, just a lackey doing his time whose Slim Jim skills came in handy from time to time. She'd picked him up at the Bellinis' offices and had followed him around all day, watching him run errands, pick up packages, and amuse his superiors. It was monotonous and tedious, just as she'd always imagined the gangster life to be.

Finally, after four more hours of chores, just when she thought her back would seize up like a rusty hinge, Russo was cut loose. Marti followed him into nearby Paterson to a hulking apartment building. He disappeared inside for a half hour and Marti was contemplating what to do. She needed to eat and was looking around at nearby options when he exited again and stood on the sidewalk looking down at his phone. A minute later an older model Nissan pulled up and Damian jumped in. The car was painted a deep glossy black and had shiny chrome details on the grille and wheel rims. It had been modified for performance, with a wide body kit and a lowered suspension that gave it an aggressive stance. Marti could hear the turbocharged engine, humming with latent power, from her spot down the street.

Russo and the Nissan led her to a drifting spot at the old Meadowlands Raceway in East Rutherford. Once the site of thunderous horse races, the sprawling complex had been repurposed by a new generation of racers.

While the cab was perfect camouflage on the city streets, it would stick out like a sore thumb amongst the high-performance sports cars and modified drift machines. She decided to hang way back as the Nissan pulled through the old gate. She followed but went left, instead of following the Nissan right, and parked the cab at a distance, blending in with other nondescript vehicles that were there for the spectacle rather than to participate in the racing.

She exited the cab and walked to where the crowd had congregated along an old section of grandstands at the south end. People were drinking bottles of beer and a few people had small propane grills. The smell made Marti's stomach lurch but she kept her distance. Sitting in the shadows, she was able to keep an eye on Russo and his activities without drawing attention to herself. The expansive parking lots and serpentine access roads had become a nocturnal playground, an unofficial drifting course. The sounds of revving engines and cheering crowds mixed with the aroma of burning rubber and gasoline.

Eventually, Russo slipped away from the crowd with a woman who was clearly intoxicated. She was a petite brunette, dressed in a tight, bright-green minidress that glowed in the dark as she stumbled along under the fluorescent lights and Russo propped her up.

"Shit," Marti said, standing up. She trailed them from the track and the cars to a dark corner on the edge of the parking lot.

Once they were isolated, Marti made her move. She wasn't going to let things go any further.

"Hey, your friends are looking for you," she called out to the woman, gesturing back toward the party with a casual nod. The woman squinted at Marti, her hazy gaze unfocused.

"Really?" she slurred, looking toward the noisy crowd.

"Yeah, really," Marti assured her. "They said something about your ride leaving."

The woman cursed, staggering back toward the stands without a second glance at Russo. Russo watched her leave, a puzzled expression on his face. Maybe he'd had a few drinks himself. When he turned back to Marti, she was already moving.

"Who the hell are—" He didn't get to finish his sentence. Marti had pulled a Taser from her jacket pocket and pressed the trigger as she stepped into his personal space.

The electrical crackle of the Taser filled the air and Russo's eyes widened in surprise. It was the last expression he wore before his body convulsed, crumpled, and fell to the ground. Marti looked down at him, her face impassive. She hated men who took advantage of certain situations. She glanced around. No one was moving in their direction. Tight Green Dress had probably already tripped into someone else's arms. Marti couldn't stop them all. She holstered the Taser, grabbed Russo under the arms, and began the difficult task of dragging him back to the cab.

Lucky for Marti, his rendezvous spot was partway to where she'd parked the cab. She managed to get him around to the trunk without being seen. He was of average height, with a lean, wiry frame that suggested more strength than his build would initially reveal, but it also meant he was light enough for Marti to wrestle into the trunk. She wasn't exactly gentle but she wasn't that concerned. Before she closed the lid, she secured his hands and ankles with plastic zip ties and stuck a rag in his mouth.

She quickly moved around to the driver's seat and navigated out of the lot. She kept checking the mirrors but her luck had held. It was risky but necessary in her opinion. She couldn't afford to interrogate him at the party—he'd put up a tough front, might even make a scene and get others involved. But she needed information.

She had a better place in mind to chat.

Chapter Seventeen

The autumn air carried an electric tension as Marti pulled up to the understated bail bonds office in Jersey City. A buzzing neon sign reading Atlas Bail Bonds illuminated the nearby night, casting an ethereal glow onto the brick façade of the building. As she came to a stop, the colossal figure of Benjamin 'Bear' Wachowski stepped out onto the pavement, his silhouette forming an imposing counterpoint against the modest backdrop of the office.

"Hey, Bear," Marti greeted as he climbed into the passenger seat, the cab noticeably dipping under his weight. He grunted in response.

She admired Bear for his willingness to help with no questions asked. He owed her one after her work on the Earl Monroe case, but she thought he would have likely got in the car regardless. Marti knew Bear's secret. He was more teddy than grizzly. He'd earned his nickname not from his intimidating stature but from his distaste for violence. Instead of drawing his gun, Bear preferred to incapacitate the fugitives he was hunting in a bear hug that few could escape from. But he still looked like a grizzly.

He stood at a towering six-feet-six inches, with broad shoulders and arms that looked like they could bench press a small car. His skin was marked by various tattoos, each one a testament to his past life. A thick beard, more salt than pepper these days, enveloped his face, framing a pair of soft, brown eyes that were often filled with warmth and humor. But he could put on a game face when needed. He was the brawn, and his wife Vivian was the brains, behind Atlas Bail Bonds.

Marti pulled back into traffic and headed for the Holland Tunnel entrance. "There's a kid in the trunk. Damian Ross. He stole a car that ended up being used in a kidnapping attempt on my client. I don't think he was involved in the actual attempt, but I reckon he knows something useful. He's a low-level gopher for a Bellini brothers crew."

Bear let out a low whistle, his eyes widening. "The Bellinis, huh? You sure you want to get tangled up with them?"

Marti grimaced, her grip tightening on the steering wheel. "I hope not. Whatever Damian knows, I hope it doesn't pull us into their orbit. The car theft and kidnapping don't seem like their style, right? Not anymore. They're too busy acting legit to try a street grab. I'm hoping this was more of a side gig for Damian. Maybe trying to get noticed."

"Maybe," Bear said. "They certainly weren't above it back in the day."

"Tell me."

"Back in the late 1980s, the Bellini brothers, they weren't much of anything yet," he began, his voice a deep rumble that almost echoed in the quiet car. "They were just a pair of roughnecks from Little Italy. Small-time crooks mostly, but they had ambition. Frank, the older brother, had a mind for strategy. And Tony, he was the muscle. They decided they wanted a piece of the big time, the real mafia action. The problem was, they weren't made men and the families didn't take them seriously."

Bear paused, chuckling to himself without much humor. "Well, those boys decided to change that. There was a man named Vito Scalise, a capo in the Gambino family. The Bellinis cornered him in his own restaurant, in front of his crew and the customers. Frank walked up to him, cool as a cucumber, and shot him in the head. Tony, he took out two of Vito's bodyguards before they could even reach for their guns."

Bear shook his head, a far-off look in his eyes. "I was just a kid when it happened, but I remember the talk. It was a statement, you see. The Bellinis were saying they weren't scared, that they were ready to take on anyone. After that, the families started to take them seriously but it was too late. They were ruthless, not afraid to spill blood and break any of the so-called rules to get what they wanted."

"Why didn't the Gambinos retaliate?"

Bear shrugged. "You'd think they would, right? But the Gambinos were in a tough spot. Their boss at the time, a guy named Tommy 'The Bull' Santoro, was under heavy scrutiny from the Feds. He was trying to keep a low profile and avoid any kind of violence that could draw more attention to the family. Plus, there was some internal strife, different factions within the family fighting for power."

He sighed, shaking his head. "But the real reason, I think, was fear. The Bellinis had shown they were willing to take extreme measures. They had the element of surprise and they were ruthless. The Gambinos were established. Critics would say they were soft. They didn't want to start a war they weren't sure they could win. So they waited. Bided their time. It was a calculated move, but it backfired. They never hit back, not hard enough, and it allowed the Bellinis to grow in power and influence."

Bear fixed Marti with a serious look. "They're old men now, but don't underestimate them. They've got years of power and violence behind them. They won't make the same mistake as Santoro. You don't want to get on their bad side, Marti."

***

When they arrived in the Village, Gwen was waiting for them at the back of her building. The basement, soundproofed for her fitness and self-defense classes, served a dual purpose on occasions like this. The studio was spartan in its decor, with just enough room for a few exercise mats and, today, a single wooden chair in the center of the room.

Bear easily carried the still unconscious Damian down the short flight of steps and put him in the chair where Gwen secured him further with lengths of rope. Then, they finally woke him up. The sight of Bear, his game face on, was enough to make the young man flinch back in fear before he tried to regain his composure.

"Are you guys crazy?" Damian sputtered, his eyes darting between the three of them. "Do you know who I am?" His bravado, however, rang very false as he tried to make sense of the situation, all the while in the shadow of the teddy bear-turned-grizzly. He writhed against the rope. They watched in silence until he exhausted himself. Gwen, always meticulous, had secured the knots. There was no chance of escape. "You know what happens if I don't show up tomorrow, right?" he spat out.

Marti smirked. "What? A couple of goons miss their lunch? Have to fetch their own dry cleaning?" She leaned back. "Damian, let's be clear. You're a tiny pawn in the Bellini operation. If you don't show up tomorrow, there might be a few raised eyebrows and a few questions. But eventually, you'll only be a memory. 'Remember Damian?' they might ask, 'Whatever happened to that guy?'"

Defeat swept over Damian as he slumped lower in his chair. Realizing his own insignificance was a bitter pill to swallow.

"What do you want?" he muttered, his voice barely above a whisper.

"We're not interested in the Bellinis, Damian. Or even you, for that matter," Marti said. "We're interested in a car you jacked recently."

Confusion crossed his face.

"Are you telling me that you steal so many cars that you can't remember?" Marti asked.

"No, I remember. A black Town Car, Second or Third Avenue."

"That's right. Who asked for it?"

"I don't know."

"Really?" Marti's eyebrow arched skeptically.

"Really." Damian insisted. He was insignificant and defeated but he wasn't going to snitch.

"Here's the thing, Damian," Marti said. "That car was used in a shooting. A woman is in the hospital. If she dies, you're an accessory to murder. That's a long sentence for a young car thief. But maybe you get out by the time you're fifty or sixty. Collect a little Social Security."

"What? Shit!" Damian's eyes widened. "For Slim Jimmying a car? I didn't know anything about a shooting or a murder. I was just told to lift a car, a generic sedan, and deliver the keys to an address."

"And what address would that be?"

"28 West 43rd Street, down in Hell's Kitchen."

"That's it?" Marti asked.

Lowlifes always snitch eventually. It's in their DNA.

"Drop off the keys at the front desk, tell them they're for 'The Wall,' then forget all about it. Which I was doing a good job of until you showed up."

"The Wall?" Marti froze, her eyes narrowing. "You sure that's what they said?"

"Yeah, I thought it was weird too, but the guy at the desk didn't blink. Just nodded and took the keys. That's all I know. Honest."

Marti swallowed. 'The Wall.' A nickname she hadn't heard in years. A name she'd hoped to never hear again.

Chapter Eighteen

B ear glanced at Marti, his eyes brimming with questions. "The
Wall? Like ..."

Marti subtly shook her head and gestured toward the stairs.

Meanwhile, Damian, oblivious to the growing tension, fidgeted
uncomfortably in his chair. "So ... am I in trouble? I swear, I didn't
know anything about a shooting!"

Marti ignored his question as she ascended back to the street.

"Robert 'The Wall' Herschel," Marti said to Bear as she paced a
short distance up and down the alley. Bear, knowing Marti's history,
stayed silent and just nodded. Herschel's name was a dark chapter
from Marti's past that she had long tried to erase. Herschel was a
phantom, a haunting figure who had left a trail of destruction in his
wake. How could he be involved in this?

"We're finished here," Marti said.

***

Leaving Damian securely confined in the basement, under Bear's vigilant watch, Marti first dropped Gwen back at the clinic to watch over
Cassidy and then made her way back to her own apartment. After

hours of hunching in the cab, her body protested vehemently as she climbed the stairs, but her mind refused to slow down.

Marti selected a bottle of medicinal red wine from the small shelf near the fridge, filled her bathtub with hot water, and immersed herself in its soothing warmth. The combination of the steaming bath and the comforting effects of the Cabernet gradually lulled her restless mind into a semblance of serenity. After drying off, she managed to slip into an uneasy slumber.

Morning light filled her room when she woke up, and she attempted to shake off the remnants of sleep and wine with an invigorating run along the waterfront. The rhythmic thud of her sneakers on the pavement and the cool morning breeze against her skin served as a much-needed wake-up call. It wasn't her best run, but it was better than nothing and it loosened some of the knots in her back from her cab stakeout.

Half an hour later, after a shower and attending to Rita Mae's needs, Marti found herself back in her favorite corner booth at Cafe Grand. She cradled a tall Americano, taking occasional sips, and indulged in a pastel de nata. The small Portuguese tart was a rare treat, a cafe specialty served only on select days. Its flaky pastry shell, filled with creamy egg custard, held a special place in Marti's heart, second only to a decadent chocolate croissant. While she savored her pastry, she idly watched the morning traffic flow past the cafe's window, her thoughts focused on Herschel and what she would, or could, do with this latest piece of information.

When she'd finished the pastel de nata, Marti reluctantly left the cozy warmth of her booth and the comforting cafe aromas. She took the remainder of her Americano to go, headed back to her apartment building, and descended to her basement office. While she waited for the worst of the rush hour traffic to subside, she lost herself in a review of her case notes. Each piece of information went up on her whiteboard, creating a sprawling visual mind map of the case. Her chronological notes provided structure, but the whiteboard allowed for a more fluid approach and could reveal potential connections she'd miss in her notes.

***

An hour passed, and with no new leads materializing, Marti decided to contact Dr. Benjamin Ackerley, Rathbone's former business partner and now an academic at Stanford. In the rush of trailing Damian Russo, she had neglected to do so the previous day. It was still early in California, and Marti was prepared to leave a voicemail, but to her surprise, he answered.

"Hello?"

"Oh. Good morning. I was expecting to leave a message for Dr. Ackerley."

"Well, you've got me in person," he replied. "I like to swim at the university pool before it gets busy and too hot. So I'm almost always at my desk by seven. What can I do for you?"

"My name is Marti Wells, I'm a private investigator in Jersey City. I was hoping you could tell me a little bit about NeuraLynx Technologies and Victor Rathbone."

"What a waste," he said, his initial liveliness replaced by a more somber tone.

"Which one?"

Dr. Ackerley chuckled lightly. "Both, I suppose. NeuraLynx was our dream, Victor's and mine. We saw the potential of AI and the vast possibilities it held. But somewhere along the way, our visions diverged."

"How so?"

"Well," Dr. Ackerley began, "I saw the future of AI as a tool, something to augment human capabilities, to aid us. Victor ... he had grander, more ambitious visions. He wanted to push boundaries, to create something more ... autonomous, sentient even."

"And this disagreement ... did it lead to a falling out?"

"Yes. Victor was charismatic and persuasive. He managed to sway the board members and our early investors. Before I knew it, my voting shares were rescinded."

"And you left the company?"

"You could say that. I was forced out."

"And what happened next? What became of NeuraLynx?"

"A couple of years later, Victor sold the IP."

"He abandoned his vision as well?"

"No. You have to understand that this was the late 1980s. Much of AI was theoretical and any practical applications, involving hardware, were prohibitively expensive. Victor essentially ran out of money. He needed a partner with deep pockets."

"Calderone Innovations."

"The buyer's identity was never disclosed," he said with a tone that hinted at the answer. "But the timing was suggestive."

"I've read some of your papers," Marti said. It was mostly true. She'd read the abstracts. "You're still involved in the field. Do you maintain contact with Rathbone?"

Another laugh. "No. I have no use for Victor. Though it might be more accurate to say Victor has no use for me. Not since I lost those shares. Sometimes I used to joke that he was more machine than man, which later made me worry about his vision of AI. The man is brilliant, but he seems to embody the cold cunning and calculation of humanity, without any warmth."

"So his vision of AI was deceitful and manipulative?"

Another laugh, this one tinged with genuine humor. "That's a bit blunt, but might be pretty close to the truth."

***

After ending the call with Dr. Ackerley, Marti took a moment to digest the new information. Victor Rathbone's maneuvering, ambition, or perhaps something else had not only shaped the trajectory of Neura-Lynx but had also fomented a deep-seated resentment from his former partner, even decades later. That might be significant to remember.

Shaking off her contemplations, Marti dialed Gwen's number. They had agreed that after two days, it was unlikely that Cassidy had been traced to the clinic and that Gwen would only stay nights at the clinic with Cassidy until they moved her again. She picked up on the second ring.

"Hey, Marti. No change with Damian or Cassidy," Gwen reported. "I talked to Bear and he told me Damian was still asleep in his chair when he checked in before opening the shop this morning."

"Bear is running the store?"

"I'm on my way back, but I think he likes it."

Marti tried to picture the big man snipping thorns off roses or ringing up a bouquet of lilies but failed and then stopped trying. Just trying to conjure the images was giving her a headache. "Thanks, Gwen," Marti replied.

Next, she contacted Dr. Kramer at the clinic.

"This is Elise," came the doctor's recognizable voice.

"It's Marti. How's Cassidy doing?"

"She's awake," Dr. Kramer informed her. "About what you'd expect two days after being shot. She's still on heavy pain medication and a sedative to help her sleep at night. You remember what we talked about, right?"

"Yes, I'm working on it. I should have more information on a long-term plan today."

"Okay, Marti. You should come see her."

"On my way."

Marti retrieved her coat and keys and headed to her car. The drive to the clinic was a blur of brake lights and the fluorescent lights of the tunnel. As she drove, she pondered the best way to support Cassidy's recovery.

Upon her arrival, Marti found Angela by Cassidy's side. The sight of Angela, marked by concern and relief, provided Marti with some comfort. Cassidy might not have any immediate family but she wouldn't be alone in this battle. As she entered the room, Cassidy turned her head to gaze at her, mustering a weak smile. Marti could see her eyes were still cloudy and swimming in the pain meds.

"Marti," she murmured, her voice frail but clear. Her blankets were pulled up to her chin, concealing most of the bandage that wrapped up her shoulder. Various machines surrounded her, their rhythmic beeps and hums creating a background chorus.

"Hey," Marti responded. "Nice to see you awake. How are you feeling?"

"Have you ever been shot?" Cassidy asked.

Marti paused. "Yeah, a couple of times."

"Then you know that's a stupid question."

Marti smiled. "You're right."

"Is Gwen coming back?"

"She'll return tonight. We're hoping to get you out of here tomorrow."

"She's got dead eyes, Marti."

Marti didn't know how to respond. She wasn't even sure if she wanted to. She knew some people were uncomfortable around Gwen or sensed something slightly off, but no one had ever said that to Marti about her friend before. Perhaps it was the effect of the morphine, or maybe a brush with death had provided Cassidy with a new perspective. Marti didn't think she was wrong.

"She'll take care of you," Marti eventually replied.

"I know," Cassidy said before closing her eyes.

Marti motioned to Angela, and they exited the room into the hallway.

***

"What's happening with the paternity suit you filed in California? Any updates on that?" Marti inquired.

Angela sighed, running her fingers through her hair. "It's still in the initial stages," she explained. "We're just beginning the discovery process. We've requested certain documents, and they've made requests of us. It's ... a lot."

Marti nodded. Burying the opposition in paper was a common tactic. "What about the paternity test?"

"That's the first significant hurdle. Cassidy is contesting the will based on her status as an unacknowledged heir. The initial step is to prove her paternity claim, which means establishing her as the biological daughter and, consequently, a potential heir to Calderone's estate. They're, of course, disputing our previous results, so a new test has been ordered by the court. Once we have those results, we'll have a clearer picture of where the case might go."

"And if the test confirms Cassidy's claim?"

"Then it gets more complicated," Angela acknowledged. "The court will need to consider the terms of the existing will, specifically whether it explicitly excludes Cassidy. It doesn't, as Calderone was unaware of her existence. If that fact is established, she could have a rightful share of the estate as an unacknowledged heir."

"What about the current beneficiaries of the will?" Marti asked. "What happens to their inheritances?"

"It depends on the terms of the will and the laws of the jurisdiction," Angela responded. "If Cassidy is recognized as a legal heir, she might potentially inherit a portion of the estate. In her case, it could be a substantial portion, given that she would be the sole direct heir. This could reduce the shares of other beneficiaries, or it could even invalidate the will, leading to an intestate situation where state laws determine the distribution of assets."

"That's likely to upset a lot of people. Like a brother-in-law."

"True, but even worse, it might take years to resolve," Angela added.

Marti understood that the board meeting would take place long before any of this legal tangle was unraveled. She had a feeling this was only the tip of the iceberg. This was Rathbone, if it was Rathbone, acting cautiously. He couldn't outright expose his involvement, but if Rathbone seized control of the board, he could make it more official and utilize the full resources and power of Calderone Innovations to squash Cassidy's claims or simply hold out and slowly grind her to dust.

***

Changing direction, Marti asked, "Did you know about Cassidy's history of drug use?"

Angela appeared to deflate, her eyes momentarily dropping to the floor before returning to meet Marti's gaze. "Yes, I did," she admitted. "But she's no longer using. Cassidy completed her rehabilitation six months ago, and she's remained clean and sober since."

Marti absorbed this information and what Elise had told her yesterday. Some of the needle marks were fresher than six months. Cassidy might have slipped. "That's going to make her recovery more challenging, you realize that, right?" she remarked. "Furthermore, it's likely to become public knowledge, especially when the media latches onto this story."

"I'm aware," Angela replied, her voice tinged with emotion. "But I'm prepared to support her in any way necessary. She's my sister, not by blood, of course, but in every other sense. I'm not going to abandon her."

"Neither am I," Marti said, nodding and making a decision. "I might know someone who can help. She's unorthodox, to say the least, but the program is effective. When she leaves, she won't want to go back."

This time, it was Angela who nodded. "I'll try anything."

"Okay, I'll set it up and let you know."

Chapter Nineteen

M arti exited the clinic and glanced at her car parked in a miraculously convenient spot on the street. The idea of abandoning such a prime parking spot almost made her physically ill. She decided to leave it there, opting instead for the city's subway system.

Descending into Christopher Street station, she was immediately enveloped in the distinct miasma of the NYC subway. The air was a mix of hot electronics, oil, and a million different human stories. The clamor of chattering voices, echoing footsteps, and the distant rumble of trains was a calming balm to Marti.

She rode north for twenty minutes, exited at Times Square, and then walked west. She navigated the streets with a seasoned familiarity, stepping around sidewalk vendors and weaving through the throngs of pedestrians. Hell's Kitchen, despite its menacing moniker, was an area of contrast. A symphony of city life, it was a place where the old grit of New York blended with the gleam of gentrification. The crowds thinned as she crossed 9th and she was almost alone when she passed 10th.

The street she was heading to was a fusion of this diversity: Grimy dive bars and second-hand stores nestled side by side with upscale eateries and glitzy high-rise condominiums. The buildings were a mishmash of styles, from old brick and stone structures whispering stories from the last century to sleek glass and steel towers reaching for the sky.

When she reached number 28, she casually glanced over but maintained her pace. The building housing the supper club struck her with its understated elegance. Tucked comfortably between a laundromat humming with activity and a family-owned bakery emanating comforting aromas of fresh bread, the supper club resided in what appeared to be a standard four-story New York City walk-up. One might easily mistake the building for a residential home or an apartment complex. The building was made of old brick with an unassuming black door, its anonymity preserved, save for a small brass placard displaying the address number at street level. She spotted a diminutive camera tucked into the cornice above the door and she was sure there were more she didn't see and never would. The building may have appeared ordinary, but she knew it held many secrets within its walls. She was only interested in one of them.

She found a bus stop halfway up the block, an unassuming plastic alcove that provided a direct line of sight to the club's entrance. She seated herself, her eyes never leaving the black door. She had no idea if Herschel would show up today, but she had to hope he was a man of habit.

***

Luck was smiling on her today. Marti had barely settled onto the hard plastic bench of the bus stop when she spotted him making his way down the street. Even from a distance, she could recognize his distinctive gait, a confident stride that spoke of authority and power. As he moved closer, the telltale port-wine stain splashed across the left side of his face came into view. Time had etched lines into his face and grayed his hair, but he still emanated a palpable sense of strength.

With a casual practiced ease, Herschel stopped at the black door. He pressed the doorbell set into the frame. There was a momentary pause, long enough for an unseen observer inside to verify his identity, then with an almost imperceptible nod Herschel pushed open the door and disappeared inside.

From her vantage point at the bus stop, Marti watched the door close behind him. The man who had once loomed so large in her life, and had caused so much damage, was now once again within her reach. She just had to get through that door.

Marti's mind began to drift back to the past, to the aftermath of the night that had changed her life forever. She had woken up in a sterile hospital room with the steady beep of a heart monitor her only companion. It would be two days before someone told her that Joel hadn't been so lucky. He had died on the floor of the bedroom within arm's reach of her.

The intruders that night had been the golden boys of the department, members of the Violent Gang Task Force, known as the Vig. Their job was to clean up the streets, take guns off the streets, and reduce violence. But in the shadows, they led a dual existence, plundering money, jewelry, drugs, and weapons from the very criminals they were supposed to apprehend. They gouged the already cash-strapped city for overtime and hours they never worked.

Did they face justice? No. The truth of their misdeeds came out in an internal review report, a document that was quickly buried deep within the department's archives, never to see the light of day. The chief and his staff made sure of that. The main players eventually lost their jobs, and their badges, but no one went to jail. The real story never made it to the public; even within the department, not everyone knew the full extent of it.

All most of the rank-and-file saw was the disbandment of the Vig, a dead officer, and a rookie who had barely started her career. You can guess who bore the brunt of the department's anger, and who became the scapegoat in the aftermath. The events of that fateful night had ended her career almost as soon as it had begun, leaving her with a legacy she hadn't earned and didn't deserve.

***

She stood. Her heart raced in her chest as she walked down the block, her mind still clouded with the bitter memories of the past. Each step felt heavy as if she dragged the weight of her past behind her. But there was no clever or covert way to navigate through this, not that she could see. She heard the voice of her Nana echoing in her head: 'Darlin', in my day, we didn't have time for fancy talkin'. We said what needed sayin' without all the fluff and feathers.'

The direct approach was all she had left. She didn't have much to lose, after all.

Taking a deep breath, she rang the bell. She waited, each second ticking by with agonizing slowness. It was much longer than it had taken for Herschel, and for a moment, she thought they might not let her in. But then she heard it, the soft click of the lock disengaging.

She opened the door and stepped inside.

***

The dim light from the interior washed over her, and for a moment, she stood there, letting her eyes adjust. It was quieter than she had expected, the hushed murmur of conversation barely penetrating the jazz playing in the background.

She was in. Now came the hard part.

She stood in a small foyer with a tall desk positioned directly ahead and an open door just behind and to the left of the desk. She could discern the edge of a dark, wooden bar and an array of hanging glasses through the door but nothing else. A man stood behind the desk. He could be anywhere between forty and seventy. His face was smooth and unlined. His gray hair was styled short. He wore what appeared to Marti's eye to be an expensive tailored suit. There was no nametag or even tasteful lapel pin.

As he turned his gaze toward Marti, she half expected him to arch an eyebrow in inquiry, his mouth twisted into a British-accented sneer. But his facial expression remained neutral and when he spoke, his voice was devoid of any particular accent, his enunciation precise.

"I'm sorry, madam, but a membership and a reservation are pre-requisites to dining here." His smile was professionally neutral, a trait honed to perfection, reminiscent of a seasoned airline gate attendant.

"Yes, I realize that. My name is Marti Wells. I'm here to meet with Mr. Herschel."

He didn't break eye contact. "Mr. Herschel's reservation is for one."

"It was a last-minute decision. He might not even be aware himself, but I know he just sat down. I doubt the soup is even cold. Could you ask him?"

His gaze on her lingered and she felt him assessing the situation, weighing the pros and cons of either turning her away and potentially upsetting a member, or admitting her and risking having to apologize later. Ultimately, he opted for the path of least resistance. "Please wait here a moment, madam."

"Of course."

With a swift practiced turn, he disappeared through the doorway and past the end of the bar. Marti immediately seized the opportunity to take two steps forward and peer over the desk. She argued it was professional curiosity—after all, she had a knack for snooping since childhood. She blamed her fondness for Harriet the Spy. But in this case, her curiosity was disappointed. The desk was austere; she doubted even dust was permitted to linger. The only items present were a ledger-style book, currently closed, a multiline telephone, and a small monitor divided into four squares displaying various views of the street outside. Nothing more. No flashing clues. With a sigh, she stepped back.

While she waited for No Name to return, she wondered what she'd do if she was not allowed inside. She didn't think it was the type of place she could force her way into. She decided that even if she was turned away, a type of message would get through to Herschel. He would know that she was onto him and it might force him into more action. That could be useful to Marti.

No Name returned. "Mr. Herschel would be happy to have you join him, Ms. Wells."

The space tucked behind the bar was more intimate than she had anticipated. The lighting was subdued, casting a quiet glow against the dark paneling of the walls. An assortment of small tables, their delicate legs lending an air of elegance, were scattered thoughtfully for privacy. Three plush booths lined the back wall, offering a more secluded setting. The room was speckled with members, their conversations coming to a standstill as No Name guided her past the bar to a reserved table on the right.

"Lieutenant," Marti said.

"No one calls me that anymore."

"What do they call you?"

He nudged the chair opposite him with a foot. "Have a seat, Ms. Wells."

There was a thick, center-cut sirloin on the plate in front of him along with a knife, a pat of butter, and four onion rings. A glass of brown liquid with a large ice cube sat at his elbow.

Marti took in the man as she settled opposite him and he picked up the knife to cut his steak. Decades later, even without the vivid birthmark on his face, Marti would have recognized him instantly. He had the same commanding presence, same broad shoulders and barrel chest. She could see the thin blue line tattoo at the base of his throat. His face was creased with the years, but he still had that same piercing gaze that made her feel like a rookie cop all over again.

"What brings you here this afternoon, Ms. Wells?"

"My current case."

"And that is?"

"My client is involved in a legal matter with Calderone Innovations."

"Powerful people, Smartie. Be careful."

A subtle jab that he remembered her. She took a moment. She looked around the room and wondered how Herschel became a member. He was dressed in a dark suit, but he still stuck out in the room of businessmen and politicians. There was something hard and alien about him. He didn't belong, yet here he was.

"I need to know who sent you up to the Upper East Side two days ago to try to snatch a young woman."

He stabbed a triangle of meat and chewed. "Dominic Blackwood," he said.

Marti hadn't expected a direct answer. She blinked.

"You know him?" Herschel asked. The edge of his lip might have twitched into a grin.

"Never met him."

"Can't imagine you ever will either."

"That who you work for now?"

The steak was gone. He kept his hand on the hilt of the knife and picked up his drink with the other before he took a sip. "One of many."

"Whoever's paying, huh?"

His eyes sparked briefly at that but then he continued, "Not much different than you. People have a problem, I help them fix it."

Marti thought there was a world of difference between what they did but she wasn't going to press her luck. She'd made it inside and she'd learned a name. It was time to go.

"Thank you, Mr. Herschel. You've been quite helpful." Marti stood.

He tipped his glass and popped an onion ring in his mouth but didn't respond.

***

No Name gave her a brief nod and opened the door for her. "Please call next time, Ms. Wells," he said as she went through. Marti resisted the urge to give him a proper New York City salute.

Chapter Twenty

"Dominic Blackwood," Gwen said.

Marti, Gwen, and Angela were sitting around the prep table at the back of Gwen's flower shop. They were alone in the shop. It was after hours and Gwen was finishing up a selection of centerpieces featuring lilies and peonies. They had cut Damian Russo loose from his basement chair and Bear had driven him back in one of the shop's delivery vans to his apartment building in Paterson. Marti didn't expect any more trouble or a peep from Damian. It would be too hard for him to explain to fellow gangsters how a woman got the drop on him. And too dangerous for them to wonder what he might have told her. Marti was sure he'd lay low and hope it all blew over in time.

"Who's Dominic Blackwood?" Angela asked.

"The Rainmaker," Marti replied. "I'm not sure what you'd call him exactly. Is powerbroker an actual thing? He made his first fortune in the initial dot com boom but he didn't get caught up in the bubble bursting. He had a knack for recognizing potential and was not afraid to take risks, which paid off handsomely. Over time, he diversified his portfolio, investing in everything from real estate to pharmaceuticals, and even ventured into media ownership. Today, on paper, he's the head of Artemis Capital Management, a hedge fund and investment firm. In reality, he's a man with a lot of money and a lot of influence."

"The CEO of ACM? That Dominic Blackwood? Why's he interested in Cassidy?"

"He's probably not. Not for himself. Blackwood's real power comes from working behind the scenes. He trades influence and power for favors. I'm guessing Rathbone hired him and the job eventually trickled down to Herschel."

"So he's an upscale gangster?"

"You'd probably find a lot of people that would agree with that assessment."

"If I've got this right, you're up against Rathbone and Blackwood, two men with almost unlimited funds and reach, plus Herschel, an amoral asshole that we know will do just about anything for money. I think the safest thing to do would be to drop the whole thing and ship Cassidy back home to Europe."

"You're probably right but I'm not sure it would be that simple," Angela said. "Rathbone knows about her, maybe even believes she really is Alex's biological daughter. Maybe he even told Blackwood as part of their deal. That's a very powerful secret. I'm not sure he would just let her go."

Gwen nodded her head. "She's right."

Marti agreed with both of them. "The good thing about being between a rock and a hard place is the choices aren't difficult, they are inevitable."

***

After saying goodnight to Angela and Gwen, Marti slid behind the wheel of her car and bid goodbye to her sweet parking spot. You had to celebrate the little things.

As she exited the tunnel and navigated the local streets, her cell phone buzzed from the cup holder. A glance at the screen showed a blocked number. She was busy with the Calderone case, too busy, but she hated to turn down work. At the very least, she might be able to refer a job to a colleague. She plugged in her Bluetooth earpiece and answered the call. "Hello?"

The voice on the other end was raspy and muffled, like someone talking through their hand. "Someone's put a contract out on you." The statement, blunt and chilling, hung in the air. Before she could respond, the voice was gone.

Someone putting out a hit on her given everything involved in this case was not that surprising. The surprising thing was that Detective Klein had warned her about it. A hand over the mouthpiece wasn't enough to hide his native New Yorker vowels. It was a lifeline thrown her way from someone who might just care more than she thought.

She removed the Bluetooth from her ear. Suddenly everything around her felt suspicious. The car next to her. The truck going in the opposite direction. The two men chatting on the sidewalk. She pushed the paranoia away. It wouldn't help. She had to be careful, yes, but not irrational. And for the moment, she had to focus on driving. She'd think about the implications of the call later.

Inside the familiar walls of her apartment building, she felt better, more secure. Pedro kept the locks and front doors well maintained. She'd taken extra measures to secure her own door, too. It was fortified with a steel core, like her office door, and outfitted with additional locks. She was confident it would stand up to anything short of a medieval battering ram. For added reassurance, after she changed into sweats and her St. Peter's sweatshirt, she retrieved her Glock from the bedroom safe, keeping it within arm's reach.

In the cozy confines of her kitchen, Marti set about making a simple late dinner. Tonight's fare was a comforting classic: Grilled cheese and vegetable soup. Marti loved to eat but was a terrible cook. She considered it a personal strength that she knew her limitations. Soup and a sandwich was a regular staple for her and close to the pinnacle of her culinary talents.

Rita Mae lounged nonchalantly on the seat of one of the kitchen chairs, watching Marti's movements with a half-lidded gaze. The enticing smell of melting cheese filled the apartment, causing Rita Mae's ears to twitch in anticipation. Once her own meal was ready, Marti filled a dish with Rita Mae's favorite cat food and placed it on the floor next to her water bowl. The cat gracefully descended from her perch to examine her dinner.

Once dinner was taken care of, Marti slipped the gun into the sweatshirt's front pocket and went downstairs to her basement office. Her office was a sanctuary, a space where she immersed herself in the world of research, case files, and planning. The separation of floors, she felt, provided a necessary boundary between her personal and professional lives. Not that she often felt like she had a personal life, she tried not to bring work upstairs, but tonight, she was bending her own rules.

Retrieving her laptop, she retraced her steps back up the stairs and settled onto her worn but comfortable sofa. Rita Mae, full of kibble, purred contentedly beside her. She opened her laptop and began her research. The Calderone board of directors was a list of names each linked to their own share of power and influence. She needed to understand them, their motivations, and their vulnerabilities. She needed allies, board members who might be open to Cassidy's cause. Or, at the very least, a sympathetic ear in the boardroom to let her state her case, should she manage to get herself into the upcoming meeting.

She spent an hour reading as much as she could find on public sites. Calderone's penchant for secrecy did not make the research easy but she eventually winnowed the 10-member board down to three potential candidates.

Maria Rodriguez, 57, started her career as a financial analyst at a prestigious investment firm before climbing the ranks to become the youngest female partner in the firm's history. Her commitment to fair and ethical business practices earned her a reputation as a maverick in the male-dominated world of finance. Maria was a close confidant of Alex Calderone, and the two shared a vision for the company that prioritized both profit and people. In a rare *Wall Street Journal* article that touched on her work for the Calderone board, Maria had been vocal about her skepticism of the company's often aggressive business tactics.

Audrey Chen, 49, served as a legal consultant to various Fortune 500 companies before joining the Calderone board. Audrey was instrumental in advising Alex Calderone during the company's early expansion stages. She was known for her sharp intellect and unyielding principles inside the courtroom. Marti thought she might be able to appeal to Chen on the black-and-white legal grounds of Cassidy's paternity claim.

The last one was the most tenuous in Marti's mind, but there was something between the lines that made her jot Dr. Anil Sharma down on her list. Maybe it was the professional resemblance to Dr. Ackerley. Or maybe she was desperate and clutching at straws. Sharma was 62 and a respected figure in the tech industry. With a doctorate in Computer Science from CalTech, he was a pioneering force behind several breakthrough innovations in the early days of the internet. He'd made a name for himself as a tech entrepreneur and venture capitalist, investing in socially responsible tech startups. Multiple articles mentioned Dr. Sharma's talent for acting as a mediator during difficult negotiations. He might not side directly with Marti, but he might be open to hearing what she had to say. He was also the newest member of the board and perhaps not as entwined in personal histories as other board members.

As Marti built profiles and connected dots, a plan began to take shape in her mind. Before she closed her laptop and went to bed, she added one more name to her list. Dr. Richard Lancaster, 66, was a recently retired member of the board. Maybe any strict NDAs that he'd been held to as an active board member expired when he stepped down. Judging by his active social media feed, the man had opinions. And he was nearby, too. He was a professor emeritus at Cooper Union just across the river. And, thanks to his just as active Instagram feed, she knew how and where to find him, too.

Chapter
Twenty-One

The next morning arrived far too soon for Marti's liking. The buzzing of the intercom was an unwelcome alarm, its shrill and unceasing drone pulling her from the warm depths of unconsciousness. She was typically a morning person, but this case was throwing her off. She groaned and tried to muffle the noise by burying her head under her pillows, much to the chagrin of Rita Mae, who was comfortably ensconced on top of the pillows.

Then the memory of the late-night phone call/warning from Klein jolted her awake. She sat up abruptly, her heart hammering in her chest, all traces of sleep instantly banished. She reached for her phone, its screen illuminating the dark room with a soft glow: 8:30. She had slept far longer than she had intended, the long hours from the past few days finally catching up with her. It was still early, but not outrageously so. Still, she wasn't expecting anyone.

Feeling a tinge of apprehension, Marti reached for her Glock on the bedside table. Holding the pistol firmly in her hand, she padded softly into the main room, her bare feet silent on the cold wood floor. She approached the intercom with caution, her mind racing through all the possibilities of who could be on the other side of the door.

"Yes?" she said, pressing the intercom button.

"Package for you," a gruff voice replied from the other side.

Marti almost snorted. As if she would fall for that old trick. "Please just leave it on the step," she said, attempting to keep her voice calm and steady.

"I need a signature."

She wished she had a video feed from the front door to check this guy out. That was something to think about for later. She jogged the few yards to the window and looked down. There was a FedEx truck parked up on the curb near the building. That pushed the needle closer to a legit delivery but she was still not convinced. The buzzing started up again. She returned to the intercom.

The guy was getting impatient. That also felt legit.

"Who's it from? What's the return address?" she asked.

"Reynolds Security. Look, lady, what's with the 20 questions? You want this or not."

If this wasn't legit, they'd gone to a lot of effort.

"Stay there, I'm coming down."

Marti quickly threw on a pair of jeans and a T-shirt. She slipped her feet into a pair of old running sneakers, grabbed her keys, and headed out the door, then ducked back inside and grabbed the Glock. She tucked it securely in the waistband of her jeans, hidden under her shirt. She made her way down the three flights of stairs, her heart pounding with a mixture of anticipation and unease.

As she approached the building's entrance, she could see the FedEx driver through the glass door. He was looking at his watch impatiently, a clipboard in his other hand. He was a middle-aged man with a receding hairline and a slightly paunchy build. He looked harmless enough. He didn't look like a hitman, but what did she know?

Marti opened the door and stepped outside, one hand on her hip, never far from the Glock.

"Just need your John Hancock here," he replied, holding out the clipboard for her to sign.

He looked bored and slightly annoyed. She took the clipboard and signed quickly. He took it, made some notations, and then started down the stairs back toward his truck. She resisted the urge to apologize for her questions or caution. Women apologized too much. She watched him climb inside and drive off. Marti's heart rate slowed.

She looked down and studied the package he'd handed her. It was a standard size. Thin, longer than it was wide like you get from a clothing store. She looked up and down the street but saw nothing unusual. She went back inside.

Once safely upstairs in her apartment, Marti sliced open one end of the package with a kitchen knife. Inside was a Reynolds Security uniform, a nametag reading Marcia, a keycard, and a note from Frank. The note read: You are Marcia Brown. A recent hire who typically works at 14 Park Street. But you are filling in at Astral Tower. Be careful. Burn everything when you're done.

She smiled. Frank had come through. Left unsaid was the fact that he now considered them square. His debt was paid. Marti wouldn't disagree.

***

Dr. Richard Lancaster's Instagram feed was an eclectic mix of pictures, but one detail stood out to her—an uncanny number of posts from Union Square each weekday, each one time-stamped between 10 and 11 in the morning. She dressed, took the PATH train to 14th Street, and then walked the last half mile in the late-morning sun.

Union Square was a beloved landmark in the heart of the city, a public plaza that served as a bustling meeting place for locals and tourists alike. Known for its vibrant atmosphere, the Square was a hub for various activities including art shows, live music performances, and political rallies. But perhaps its most charming feature was the weekly farmers' market, a tradition that had been in place for as long as Marti could remember, a haven for chefs and locals alike to get fresh produce in the city.

The park was already teeming with life. The farmers' market was in full swing, the area awash with the colors of fresh fruits and vegetables and the chatter of morning shoppers. Stalls lined the park, vendors calling out their wares while customers browsed the fresh flowers, artisanal cheeses, and homemade bread. The scent of coffee wafted from a nearby stand, mixing with the earthy aroma of the market.

Marti purchased a cup of coffee from one of the stalls, the warm paper cup warming her hands. On an impulse, she also bought a cookie—a small indulgence to make up for the rough wake-up call of the intercom. Marti was great at rationalizing, especially when it came to cookies.

With her hot drink in one hand and the sweet treat in the other, Marti started her saunter through the park. Her eyes scanned the crowd, looking for the familiar face from the pictures she had studied the night before. She walked past the playground, the fountain, and the chess tables, her gaze sweeping over each area before moving on. She finished the cookie with some regret, sweet things rarely lasted long enough for her, and kept walking

Finally, she spotted him in the northwest corner of the central square, engrossed in feeding the pigeons that had flocked around him. She approached cautiously, not wanting to startle him or the birds.

"Dr. Lancaster?"

The man turned his expression to one of polite curiosity. "Yes, and you are?"

"Marti," she said, extending a hand, which he shook. "I just moved to the area. I've seen you around here a few times. You seem to enjoy feeding the pigeons."

"I suppose I do. It's a peaceful way to start the day before the madness begins."

Marti nodded, taking a sip of her coffee. "I can imagine. I hear the world of technology and academia can be quite intense. Even for retired board members."

He raised an eyebrow, his interest piqued. "And how would you know about that?"

"I have a client involved in it," Marti replied, careful to keep her tone casual. "They're having some issues at the moment. I think part of it might come down to a boardroom dispute."

"I see," Dr. Lancaster said, his gaze thoughtful. "Boardroom disputes can be tricky. It's all about alliances and power dynamics."

"That's what I thought," Marti said, her gaze steady on his. To make any sort of progress, they were going to have to ditch the hypothetical and discuss specifics. Could she trust him? Marti didn't think she had any other choice. "I represent someone with a potential interest, both personal and professional, in Calderone Innovations. An interest that is likely to be at least partially decided in the board meeting."

"I'm no longer on the board, as you said."

"But I think you might have some valuable insight into any board members who might be more ... open-minded, more inclined to see my client's point of view."

Lancaster glanced around, then looked down and was quiet for a long time. He turned the small brown bag he was holding upside down to dump out the last of the crumbs. The birds swarmed forward to fight over the last specks of the meal.

Then he turned back to her. "Does your client happen to be from Norway?"

Marti blinked in surprise and had to work hard to conceal her shock.

Lancaster continued, "Perhaps we should continue this conversation somewhere a bit more private?"

Chapter Twenty-Two

L eaving the bustling park, Marti and Dr. Lancaster walked a short distance to a nearby cafe. The quaint establishment was nestled between two larger buildings, its exterior charmingly rustic with its brick facade and large front window. A chalkboard sign stood by the entrance, displaying the day's specials in swirling script.

Inside, the cafe was warm and inviting. The smell of freshly ground coffee filled the air, mingling with the subtle scent of baked goods. That would be the scent of the afterlife for Marti: Caffeine and pastries. Vintage photos adorned the pale-yellow walls, adding a touch of nostalgia. Marti recognized Television's debut punk album Marquee Moon playing over the speakers just loud enough to be heard over the hum of conversation and the clinking of ceramic cups and it made her think of Angela and Riot Lillies.

They found a small table near the back, offering a bit of privacy. After placing their orders with a friendly waitress, they resumed their conversation.

"Why did you mention Norway?"

Dr. Lancaster's expression softened into a wistful smile. "Alex Calderone ... he mentioned it once, after a few drinks. That was rare for him. Both the confession and the alcohol. He wasn't a big drinker, but that night he'd had a bit more than usual." His gaze became distant as if he was seeing something Marti couldn't. "He talked about a post-doc backpacking trip. The usual young man's jaunt across Europe. But he mentioned a woman he'd met in Norway. They'd spent a very intense weekend together."

Marti leaned forward, intrigued. "And he didn't follow up with her?"

Lancaster shook his head, his eyes still lost in memory. "He regretted that, I think. He never even got her full name and they lost touch. He became engrossed in building his company. Alex was very single-minded in that respect. By the time he came up for air, ten years had passed. But I think he carried that memory with him. He never mentioned it again directly, but he did talk about this feeling of a missed connection out there. A lingering thread. It was a different side of him. Away from the boardrooms and business dealings. Just a young man falling head-over-heels for a woman in a far-off country the way only the young can." He focused back on Marti, his expression serious. "I was close to Alex. Not just as a business confidant, but also as a friend. His parents ... well, after what happened to them, he didn't have many people he could trust. Maybe that's why he told me about Norway, about the woman. I've thought about that a lot in the time since his death. I was thinking about it this morning, actually, and then just a short time later, you showed up. So why don't you tell me what's going on."

Marti took a deep breath and came to a decision. It was time to burn the bridges behind her. She had to trust him. She wouldn't get through this with half measures. "There's a woman, Cassidy Calderone," she said, watching as his eyebrows raised in recognition. "She is not using that last name. She's using her mother's maiden name, but she is claiming to be Alex's daughter."

Dr. Lancaster was silent, his coffee cup halfway to his lips. He put it down, his eyes not leaving Marti's. "Cassidy," he echoed, barely a whisper in the quiet cafe.

"I'm representing her," Marti continued, holding his gaze. "She came to me with the claim, and everything we've found so far ... points to her being truthful. From what you've just told me, the timing works. She looks to be the right age."

Lancaster leaned back in his chair, his eyes thoughtful. "So, Alex had a daughter. A daughter he never knew about ..."

"It seems that way. Cassidy is seeking recognition and her rightful place in the Calderone family. And that includes a stake in the business. She's filed a paternity suit in California on Alex's estate but there's a gag order as someone, likely someone at Calderone, tries to stop it or at least drag it out until control of the company is already decided."

The implications of her words hung heavily in the air. Lancaster seemed to grasp them immediately. His eyes narrowed in understanding as Marti's words sunk in. The silence that followed was broken only by the faint strains of jazz and the distant clatter of dishes from the cafe's kitchen. "This ... changes everything," he finally said, his voice barely above a whisper.

***

He sighed, scratching his chin. "Calderone's board is a tough crowd. Alex liked to be challenged and he believed that companies often died or were eventually disrupted in the market because they stagnated. He didn't want that for his business. He made sure the board included people who would push back against ideas and future directions.

People who would challenge the status quo and not just rubber stamp things to keep the gravy train going. That worked well when Alex was there, but it also promoted some palace intrigue. Different factions and alliances."

"Led by Victor Rathbone?"

"He was certainly a loud voice and getting louder even when Alex was around. I can only imagine what it's like now without Alex's stabilizing influence."

"And what does he want?"

"That is a very good question and not one with an easy answer. Victor Rathbone possesses a shrewd intellect and an almost preternatural gift for manipulation whether it's machines or people. Often what he wants is not what he's asking for. He views almost everything like a game of three-dimensional chess."

"I've heard his interests lie with advances in artificial intelligence."

"Yes, that's true. That's always been an area of interest since he started with Calderone. He sees artificial intelligence as a tool, maybe eventually a sentient tool, that will have the greatest impact on humanity since, well, since nothing. It will change our future as a species."

"For better or worse?"

Lancaster smiled. "I don't know and don't believe anyone that tells you they do, but Victor was determined to find out as fast as possible. He wants no guardrails and no cap on the funding Calderone allocated toward AI."

"But not all the board felt the same?"

"I shudder to think of a topic where the entire board might agree, but no, not everyone shared Victor's enthusiasm."

"And what does he want to do with any advances? What is his ultimate goal? A monopoly on AI robots? Calderone as the unchallenged business in an AI-dominated world? A modern-day robber baron?"

Lancaster shook his head. "I was honest when I said I didn't know. Rathbone is exceptionally secretive about his plans, but I fear your ambitions might be too small. Calderone is already one of the top businesses in the world by any measure. Much of the recent public advances in AI are on the backbone of Calderone's patents. A simple monopoly or more money to line his pockets wouldn't be enough to drive Rathbone. It would have to be something bigger. He truly believes embracing AI will be the next advancement for our species. Maybe even save our species from extinction."

Marti nodded. "And what about you, Dr. Lancaster? Where do you stand?"

"I was, I suppose I still am, on the skeptical side of the fence. I believe it will have an impact, but I'm more nervous than some about whether it will be positive or negative. It is easy to see some of the early negative impacts already: Job displacement, certainly. Potential security risks. The ethical dilemmas and potential loss of even more privacy as our dependence on AI grows. I could go on. I did go on at the board meetings which is probably why I was forced to resign."

"I thought you retired."

"A more polite euphemism. But my biggest concerns were the things we couldn't see yet. Unintended consequences. The complexity of AI systems makes it difficult to anticipate and predict all possible consequences. We just don't know what the ultimate impact could be on a social, economic, or cultural scale."

Marti finally was able to get to the crux of this meeting. "Are there any active board members who share your views?"

He sipped his drink and thought about the question. "I can think of two who might share similar views to mine. Maria Rodriguez and Audrey Chen. I don't know for sure, but they'd voiced some skepticism of Rathbone's proposals in the past for different reasons. If you plan on approaching either of them, you might need different strategies. Maria is a woman of the people. She would always insist on looking at the impact on our employees or end users while Audrey's primary concern is the law."

Marti finished the last of her coffee. She felt good that Lancaster had named two of the three people she'd picked out from her research. "Thank you, Dr. Lancaster. You've been very helpful. I might be in touch later."

"Be careful."

It was a refrain Marti was hearing from more and more people.

Chapter
Twenty-Three

The faded paint and rust patches of Marti's old Subaru blended seamlessly with the grit and grime of Red Hook as they pulled off the highway. Old warehouses rose like steel skeletons, adorned with faded graffiti and the patina of hard times. Between them, the cobblestone streets of Brooklyn stretched out like arteries, veining out in all directions. Angela's eyes narrowed as she surveyed the scene, her disbelief palpable. Marti hooked a quick left at the bottom of the ramp and pulled into a large parking lot.

"That's the place?" Angela asked, her tone laced with skepticism as she regarded a sizable warehouse-like building ahead. A few motorcycles were parked outside in a display of shiny chrome, while the distant thrum of rock music pulsed like a steady heartbeat from behind the roll-top garage door.

"Yes, that's it. The home of The Iron Sirens," Marti confirmed. Cassidy, in the back seat, was quiet, her eyes glazed over from painkillers but maybe carrying a glint of curiosity as she peered out the windshield between Marti and Angela.

As they pulled up close to the building, a heavy metal door just to the left of the roll-top opened with a screeching protest. A short, fiery-haired woman emerged, her vivacious energy cutting through the industrial setting like a beacon. Savvy Delgado, president of The Iron Sirens, greeted them as they stepped out of the car with a toothy smile and a set of sleeve tattoos adorning each arm. "Welcome to The Iron Sirens," she called out, her voice carrying easily over the distant hum of conversation and music from inside the clubhouse. "We've been expecting you."

Marti's friend, Savannah 'Savvy' Delgado, was an enigma wrapped in a paradox. A petite, vivacious woman with a shock of red hair, Savvy had a smile that could light up a room and a contagious laugh. She was also one of the most caring and compassionate individuals Marti had ever met. It was these qualities that made her an exceptional nurse, loved by her patients and respected by her colleagues.

But Savvy had another side to her, one that was just as much a part of her as her caring nature. Savvy was a proud member of The Iron Sirens, an all-female biker gang known for their fierce loyalty to each other, their community, and their love for the open road. Savvy's biker lifestyle might have seemed at odds with her profession, but, like Gwen, she had always been a master at balancing the two. Her Harley-Davidson was as much a part of her as her nurse's uniform.

Savvy and Marti had met during their college years and had been fast friends ever since. She was one of the few other square pegs on the round Vassar campus. Despite their vastly different careers and lifestyles, they shared a bond that had proven unbreakable over the decades. Savvy, also like Gwen, was one of the few people Marti trusted implicitly, and they had been there for each other through thick and thin.

Although Savvy's biker lifestyle often raised eyebrows, it was also a testament to her courage and determination. She had never been one to bow down to societal expectations, and her ability to juggle her profession and her passion was a testament to that belief. In many ways, Savvy was a living embodiment of the age-old saying: Never judge a book by its cover.

***

Once inside The Iron Sirens' headquarters, Savvy led Marti, Angela, and Cassidy through a labyrinth of rough-hewn corridors to a room at the rear of the building. The space was surprisingly clean and spartan, devoid of the rock-and-roll paraphernalia that adorned the rest of the clubhouse. The music had dropped to a whisper. It wouldn't be audible with the door closed. A solitary cot, a toilet, a small table with a couple of chairs, and a stark white first aid cabinet were the only furnishings.

"You probably weren't expecting this," Savvy admitted, gesturing around the room. Her fiery red hair seemed even more vibrant against the stark simplicity of the room. "But for some cases, the usual medical route or the usual treatment program isn't enough or isn't the right fit."

She moved to the first aid cabinet, opening it to reveal neatly organized shelves filled with an array of pharmaceutical and natural remedies. "We call it The Siren's Cure," she explained, her eyes meeting Marti's. "It's a blend of traditional detox treatments, holistic therapy, and biker toughness."

Savvy pulled out a small box containing what looked like dried herbs and a jar of dark, viscous liquid. "This," she said, holding up the box, "is a blend of herbs we use for detox teas. They help to cleanse the system and reduce withdrawal symptoms."

She then pointed to the jar. "This is raw organic honey. It's good for soothing the throat, especially when the nausea kicks in, and it's packed with nutrients. Plus, it's a natural energy booster."

Savvy then gestured toward a small mat rolled up in the corner. "Yoga," she said with a nod. "Helps with the physical discomfort and the mental stress. Plus, it builds strength and flexibility."

Seeing the skepticism on Angela's face, Savvy grinned. "I know it sounds unconventional. But we're not exactly a conventional bunch. And you aren't here for the conventional. The Siren's Cure isn't just about getting clean. It's about rediscovering strength and resilience. It's about becoming an Iron Siren."

With that, she led Cassidy to the cot. "The road to recovery isn't easy," Savvy acknowledged. "But here, Cassidy won't have to face it alone. She'll have her Iron Sirens sisters at her side, every step of the way."

As Savvy finished speaking, Angela turned to Cassidy, her face etched with concern. The young woman looked small in the sparse room, her gaze drifting between the cot and the boxes of herbal remedies to the yoga mat. "Cassidy," Angela said softly, her voice cutting through the tense silence. "Is this what you want? Are you ready to take this step?"

Cassidy remained silent for a moment, her blue eyes reflecting a mix of fear and determination. She glanced at Savvy, then Marti, and finally rested her gaze back on Angela.

"Yes," she said, her voice barely a whisper. "I ... I want to get better. I'm ready."

***

The old Subaru hummed quietly as it cruised down the cracked and crumbling BQE back toward the city's skyscrapers. Angela sat in the passenger seat, her fingers tapping anxiously against her purse. She stole a glance at Marti, who had her eyes fixed on the road, a determined set to her jaw. Driving on the Brooklyn-Queens Expressway was not for the faint of heart.

"Are you sure about this, Marti?" Angela finally asked, her voice barely above a whisper. "Cassidy ... at The Iron Sirens' clubhouse ... It's just ..."

Marti held up a hand, cutting her off. "One week, Angela," she said firmly. "Savvy's treatment may be unconventional, but I trust her. I've seen it work before. Many times. Plus, this will also keep her safe. No one is going to find her out here in a week. And most importantly, Cassidy wants to get better. We owe it to her to give this a shot."

Angela nodded, taking a deep breath and staring out the window at the passing urban landscape. Marti let the silence stretch for a moment before shifting gears.

"Now, I wanted to ask you about those discovery documents from the paternity suit," she said, her tone businesslike, as she tried to shake Angela out of her mood. "Do they include the incorporation documents?"

Angela blinked, taken aback by the sudden change in topic. "I think so. I'm not entirely sure, but it would be unusual not to include them."

"Okay, what about anything about the board of directors? The bylaws, voting procedures, that sort of thing?"

"Yes, that should be there as well," she said. "They slapped NDAs on everything, but they should be included as part of discovery."

Marti nodded, her hands tightening on the steering wheel. "Good. I need to understand their procedures. How they make decisions, who has voting power ... Can you get that information for me?"

Angela was silent for a moment before giving a small nod. "I can have someone look into it," she said, pulling out her phone. "I'm sure it's there, but it's a mountain of paper; it's just going to be a matter of finding it."

"Good. Email or call me when you do," Marti said. "We can't do much for Cassidy right now, but we can make sure we're prepared in every other way for what comes next."

Chapter Twenty-Four

After dropping Angela off at her West Side apartment, Marti waded through the late afternoon traffic back to Jersey City. Parking her car, Marti allowed her head to drop and rest on the steering wheel for a brief moment. She could sense a wave of exhaustion cresting over her, extending beyond the physical to the mental and emotional, as well.

With the board meeting still a week away and no clear plan, she felt a weight pressing on her even without considering the potential hit out on her. She wasn't sure what to think of that. It was difficult to wrap her rational mind around it. She'd been cautious the past two days and had seen nothing to make her suspicious. She wasn't dismissing it, but she thought it was more likely a scare tactic by Rathbone, or someone connected to Calderone, designed to get her to drop Cassidy's case. First, they tried to push Cassidy, now they were going after her.

She decided to take a break from Calderone and get a little distance, even for just a few hours. Cassidy wasn't her only client and she had bills to pay. She would head down to her office and catch up on some of the slower-burning cases that ensured the cash kept flowing for Americanos and the laundry office lights stayed on. She had a glamorous life.

As she opened the back door and made for the basement stairs, she ran into Pedro. Any time she thought she might be working too hard, she only had to think of Pedro to prove herself wrong. He was doing the job of security guard, custodian, and doorman.

"Hey, Pedro," she said.

"Marti," he nodded in response, his brow furrowing slightly. "A man was here earlier asking about you."

Marti's steps faltered. "What did he look like? Did he have a birthmark on his cheek?" She raised a hand and indicated the left side of her face.

Pedro shrugged, "No, no birthmark. Blond hair, slim, fair. Dressed in a nice suit. Just a normal-looking guy."

Definitely not Herschel, but that didn't ease her anxiety any. "Did he say what he wanted?"

"Nope. Just asked for you. I thought maybe he was a client." Pedro paused as if debating whether to say more, then continued. "But he gave off a funny vibe. At home, we used to call it the *corazonada*." He looked slightly embarrassed now. "Rosa always tells me to pay attention when I get those hunches so I didn't let him in. I watched him until he was out of sight. I'm sorry if I cost you some work."

Marti waved off his apology. "Not your fault, Pedro. If he needs my help, he'll try again. Maybe email or call. I agree with your wife. You should listen to those instincts."

With a nod and a brief smile, she continued down to her office. But as she sank into her chair and tried to focus on the files in front of her, she couldn't shake off the prickling sensation at the back of her neck. The idea of being watched, being sought out, was unsettling.

Was the man a prospective client? Typically, Cassidy being the rare exception, initial inquiries happened with a phone call or an email like she'd told Pedro. She didn't publicly disclose her office location. If she needed an in-person meeting she went to the client. Or, she met them at Cafe Grand. Could it be something else? Could it really be connected to Klein's warning?

She shook her head, trying to dispel the paranoid feeling and focus on the work in front of her. But it lingered like an unwelcome guest in her thoughts. She stood and closed her office door despite the laundry room being unoccupied. She sat back down and on a whim browsed the web until she found a YouTube stream of The Riot Lillies' debut album from 1996, 'Punk Petals.' Marti smiled again at the sight of a much younger Angela snarling on the album's cover. She pressed play. Music was always a good distraction from her inner thoughts. The opening track 'Thorned Velvet,' set the tone for the entire album. It had a fast-paced rhythm, driving bass lines, and sharp, biting lyrics that immediately grabbed the listener's attention. The lead vocals were both raw and richly melodic. Marti was pleasantly surprised. She liked it. She turned it down but left it on in the background as she looked through the other active cases she was juggling. All of the cases were more indicative of her typical workday than what she was doing for Cassidy.

First, she checked the honey traps she'd set for Figueroa. He'd slipped up once and she'd been close to nailing him, but he proved just a little too slippery, then she'd gotten involved with Cassidy and hadn't kept the heat on. She didn't think he'd be fooled again and she was right. The traps hadn't been touched. Figueroa and his pilfered millions were likely sipping boat drinks in a warm climate with a nonextradition treaty. She'd have to go back through his case and find another angle. For now, she closed the file and moved on.

Next up was a missing persons investigation which, in reality, and less politically correct language, was tracking down a deadbeat dad. Marti loathed and loved these cases. She hated that they were necessary but she loved running these pricks down. Robert 'Bobby' Daniels, a 40-year-old father of two, was a typical case. He'd done a runner and his ex-wife, Laura, hired a lawyer when the court-ordered alimony and child support payments stopped coming. The lawyer hired Marti. She'd spoken with Robert's last known employer, a construction company, where he worked as a laborer. They confirmed he no-showed his job without notice at about the same time the payments stopped.

Marti had plans to reach out to Bobby's known associates, friends, and family and interview them but that would have to wait. Today, she sent off emails to the local shelters, bars, and other construction companies based in neighboring towns. She also checked her databases for any new addresses, licenses, or recent legal activities involving Daniels, but came up dry.

She moved on to Lakeside Electronics, a local electronics wholesaler, who had noticed an unusual shrinkage in their warehouse inventory. They suspected employees might be stealing goods. So far, Marti had interviewed the warehouse manager and some employees, focusing on those with access to the inventory. She'd also reviewed security footage but hadn't spotted anything suspicious.

She'd have to eventually conduct discreet undercover surveillance at the warehouse during various shifts, but she could still put in some billable hours cross-referencing the timing of missing inventory with employees' work schedules to see if any patterns emerged. She did that for an hour and didn't find any obvious patterns, but did end up with a list of employee names that might be useful later.

Her stomach reminded her that she hadn't eaten dinner yet, but she had one more case file in her pile. This one pertained to insurance fraud. A PI's bread-and-butter. Patricia Thompson, a 35-year-old office worker, had claimed a severe back injury following a minor auto accident. SureGuard Insurance had flagged the claim due to the minor damage to the vehicle and the high cost of Patricia's medical bills. Marti received a copy of the accident report and spoke with the responding police officer. Next, she wanted to interview the other driver involved in the accident. She got the details from the report and tried to call, but it went to voicemail. She left a message and then followed up with an email.

Unable to think of anything more to do, she shut down the laptop, locked the office door, and went upstairs to search for food in her forlorn cupboards.

She knew something was wrong before she put the key in the door, but it took time to register in her brain. She turned the knob and the smell of olive oil, garlic, and oregano almost made her fall to her knees. She glanced at the door. Yes, it was the right apartment but something was off. Then she heard Rita Mae purring. Definitely off. She stepped inside and despite the decadent smell of an Italian market enveloping her, she had the presence of mind to put her hand on her gun.

"Hello?"

"Do you prefer a chianti or a Barolo?"

Chapter Twenty-Five

What had Pedro said? Just a guy. Blond hair, slim, fair. She should have known.

Miles Rothchild.

A locked door in Marti's mind sprung open and she was once again on York Street staring at that house where everything had gone so wrong.

***

She sat in her car across the street. She was alone. Her ribs ached. She fingered the top of the aspirin bottle in the cup holder but held off on taking any more just yet. The elastic bandage from the hospital gave her a sense of support, but it still hurt like a bitch to take a breath. She did her best to ignore it but she had to keep breathing. Her eyes flicked to her rearview mirror, at least the swelling around her nose and left eye had lessened, and her face no longer looked like a purple marshmallow.

She turned her attention back to the house. In her mind, it was not 126 York in Paulus Hook. It was simply The House. With a capital T and a capital H. She stared at it, but no longer saw it. It was imprinted on her mind. When she closed her eyes, she could still recall all the intricate details. A sprawling, classic northeast townhouse with a brick facade and ornate scrolling at the cornices and large windows that took up three-quarters of the block in this tony enclave of Jersey City. She knew each inch. It was the scene of the incident that had altered her life forever.

The gears of the political machine turned slowly but she could see where it was headed. She knew, even half loopy on morphine, when they came to visit her in the hospital that the fix was in. A plan had been made. She didn't know the specifics quite yet but she heard the rumors, the whispers, the side glances. Her career as a cop was over. It was just a matter of time. But she was determined to find out why. So, while the brass covered their asses, she watched the house.

She had been sitting there for hours, over the past two days; her gaze rarely leaving the building. The sun had risen and set, casting long shadows that danced and flickered with the passing day. Yet the house remained still, almost as if frozen in time.

***

As she watched, she kept replaying the night of the attack over and over in her mind. The masked figures in the bedroom, the third man emerging from the closet, the sound of gunshots and Joel's shout that abruptly turned into a gasp. The memories were still raw and vivid, and she could almost feel the phantom echoes of her attacker's punches pounding her in the ribs.

Every so often, she would glance at the passenger seat, half expecting to see Joel sitting there, ready with a stupid remark to lighten the mood. But the seat remained empty. Her father and sister had stopped by the hospital but she'd sent them away. Too ashamed to look her father in the eye. The silence was deafening and she felt a deep, gnawing loneliness.

She had tried the direct approach. She had knocked on the door, peered through the windows, and even circled around the back. But it was as if the house was holding its breath, refusing to give up its secrets. The place had been cleaned up since the police had been through and now it stood as a lifeless shell, bearing no signs of the trauma that had taken place on the second floor. And no sign of the man who had been the target of the attack. She found no information about him in the police reports. No witness statements. The envelope the man said he left on the bed had disappeared. Whatever it contained and whatever he'd wanted her to do with it was lost. It was as if she imagined him, but she knew that wasn't true. He was real. He existed. Just like the house across the street. The man and Marti were connected now.

She felt a wave of frustration and anger. There was something there, something she was missing. She needed to know who the stranger was, why he was there that night, and where he had gone. She knew it would make no difference, change nothing in the long run, but not knowing was eating at her; a constant, gnawing hunger that refused to be satiated.

***

A day parked in the summer heat had transformed her car into a sweltering greenhouse. In the growing twilight, the streetlights cast a soft glow on the empty street but offered little relief. Sweat trickled down Marti's forehead. The car was filled with a hot sourness that even the fast-food wrappers and acrid coffee couldn't mask. She knew she should probably go home, get some rest, and try again tomorrow. Or not try again. Many people close to her would like to see her drop it, but she couldn't shake the feeling that what she needed started within the walls of that damn house.

She had lost eight days in the hospital, two more burying and mourning Joel. Now, she was on borrowed time, every passing day taking her further away from the incident and closer, she was sure, to losing her job. Without the access and authority of her badge, this endeavor would only get harder. The house was her only lead, her only connection to the mysterious stranger, and she wasn't going to give it up without a fight. Even if everyone told her it was a bad idea, she couldn't just sit back and do nothing. She'd end up guzzling Merlot at 11 a.m. and trying to drown herself in self-pity.

As the day faded, she settled in, ready to spend another long night watching the house. She would not be the first to crack. She had nothing to give up, so why stop? The emptiness within her was mirrored in the emptiness of the house across the street. But she was determined to beat it, to find answers, to find justice for Joel, if not for herself. She was confident the secrets would come if she was patient.

She woke with a start. She had fallen asleep slumped against the window, the unforgiving hardness of it now a painful imprint on her cheek. Her injuries throbbed with a dull persistence without the mask of painkillers to cover them up. Sweat clung to Marti like a second skin, her clothes sticking uncomfortably to her back.

A grating rumble jolted her awake, the sound of heavy machinery echoing down the quiet street. The early-morning darkness was punctuated by the intermittent flash of yellow and red lights. Marti blinked against the glare, watching as the garbage truck trundled slowly toward her.

A spark of an idea ignited in her mind. The garbage. She checked on the first day and the trash had been emptied since that night and the house had been cleaned since the crime scene crew went through, but maybe there was still a lead there. The chance was slim, yet with nothing but time stretching before her, slim was all she had.

With a grunt of pain, she pushed open the car door. Her muscles screamed in protest. She almost buckled under the sudden wave of dizziness that washed over her as she tried to stand. The world tipped dangerously and she staggered against the car for support, her breath coming in short, sharp gasps. Her body was not yet healed and it was not shy about reminding her.

She should go home and sleep for three days. She didn't.

She forced herself to take one step, then another, her gaze locked on the slow-moving truck ahead. The effort sent fresh waves of nausea rolling through her, but she gritted her teeth and pushed on. The stench of garbage grew stronger as she neared the truck, a smell she would usually find repulsive, but now held the potential promise of answers and, she sheepishly realized, would likely mask her own rank odor.

She approached the garbage truck where two men were busy emptying curbside cans into the compacter in the back.

"Excuse me," she called out, her voice hoarse. The men paused and looked at her. "Do you service that house up the street?" She half turned and indicated 126 York.

One of them, a burly guy with a scruffy beard, shrugged. "Sure, we do the whole street. Why?"

"Just trying to find out who owns it," she said, forcing a casual tone.

"Sorry, lady," the bearded man replied with a wry smile. "People don't usually strike up conversations with their garbage men, let alone friendships, and we don't read the discarded mail. I couldn't tell you who lives in any of these houses."

Marti nodded, deflated but not defeated. An idea sparked in her mind. "What about the bill? Who pays for pickup services?"

The other man, lean and tall, laughed. "Not our department. Do we look like accountants? But you could try our office." He pointed to a number printed below the company logo on the side of the truck.

"Thanks," she said, her voice barely more than a whisper. The men nodded and jumped back onto the truck as it rumbled off down the street.

As she hobbled back to her car, she noticed a small sticker, almost shaped like a badge, in the lower window of one home. She paused and moved closer until she could read the words: Paulus Hook Historical Preservation Association. That was a mouthful, but Marti realized she'd also seen the sticker before on the block. She made her way back to the car and found four more stickers. Not on every townhouse but on the majority. If she'd learned one thing during her time on patrol it was that those neighborhood associations always knew the gossip.

She painfully sat back down in her car and swung her legs in. If she was playing long odds, it was better to have two chances than just one.

Chapter Twenty-Six

M arti reluctantly returned to her apartment. It took almost fifteen agonizing minutes that left her breathless and sweating, but she made the climb up the five flights to her door and then collapsed onto her couch. Marti pulled out her phone and dialed the number she got off the side of the garbage truck. The garbage might be picked up before sunrise, but the office didn't follow a similar schedule. An automated message politely informed her that Haul in One Sanitation office hours were 9 a.m. Monday through Friday. She'd lost all sense of time in the last few days. She only recognized night and day. A glance at her watch confirmed she was calling far too early.

Seeing the futility of also trying the Historical Preservation Association number, she abandoned the idea and focused on standing back up. When she'd accomplished that, she made her way to the bathroom, her body aching with every step. She felt like her internal organs had been beaten with a hammer. She stepped into the shower and let the scalding water wash over her until her skin glowed an angry pink. When the water eventually turned cold, she stepped out and gingerly toweled off while she tried to avoid catching glances of her purple and yellow mottled skin in the mirror.

She slipped into her old police academy sweats—the softest and most comfortable thing she owned. Getting dressed was an ordeal with her injuries; pulling on her socks was the hardest part of all. Sitting on the edge of the bed, hunched over, grimacing as pain shot through her body, she tried to hook her socks over her toes. She failed three times, gave up, and lay back on the bed exhausted.

The next thing she knew, the sun was streaming through her small bedroom window, bathing the room in a warm, golden glow. She blinked, disoriented, and looked at the clock. Four hours had passed. With a groan, she pushed herself upright and started her day for the second time.

***

Marti sat at her worn wooden kitchen table, squinting against the perky sunshine, and nursed the cup of instant coffee she'd heated up in the microwave. Her second one, to be precise. The first had merely opened her eyes; the second she hoped would kickstart her foggy brain into gear. She tossed back four aspirin like candy, the chalky residue sticking in her throat. The muddy water of the coffee washed it down, leaving behind a faintly bitter taste that she was too familiar with these days.

She had no appetite but knew she should eat and forced herself to prepare breakfast: A couple of eggs scrambled to the edge of rubbery and two slices of toast burnt just beyond golden. She stared down at the plate for a moment then carried it back to the table. Good enough, she thought, but her stomach rumbled at the sight of it. She slowly worked her way through the meager meal and felt the aspirin and food begin to dull the sharpest edges of her discomfort.

Pushing the plate aside, she picked up her phone and dialed the number for Haul in One Sanitation. A chirpy voice on the other end of the line answered, "Good morning, Haul in One Sanitation, how can I help you today?"

Marti felt a wave of irritation at the woman's perky energy but forced herself to remain calm. "Hi there," she began, trying to pitch her voice to sound like a harried property manager. "I'm taking over the maintenance of a property and I just wanted to make sure you have the correct contact and billing information."

She might get easier answers if she used her badge but something told her to hold back. That she might not want this coming back on her through official channels.

The woman's response came quick and breezy, "Oh, sure thing! Could you just confirm the property address for me?"

"126 York in Paulus Hook."

Marti could hear the tapping of keys as the woman pulled up the account. "Okay," the woman said, "we have the billing under the name of Phoenix LLC. The contact person listed is Mr. Ash Featherly. Is that the information you have?"

Marti's heart sank. Phoenix LLC was the same shell company name she'd run into during her initial deed searches. And 'Ash Featherly' was made up. Someone with a sense of wordplay based on the idea of a company named after the mythical phoenix.

"Yes, that's correct," Marti replied, her voice flat.

The woman, oblivious to Marti's disappointment, wrapped up the call cheerfully, "Great! Well, if you have any other questions or changes, just give us a call. Have a nice day!"

Marti set her phone down, her gaze unfocused as she stared at the snaking wood grain of the table. Yet another dead end. Someone had been extremely careful. But why? What was so special about that house?

She'd been up for barely an hour but could feel the exhaustion stalking her already. She punched in the number for the Paulus Hook Preservation Association before her body and mind could betray her into taking a nap. The call connected almost immediately, and a woman's voice boomed through the line. "Paulus Hook Preservation, this is Evelyn speaking. How can I assist you today?" Evelyn's voice was sharp and businesslike and felt like a paring knife being inserted between Marti's ears.

"Hello, Evelyn," Marti greeted, gritting her teeth. "I'm calling about the property at 126 York. Do you know if that property is a member of your association?"

Evelyn gave a derisive sniff. "No, that property is not a member."

The way Evelyn's voice hardened told Marti there was more to the story. "Interesting," Marti said, keeping her tone light and professional. "I'm a property manager, and my client is potentially interested in acquiring that property and I'm doing my due diligence."

Evelyn's tone changed again, becoming warmer. "Oh, it's a wonderful property. Truly a cornerstone of our neighborhood. Its location and colonial aesthetics are key to preserving our historical roots."

"But?" Marti prompted, sensing there was a problem.

"But the current owner. He's been attempting to make changes that are not in compliance with our guidelines."

Marti's pulse ticked up. "Do you know who the owner is?" she asked.

"I'm afraid not," Evelyn replied, "I've seen him a few times going in and out, but have never had the chance to introduce myself. All I know is it's held by some shell company. I can't recall the name right now."

"Phoenix LLC?" Marti said, already knowing the answer.

"Yes, that's it."

Marti's frustration bubbled up again. Another dead end. Then she thought of something. "You said the owner was attempting to make changes."

"That's right, but the association is currently suing the bastard," Evelyn replied, her feelings bubbling over. " We can't let him ruin our beautiful neighborhood."

Marti's pulse quickened. A lawsuit could mean names. Real names. Not aliases. "Thank you, Evelyn. That's helpful information," she said before ending the call.

***

Marti was eager to take advantage of any sniff of a lead so she decided to drive to the local state court building in Jersey City to see if the lawsuit angle would bear any fruit. Despite being just a mile away, and easily walkable under normal circumstances, she knew trying it today, given her physical state, would wipe her out.

She changed out of the sweatsuit and managed to get some socks on her feet before she left the apartment and descended the back stairs to the parking lot. She eased her car onto the road, navigated over to Newark Avenue, and then immediately hit a tangle of traffic. The one-mile journey morphed into a drawn-out 15-minute ordeal, and by the time she finally parked her car, she was $20 poorer and still a half-mile away from her destination.

Still, even in her rundown mental and physical state, she had to pause for a moment at the base of the courthouse steps. It was an impressive building that featured a Beaux-Arts architectural style constructed of granite and limestone with elaborate detailing, symmetry, and large columns.

She climbed the steps and stepped inside to more marble and detailed plasterwork. It was only once she encountered a human being after waiting in a queue for 20 minutes that the spell was broken and things went downhill and her frustration mounted. The structure housed multiple civil court divisions, each one a hive of bureaucratic activity. The labyrinthine layout and cold, unresponsive clerks she encountered were like wading through a frozen maze of indifference.

Her energy was dwindling with each encounter. Marti was no stranger to persistence, but she was painfully aware of her limitations today. If she had been at full strength, she would have bulldozed her way through, but today was not that day.

Recognizing the futility of her solo effort, she swallowed her pride and decided to enlist a little help. She didn't know who yet, or how, but she was determined to find a way to eyeball those court records.

Chapter
Twenty-Seven

As if on autopilot, Marti found herself steering her car back toward York Street. She hadn't intended to return, but some unseen force seemed to draw her back to the silent house. The only change on the street was that the garbage cans, which had been waiting to be collected in the morning, had now been returned to their places. Evelyn probably demanded it. Everything else was as still as it had been when she left earlier. She parked across the street and watched until the heat and the boredom caused her to drift off again.

She woke up feeling lousy with a headache and her various aches and pains all turned up to eleven. She exited the car, tried to stretch, thought better of it, and shambled down to the convenience store on the corner. She'd been in before for coffee and candy. The woman on the night shift took pity on her and allowed her to use the restroom. She likely believed Marti to be homeless. If the teenage clerk working today recognized her, he didn't say anything. She bought a bottle of water and returned to her car. She rolled the cold bottle along her neck and forehead and then drank it down in two long draughts, pausing only to swallow more aspirin. She tossed the empty bottle into the passenger footwell where it joined the other empties.

Marti pulled out her phone and dialed her father's number. He was also a cop, a detective based in Paterson, a dense and diverse city 20 miles to the northwest. Their relationship had been strained since Marti's mother passed, then thawed when she'd joined the academy, but had been stretched further with this latest incident, but she was hoping he could help her now.

His voice, gruff and concerned, filled her ear as he picked up on the other end. "Marti, how are you feeling?" he asked, a hint of worry lacing his words.

"I'm okay. A little better every day."

"You taking it easy?"

"Trying to."

"What does that mean?"

"It means I buried my partner a week ago, it hurts to breathe, and somehow this is my fault."

There was a beat of silence before her dad asked, "Any news on the investigation?"

He was trying to be supportive, she knew that, but to Marti, his words sounded more like judgment. Whether it was intended or not, it rubbed her the wrong way.

"No, nothing new. Listen, I need some help," she replied, curtly. The conversation was not going the way she wanted. She pressed on. "Do you know any private investigators? I need someone good and discreet."

There was a pause, during which Marti could almost hear her father's concern morphing into resistance. "Marti, I'm not sure that's such a good idea. What happened to Joel—" he began, but she cut him off.

"I'm not asking for your opinion, Dad. I just need a name," she snapped. She knew her father wouldn't approve, but she also knew he would give in.

Her father sighed heavily into the phone. "Try Carla Mancini," he revealed, the years audible in his voice. "She was a detective over in North Bergen. We worked together on that task force investigating the prostitute murders back in the mid 1980s. She was sharp and relentless. The kind of cop too stubborn to know when to quit. You'll like her." He paused, another sigh rustling over the phone line, but then continued. "About five years ago, she had her 20 and walked away from the force, started her own PI firm. She's still in Bergen as far as I know. You should be able to find her. Carla's got a reputation for being discreet, and thorough, and she's got no patience for any kind of nonsense."

"Thanks."

"Just be careful, Marti," he urged, his voice thick with worry. "You're not in this on your own, kid. You don't have to shoulder all of this by yourself."

She knew her father meant well and he was a fellow officer, but he was an outsider in this. He couldn't see the details. If she didn't shoulder this, she was going to get buried. She'd tried to tell him that in the hospital but he didn't believe it. Not really.

The silence that followed was deafening, a chasm filled with a thousand unspoken words. Unable to formulate a response, Marti ended the call abruptly and dropped the phone in the cupholder. She had a name. The silent house on York Street glared back at her through the windshield. She flipped it the middle finger and drove off.

***

She knew if she went back to her apartment she'd likely open a bottle of something and not be able to stop until she ran out. Two days might pass in a muddled haze, so she drove on Route 1 until she could transition to Route 9 and crawled her way north toward North Bergen in the afternoon traffic.

As she waited at the light to turn onto 79th Street, she used her phone to search for Carla Mancini's contact details, finding a simple web page with a business address listed for Mancini Investigations, LLC. The address led her to a quaint brick building nestled amongst a row of similar structures on Bergenline Avenue, a lively artery that cut through the heart of North Bergen. The street was lined with shops and cafes, a bustling hub of activity that felt like a different planet from the silent, watchful stretch of York Street she'd become accustomed to.

She found street parking nearby and walked back to the brick building. Mancini Investigations occupied a small office on the second floor of the building. She was beginning to hate stairs. She climbed up and found a door with the name of the firm discreetly etched on the glass pane. A woman was visible inside at a big desk; she waved Marti in before she could knock.

Inside, the office was surprisingly airy. Large windows overlooked the vibrant street below, bathing the room in a warm natural light. The modern computer and sleek monitor on the desk were a stark contrast to the otherwise classic decor. A pair of comfortable leather chairs sat in front of the solid oak desk, its surface organized with stacks of neatly piled documents, a notepad, and a coffee cup with a bold 'World's Greatest Detective' printed on it. Behind the desk, a row of filing cabinets stood like silent guardians. Black-and-white cityscape prints hung on the walls along with various commendations.

Marti guessed Carla Mancini was in her late 50s, her hair a rich blend of chestnut and silver, cut in a practical bob that framed a face with sharp, intelligent eyes, high cheekbones, and a strong jawline. Her mouth gave off a hint of a smirk which lent an air of authority mixed with a sense of humor. She was dressed in a simple crisp white blouse and dark slacks.

The entire set up—the office, the decorating, and Mancini herself—exuded professionalism. Marti suddenly felt woefully inadequate in every way, like a tardy pupil called into the principal's office.

Mancini indicated a chair and Marti sat as Mancini leaned back, a thoughtful expression on her face. "You look familiar but I'm sure we haven't met."

"No, we've never met. My name is Marti Wells. My father is John Wells. He's a detective up in Paterson."

Carla slapped a hand down on the desk. "Jack Wells. Yes, of course. You have his eyes and a bit of his nose. Please, have a seat. How is Jack?"

Marti was a bit taken aback. Few people called her old man Jack. Marti suspected that perhaps they had more of a history than her father initially let on. "He's doing all right. Still chasing the bad guys."

Mancini shook her head. "Good for him. He's a good egg. The department needs more guys like him. Guys like Jack are not the reason I pulled the pin."

"Why did you? If the department needs more of him, they definitely need more like you."

Carla eyed her. "You on the job?"

"Yes, second year. In Jersey City."

"Well, you can probably already guess. It's not an original story."

"One too many dick jokes?"

She gave a small smile. "Sure, though you sort of build up some armor or learn the best way to disarm those guys. Still, you do get sick of it. Every guy thinks he's the first one to make the same joke.

It probably contributed to the burnout, but I wouldn't have stuck it out long enough for my pension if that was it."

Marti found herself interested. There were not a lot of female officers to talk to and even fewer with Mancini's age and experience. "So what was it?"

"You're a lot like your father, you know that?" Carla said, her voice soft and low. "A dog with a bone."

Marti frowned slightly, unsure whether that was a compliment or an insult.

"Politics," she said simply. "I didn't join the force to play office politics. I joined to make a difference and to help people. I know it sounds naive and too idealistic, but it's true. I really felt like being police was my vocation. But the higher up the ladder you go, the more the job becomes about keeping your superiors happy and less about actual police work." She paused, running a hand through her hair. "Eventually, I had enough. I was tired of the red tape, the bureaucracy, and the petty backstabbing. So I quit. Hung out my shingle. I figure this way, I can do what I wanted to do in the first place—help people, without having to answer to anyone."

Carla leaned forward, her gaze refocusing on Marti. "So, Marti Wells, how can I help you?" she asked, her tone businesslike once more.

***

Marti took a deep breath, mentally preparing herself for the story she was about to recount. She told Carla everything—the house on York Street, Joel's untimely death, her time in the hospital, the unknowns, the feeling that a coverup of some kind was underway, the enigmatic stranger, and her unsuccessful attempts to uncover his identity.

As Marti spoke, Carla's eyes never left her face. She didn't interrupt, didn't ask questions. She just sat there, listening, her expression unreadable. When Marti finally finished, there was a moment of silence as Carla processed everything she'd just heard.

"You've done well," Carla said finally, her voice filled with a grudging respect. "Most people wouldn't have thought to look into the sanitation service and your idea about the neighborhood association ... that's good. It's thinking outside the box."

She paused, her gaze thoughtful. "A lawsuit could shake things up, force them to reveal themselves. And if you're worried about this coming back to you through official channels, don't be. Us PIs have access to some pretty comprehensive databases, and we know how to use them."

With that, Carla reached forward and pulled her keyboard closer, then tilted the monitor slightly so Marti could see. Marti felt a sense of relief flood through her body. Someone believed her. Someone was going to help her. More importantly, it felt like someone understood why she might feel like she needed to do this. That letting it drop wasn't an option.

Carla's fingers flew across the keys, the soft clicking sound filling the room. Then she slowed down and started reading, then she started talking. "In New Jersey, if a neighborhood or homeowners association sues a property owner, the case would generally be handled in the appropriate state court. The specific court that would handle the case depends on the nature and value of the dispute.

"For civil cases involving property disputes or homeowners association matters, the case would typically be filed in superior court, which is the general trial court with jurisdiction over a wide range of civil matters. Then, within the superior court, the specific division that would handle the case may also vary. For example, if the dispute involves a breach of contract, it might be filed in the Civil Division. If it pertains to property rights or disputes, it might be filed in the Chancery Division, particularly the Chancery Division-General Equity Part. You get the picture."

Marti thought of the lines and endless doors and hallways of the courthouse. "Yes, bureaucracy in action."

"The more you learn to live without, the more you'll have to live with." There was a period of silence as Carla clicked and typed. "Ah, or if it involved ... exterior window trim detailing. It would land in the Property Division. Does the name Harper Montgomery mean anything to you?"

"No, that name hasn't come up. Is that the owner?"

More typing and clicking. "No, I don't think so. I think it's the local lawyer representing the owner. Let's try something else. I'm going to search his name and Phoenix LLC." She typed and hit enter. "Yup, looks like he handles a lot of legal business for them."

"Does that help me at all? I can't just call them up and ask."

"You could but they'd probably just hang up. I've never met a high-priced lawyer who didn't like a little free publicity. Let's try a Lexis-Nexis search."

She switched databases and searched for Harper Montgomery's name in the newspapers for the last five years.

"Huh. Not as many hits as I would have thought. He must be a very high-priced lawyer."

Marti slumped back in the leather chair. She'd felt so optimistic that with Carla's help, she'd finally crack this and get a name but she'd just rode the rollercoaster again and ended up at another dead end.

Carla noticed her reaction. "Don't give up yet. Let's scan through these. There aren't a lot." She hit a button and the printer in the corner started humming. They divided the news stories and started reading.

Ten minutes later, Carla sat up straighter and then moved back to the computer. She typed and clicked and then swiveled the monitor around completely to face Marti. "Do you see your guy?"

And there he was. Marti was so stunned that she could only nod.

"Girl, you got a big, big problem."

Chapter Twenty-Eight

The image on Carla's screen was a classic family portrait, taken in what appeared to be a stately wood-paneled library. Marti could almost see the stone fireplace and the mounted head of a moose just out of the frame. The grand patriarch and matriarch of the clan sat in the center, their faces etched with the lines of age and success. Surrounding them was the next generation, dressed in an array of business attire, projecting an image of wealth and influence.

"Which one is he?" Carla asked.

Marti pointed to the man on the far left at the end of the row, his youthful energy making him stand out from the rest. Marti could almost feel him vibrating through the photo. His blond hair stood out sharply against his well-tailored dark suit, and his eyes, even in the pixelated image, were a striking blue. He was slim, his physique hinting at an athletic grace. A faint shadow of stubble on his face gave him a rugged edge, and the confident smile playing on his lips was almost infectious but not quite. There was something just slightly unnatural about it. Like he'd practiced it in the mirror. Or like he was wearing a mask.

The stern face of the man in the middle of the photo, standing behind the seated white-haired patriarch contrasted with the younger man's relaxed demeanor. The other family members, male and female, also looked serious, their faces set in expressions of sober responsibility, making the man's easy smile and relaxed posture even more noticeable. She studied his posture. There was a sense of assuredness about him. He knew who he was and was comfortable with it.

Carla ran a finger along the caption at the bottom: Miles Rothchild. "Don't know him," Carla said. "Don't know any of them, of course. I had one case years ago that brushed up against the family business. Like anything involving those with money who make big political donations, we were told in no uncertain terms to use kid gloves. If I recall correctly, it didn't matter that time. The perp we were looking at had worked there briefly, a low-level gig, but not for three months. He'd moved on. We did a couple of pro forma interviews with HR and that was it."

Marti had finally recovered her voice. "I don't know the name. What do they do? The Rothchilds?"

Carla leaned back in her chair and crossed her arms over her chest. "Like a lot of old New York families, the Rothchilds made their fortune in the 1800s through shipping and trade. Over the years, they've diversified their portfolio, investing in everything from real estate to technology startups. Today, the Rothchild empire spans several industries, but you'd never know it. I'm not surprised you haven't heard of them. They're known for their discretion. You won't see their names on any buildings or universities. They prefer to pull the strings from behind the scenes, away from the public eye."

Now Carla leaned forward and put her elbows on the desk. Marti could smell her light perfume. "I don't know what is going on here but, Marti, this is not a family you want to cross. If Miles Rothchild is connected to this, you need to tread carefully."

***

The drive home was a blur for Marti. Her mind was a whirlpool of new information, theories, and unanswered questions. Miles Rothchild. A name to put to the face, yes, but it was like trying to grasp smoke. The more she tried to make sense of it, the more elusive it became.

The Rothchilds were a force to be reckoned with; Carla had made that much clear. And Miles, with his blond hair, ice-blue eyes, and unsettling ability to vanish without a trace, was an unexpected puzzle piece that didn't seem to fit with the rest of what she knew.

Was he a target? A victim? Or was he something more sinister? Was his attempt at anonymity a sign of guilt, or a desperate move for self-preservation? The possibilities were numerous. Questions swirled around in her head, each as frustratingly unanswerable as the next. But now she had a name and a clear objective. She was going to find him and she was going to get her answers.

But not tonight. Tonight, her body ached for rest, and her mind craved the quiet calm of sleep. Her apartment was a welcome sight; the familiar smells, the soft lighting, and the quiet hum of the refrigerator were all soothingly normal. She dry-swallowed two painkillers from the hospital, too tired to fill up a glass from the tap, and stumbled into the bedroom. With one last lingering thought of the enigmatic Miles Rothchild, she settled into her bed and let the exhaustion of the day pull her into a deep, dreamless sleep.

***

The morning light filtered through the blinds and threw an array of thin shadows across the room. Her hand-me-down air-conditioning unit rattled in the window frame. It was struggling to keep up with the unrelenting heatwave. She had slept fitfully, her mind spinning with questions and theories, and she only felt half rested. She rolled out of bed and wandered into the bathroom, catching sight of herself in the mirror. The bruises on her face were still apparent, though less angry and red than they had been. She could breathe a little easier now, the sharp pain in her ribs now more of a dull ache on each exhalation. It was progress.

After dressing in casual clothes that wouldn't draw attention, she padded into her kitchen and poured herself a bowl of cereal. As she ate, she mulled over her plan. She didn't have much to go on, but the public address of the Rothchild office downtown was as good a place to start as any. At the very least, she might get a glimpse of Miles, figure out his routine, and find a place to approach him.

After a quick caffeine stop at the new cafe on the corner, Cafe Grand, she walked the rest of the way to the PATH station and, 15 minutes later, she found herself standing across the street from a towering skyscraper in the financial district. Their name was nowhere on it but a glance at the directory in the lobby showed they occupied the top five floors. It was a steel and glass monument to power and wealth, and it seemed to taunt her with its inaccessibility. Security hovered in the lobby and key card access gates were installed in front of the elevator banks. She wouldn't last two minutes inside without being questioned. Still, she was undeterred. She took a deep breath and chose a spot in a nearby pocket park from where she could watch the entrance.

As the day wore on, Marti saw people coming and going from the building. Executives in expensive suits, assistants juggling coffee and documents, delivery people, but no sign of Miles. Her optimism waned slightly with each passing hour, but she reminded herself that this was a waiting game.

She wasn't sure what she was expecting. A grand entrance by Miles, perhaps? But as the day wore on, and the flow of people in and out of the building continued unabated, there was no sign of the man she was looking for.

Marti's anticipation began to turn into disappointment. Was this a wild goose chase? Was Miles even in town? There were other entrances. She couldn't cover them all. She shook off the doubts, reminding herself that patience, some might call it stubbornness, was her superpower.

It became her mantra as she returned to the park and watched the building for the next three days. She showed up early. She showed up late. She never saw him until he sat down on the bench next to her.

Chapter Twenty-Nine

M arti turned, her breath hitching in surprise. Miles Rothchild had taken a seat next to her, as silent and unassuming as a ghost. The scent of roasted cashews from a small bag in his hand filled the air, but beneath it, she picked up the faint smell of soap and citrus.

He was older than he appeared in the family photo. He wore a summer suit, light in color, no tie, with the collar open. A casual elegance that seemed to mask the man who had whispered the warning to stay away as she lay on that bedroom floor. His hands, were perfectly manicured, the nails clean and trimmed. He tilted the bag toward her in a silent offer. She shook her head, her mind not on food but on the answers she craved.

"Why did those men attack you?" she asked, breaking the silence.

He shrugged; his gaze focused on the crowd in front of the building. "Isn't it obvious? My money."

"I don't think so," Marti said.

He turned to look at her, his eyebrows raised. "Why not? My family has plenty of it."

"According to the evidence log, the safe was empty," she said.

"Maybe they got in and got away," he suggested, sounding unconcerned.

"We both know that that isn't true. Plus, the detectives had the safe checked for trace evidence. It was brand new and completely clean. Like it had never been used. Like it was just bait," she said, watching his reaction carefully.

He chuckled, a small smirk playing on his lips. "Huh. Imagine that."

"Why did you run? Why are you hiding?" she asked, her voice steady.

"Who said I was hiding?" he said, turning to look at her fully for the first time. His eyes were the same vibrant blue from the snapshot, but where she'd seen infectious confidence before, now they appeared cold, almost mean. She felt like a small bug pinned under a microscope.

"You don't get mentioned in any of the statements or official reports. You never alerted the authorities about the break-in," she pointed out.

"Did you tell them about me?" he asked, his gaze scrutinizing.

"Yes," she admitted. "But my captain thinks I'm concussed. I'm not sure he believes me."

"I'm not hiding," he said. "It's just no one's come looking and, as you pointed out, nothing was taken. There was nothing to report."

The conversation felt like a game of cat and mouse, and Marti knew which she was. She had a sinking feeling that getting answers from Miles Rothchild was not going to be as straightforward as she'd hoped.

"Can I pose a question, since you've managed to track me down?" Miles asked, popping a cashew into his mouth.

"Sure," Marti replied.

"How much do you know about what transpired in that room?"

"Clearly not enough. Or, not as much as you."

"You've read the reports, right?"

"Some of them, yes."

"And who, according to those reports, is responsible for your partner's death?"

"I don't know," Marti admitted. "I blacked out at the scene and came to at the hospital. All the reports say is that Joel and I were found unresponsive in the room by first responders. Are you saying you know who else was there? Who assaulted me? Who took Joel's life? If you know anything, you have to come forward."

"Why should I?"

"What do you mean why? So we can apprehend those responsible, so someone is held accountable for what happened."

"Sorry, one more question. What do you know about psychopathy?"

"What?" The abrupt turn in the conversation lost her.

"Psychopathy. Are you familiar with it?"

"A little. It's when someone has a hard time caring about how other people feel and they may act out aggressively without feeling sorry."

Miles was nodding his head. "That's pretty good. Most people would just say a person is nuts, but it is a complex condition that exists on a spectrum, like autism, with varying degrees of severity and vast differences between individuals. If you had a bingo card it might read: Lack of empathy, superficial charm, manipulation, impulsivity, risk-taking, lack of remorse, shallow emotions, and antisocial behavior."

The feeling that she was looking at someone wearing a mask returned. Someone who played along but was slightly out of step with society. "You're saying you think you're a psychopath?"

"I don't think it. I know it. I went through a thorough assessment, very thorough, my family made sure of that, and diagnosis. My mental health passport officially has a psychopathy stamp."

"Why are you telling me this?

"Because this is likely to be the only time we chat like this, and I could sense you were having trouble with some of my reactions, and I can tell you had hoped this conversation would bring some sort of closure to what happened. I'm sorry, but I don't think that will be the case, unfortunately."

"Why not?"

"I'll be straight with you, or as straight as I can be," he said looking at her sideways and with half a smile. "You're right. It was a setup. I deal with my ... condition in an unusual way, according to my therapist. I like to scratch my darker itches while still serving society in some way. If that greater good also happens to be mostly self-serving to me or my family's business, so be it."

"You're a psychopathic vigilante with a mild case of empathy."

"I prefer to think of it as active therapy for strategic reasons. I believe that prosocial benefits can coexist with personal gain or a positive public image."

Jesus, this made her head hurt. "And Joel ending up dead is a prosocial benefit?"

He dropped his smile and for a moment Marti did see behind his mask. His jocularity was a practiced front for something very dark. "That was a mistake," he eventually said. "I'm not perfect. I try to be. I can come very close. But my plans are not foolproof."

"What happened?" she prompted.

"I hesitated. No, that's not quite right. I expected them to hesitate. That was my mistake that led to everything else. They'd gone so feral that any norms were gone. They were inside and on me before I could react. You and Joel were in place to make the discovery and arrest before it went sideways. You ended up saving my life. I recognize that."

"What do you mean they were feral? Who?"

"I had expected the police to still have some sort of ingrained norms or training, but these guys had fully embraced their roles. They were unhinged."

"Wait, you're saying the men in that room were cops?"

She was shaking her head, refusing to let her mind believe it.

"I'm sorry, but yes. I still hoped that by calling 911 and getting more cops on the scene they would go down, but it had the opposite effect. Or, I got unlucky and the wrong cops showed up. They locked down and sanitized the scene. The reason no one is looking for me is that they don't want to. They are happy if I remain a mystery. Right now, they are waiting on you."

"Me?"

"Yes. That's my guess. How much of a problem is Marti Wells going to be? They are waiting to see what you remember or maybe who you remember."

"Why?"

"The Violent Gang Task Force has become the most powerful gang in the city. They could act with impunity. They'd make legit arrests, but half the money and evidence wouldn't make it to the station. Then they just started skipping the arrest part and went straight to robbery and assault. This chief has higher political ambitions. The Vig was his meal ticket. He created it and could point to its impact on lowering crime. It would have been the major tent pole in any campaign. If this all came out, it would now be a millstone around his neck. He wouldn't survive as chief, never mind any elected office. So this will never see the light of day. The unit will be quietly disbanded because, hey, the stats are down, it's served its purpose. At best, the cops involved will be shown the door, but no one is going to jail. That would involve a trial and everything coming to light."

Marti felt the acid burn in her stomach. Her fury outweighed the pain in her body. She stood and paced in front of the bench and finally said, "And that's good enough for you?"

"No."

"That's it. No? That's where you draw the line?"

"You don't want to know where I draw the line."

Maybe she didn't but right now she wanted retribution. She wanted someone to pay. What Miles was telling her made no sense. She wasn't naive but this was too big to just cover up. Joel was dead. She'd watched him die. And Miles was saying they knew. They all stood up at his funeral and said their platitudes but all along they knew who was responsible.

Miles stood and tossed the empty bag into the nearby trash. "They will fall. Men like that don't have happy endings. It just might take some time. Take care of yourself, Marti." He turned on his heel and disappeared into the crowd.

Chapter Thirty

She looked at him now, casually cooking in her kitchen, a glass of wine at his elbow. It had been over two decades since their brief encounter on that park bench in the heart of the financial district, but time seemed to have barely left a mark on him. Sure, there were a few fine lines etched around his face, like cracks in a piece of fine china, and his hair had thinned out slightly. Yet, his eyes retained their intense blue vitality. Money might not be able to halt aging, but it certainly had a knack for slowing it down.

"How's the psychopathy going?" Marti asked.

"It's evolving," he said with a laugh. "We only had a short conversation, but I'd forgotten that I found you quite likable."

Was it good or bad when a psychopath took a liking to you? Marti decided it would be best not to delve deeper into that. "How did you get in?" she asked instead. Her door and her locks were not as old as the rest of her apartment. She'd upgraded them. Considerably.

"I have a certain facility with locks," he replied nonchalantly. Marti was too fatigued and famished to put up a fight.

"Wine, please," she requested, taking a seat at the kitchen table. Without missing a beat, he poured her a glass of Barolo, a rich Italian red, then turned back to the pot simmering on the stove, stirring it with practiced ease. Rita Mae was sitting on the counter nearby watching him adoringly. Her cat had questionable taste.

He took two plates from her cupboard and served her a steaming portion of pasta carbonara with a rich and creamy sauce. He added a slice of warm garlic bread and a caprese salad on the side.

It smelled heavenly and was the most complete meal that had been cooked in her apartment in at least a year. She had questions, plenty of them, but her hunger took precedence. She ate half the pasta and the bread before she came up for air.

"Is cooking part of your therapy, too?"

He took a sip of wine. He was eating more slowly. "No, I just enjoy it."

She raised her glass in response. "Well, cheers to the chef." He dipped his head in response to the compliment. "It almost makes up for you breaking into my apartment."

"Apologies for the intrusion. I tried to call on you earlier, but you weren't home and the super practically shoved me out the door."

"He's a good judge of character."

"Touche."

"I came back the second time and was a bit more, shall we say, circumspect because I didn't want the guy on the street watching your apartment to see me."

She paused with the fork halfway to her mouth. "Guy on the street?"

"Yes. He appears to be watching your building."

"All right," she pushed the plate back, "let's get into this. If he's watching my apartment, it's because of you. You sent Cassidy and Angela to me. Why?"

"Because I owed you."

She suppressed a sigh. She was not a child anymore and no longer wanted to joust with him. There was a man outside, if Miles was to be believed, and there was only one reason she could think of for why he would be there. "I received a call the other night warning me that there was a contract out on my life." That seemed to catch him a little off guard but not completely by surprise. "Wait, you knew?"

"I never received confirmation like a phone call, but I've heard similar rumors. It's one of the reasons I'm here."

"What are the other reasons?"

"I owe you."

"Herschel and the Vig. And Joel."

"That's right. It didn't start with him. When Angela first approached me, I had no idea Herschel might be involved with Rathbone but then, I admit, I saw an opportunity to settle my debt with you."

"If you didn't know Herschel was involved then why did you send Angela and Cassidy to me?"

"Because I believe you are good at your job and will do your best to help them."

"In other words, you didn't want your ass hanging out in the wind with Calderone."

"That might have been part of the calculus, but that does not make the other part untrue."

"How would you know I'm good at my job?"

"Since our paths crossed that night, I've made it part of my business to keep tabs on you."

Marti felt a cold wind blow across her neck. She tried to push the feeling down. This was not about her. "Why do you care? Why did you try to help Cassidy at all, even if it was just to send her to me? If

I recall correctly, your therapy," she used air quotes, "aims to serve the greater good but is mostly a byproduct of serving yourself."

"It's interesting the role that serendipity plays in our lives. Angela shows up in my office with Cassidy and her story, but Calderone Innovations was already on my radar. How much do you know about Victor Rathbone?"

"I've talked to some people who know him and read the usual bio information on the internet. Doesn't seem like the type of guy I'd be friends with."

"Maybe not, but a smart guy. A very smart guy."

"I haven't found anyone who would dispute that, but most of them said he was also sort of an asshole."

Miles nodded. "Yes, he'd probably use that same word to describe himself. He's also dying."

"What? That did not come up when I talked to anyone."

"Cancer. I don't know how many people know, and I don't know the details, but I know it's real and it's terminal. But Victor," Miles continued, "he sees his impending end not as a death sentence but as an opportunity. A chance to test his most daring project yet."

"And what would that be?" Marti asked.

"Victor wants to transcend mortality. He's been exploring AI, looking for ways to capture and transfer human consciousness into machines."

Marti's eyebrows shot up, and her wine glass paused halfway to her lips. "That's ... ambitious. Is it feasible? It sounds like science fiction, like a modern reinvention of the fountain of youth."

"The fountain of youth might be a good analogy. It might end up just being a huge money pit, but Victor certainly thinks it's feasible. He was trying before, dabbling, but I hear his diagnosis has only accelerated his plans. He calls it Project Lazarus. I wouldn't bet against him."

"And he wants control of the company to make this happen?" Marti asked, trying to wrap her head around the concept.

"Exactly," Miles nodded. "He needs the funds, computing power, and the clout of Calderone to have any chance at success. And he's prepared to do whatever it takes."

"Okay, that explains his reaction to Cassidy. He literally can't afford her to be a legitimate heir. For him, it's a matter of life and death. But what is it to you?"

"You mean beyond the host of ethical questions?"

"Since when do ethics matter to a psychopath?"

"If you prick me, do I not bleed?"

"Actually, the character of Shylock is just about perfect for you."

Miles waved a hand. "I mean it as less of a reflection of me and more as an illustration of my concerns. Even a diagnosed psychopath is still human. We all bleed. We all share a commonality of feelings and emotions, regardless of our physical or mental differences. If Victor succeeds, it calls all of that into question. What does it mean to be human if our minds can exist outside our bodies? Do we still have the same rights and responsibilities? How does this redefine our concepts of life and death or even our sense of self and identity? Losing that, becoming digital entities, we might become an entirely new or different species. It would fundamentally change us."

"Okay slow down. I see the technological risks and the potential for exacerbating socioeconomic disparities. I don't imagine this would be cheap. If only the wealthy can afford to live forever ... that might piss a lot of people off."

"You forgot one. The potential for exploitation. Who do you think will control the digital realm where the consciousness resides?"

"Ugh. A corporately-sponsored afterlife? Gross."

"Corporations or governments and neither have glowing track records on misuse or manipulation. The rich and powerful like nothing more than keeping a tight leash on the status quo."

She finished her glass of wine. "Now that is a self-serving reason that I can see Miles Rothchild supporting."

He smiled. "My two halves can coexist. That's actually what I strive most to do. It's probably what most people try to do; I'm just more honest about it."

"I spoke to someone else in the field and he said it's the unknowns and pushing too far too quickly that is his greatest fear."

"Even a psychopath like me can see that Rathbone is taking us out on a dangerous precipice." He stood and placed a card on the table. "My number. If you ever need it." Then he moved toward the door. When he turned to face her, he was no longer smiling. "Do you know what Oppenheimer said after he witnessed the first atomic bomb test?"

"No."

"'Now I am become Death, the destroyer of worlds.' It's a reference from Hindu scripture. He had a lot of regrets and complex feelings about his involvement in the Manhattan Project once he saw the consequences of his work. If Rathbone succeeds and the technology successfully allows for a consciousness transfer, it would give him control over a fundamental aspect of human existence. I believe that is too much power for one person to hold. He has to be stopped."

Chapter Thirty-One

Even after Miles left, Marti could feel the heaviness of their conversation hanging in the air, like a thick fog that refused to lift. The rich meal, the wine, and the intense discussion had left her feeling wrung out and drowsy.

She double-checked that the apartment door was locked, turned off the lights, and moved to the large living room windows. The blinds were closed, and she used a finger to part them and watch the street below. The late-night city rhythm was a comforting hum in the background, but she hadn't forgotten what Miles said during dinner. She tried to spot the man Miles had mentioned from her vantage point, looking for any signs of someone lingering on the street or sitting in a car, but found none.

She'd returned in her car and pulled around back. Did he expect her to be on foot? Or had he left already? Or was he just a figment of Miles's imagination, a story spun by a man she wasn't sure she could trust? Trusting a psychopath was like trying to hold water in a sieve—an exercise in futility. She spent 15 minutes slowly scanning the dark car windows and windshields from her window but still came up empty.

Eventually, she poured the last of the wine into her glass and retreated to the comfort of her couch. Rita Mae followed suit, curling up on a pillow at the opposite end. Marti flipped on the classic movie channel and found herself in the middle of 'Shadow of a Doubt,' a lesser-known Hitchcock psychological thriller she'd seen before.

She always enjoyed the film, written by Thornton Wilder, a Pulitzer-winning author and playwright who simply told good stories. He didn't bother with literary pretensions; he just spun a tale and let it unfold. The combination of Wilder's script and Hitchcock's direction made the exploration of the dark side of human nature in a small California town ring very true.

As she watched the tense train station finale unfold on screen, she felt her eyelids growing heavy. Once the credits rolled, she decided it was time to head to bed. She lay in the dark and felt Rita Mae's tiny heartbeat next to her. She thought about that physical sensation, the emotional connection, the process of aging, the cycle of life and death, and how losing our tether to those things might change us. Make us less human. She reached out a hand in the dark and stroked Rita Mae's fur until she stopped thinking and fell into the black.

***

Marti awoke feeling the fatigue of a night spent wrestling with her subconscious. She remembered no dreams, no nightmares, just the sense of an ongoing battle waged within the dark corners of her mind. It was a tiredness that coffee could not fix, but she brewed a pot anyway, forgoing her usual morning run in favor of extra time to nurse her weariness. And maybe wallow in a little self-pity.

After two cups of coffee and a short stretching routine, she felt better. She made the decision not to let the threat dictate her life. She would be cautious, yes, but not cowed. Her office was at least inside her building and allowed her to maintain her routine without unnecessary risks. She ate two pieces of leftover garlic bread as she cleaned up the kitchen from last night, then felt somewhat ready to start the day.

Marti took a moment to glance outside her windows again before heading to the basement. The morning was just beginning to stir, and the street outside was slowly coming alive. Ms. Jenkins, her octogenarian neighbor, was already out, of course, tending to her riotous front garden on either side of the building's front steps. Her straw sun hat bobbed along to some silent rhythm as she pruned her rose bushes with a dedication that was as fierce as it was endearing.

Farther down the street, a delivery driver was unloading crates of fresh produce at Delgado's. The early-morning light caught on the array of colorful fruits and vegetables, creating a makeshift still-life on the sidewalk. The driver, a burly man with a deep tan and a bushy beard, moved with an efficient grace, hoisting the crates onto his shoulder and carrying them inside with practiced ease. A city bus trundled by, burping exhaust.

These were the normal rhythms of the city waking up, the predictable patterns of everyday life. There was no sign of anything unusual or threatening, no shadowy figures lurking in doorways or cars parked in unusual places. The normalcy of the scene was a reassurance, a reminder that life went stubbornly on.

Despite the reassuring cityscape, she ducked into her bedroom and took her gun from its place on the bedside table. Cautious, but not cowed.

She filled Rita Mae's bowls, tucked the gun under her sweatshirt, and descended into her basement office. Diffused morning light filtered through the small windows, casting long shadows on her desk. Her email inbox contained some responses from the previous day's inquiries. Local shelters had responded with negative matches for

Bobby Daniels, and a nearby construction company also reported no one matching his description had recently been added to their payroll.

But there was good news, too. The woman involved in the Patricia Thompson insurance investigation agreed to a meeting. Marti sent back a response with a proposed time for early next week, thanking her for her cooperation. Finally, a quick text check-in with Savvy confirmed that Cassidy had made it through her first night, a sentence that Marti knew belied the struggle it likely entailed.

***

With the easy tasks out of the way, Marti turned her attention to the main challenge of the day: Contacting and convincing Calderone board members who might support Cassidy's position.

She opened two digital dossiers on her computer, one for Maria Rodriguez and the other for Audrey Chen. These were the women she had to convince to support Cassidy's paternity claim and to stand against Rathbone's Project Lazarus.

Maria Rodriguez was a financial analyst, a friend, and an ally of Alex Calderone who shared his vision for a company that served both profit and people. Marti knew that Maria's skepticism of Rathbone's aggressive tactics that put humanity firmly in the back seat could be an opening.

Audrey Chen, on the other hand, was a powerhouse legal consultant with razor-sharp intellect. Her principles were unyielding, and Marti suspected that she would respond well to arguments around the potential legal issues that could arise from misuse of the technology, especially in an unregulated environment.

For Cassidy's paternity claim, Marti decided to focus on the clear DNA evidence and the legal obligations it entailed. She would underscore the potential legal and PR fallout if the company chose to ignore the claim.

Marti stared at the screen, her fingers hovering over the keyboard. She needed to talk to Maria Rodriguez and Audrey Chen, preferably face-to-face, but neither woman was anywhere near New York City. Both had LinkedIn profiles but that was it. Nothing on Facebook or Instagram. No crack or crevice that Marti could pry open with a direct message. LinkedIn might be an option, but how often would they check there? Time was a luxury she couldn't afford. She needed to be certain her message would be received and considered. She reached for her phone. This was a job for Neon.

Neon's talent for uncovering buried internet treasure made him the perfect person to track down contact information for Maria and Audrey. The only downside was his aversion to early-morning calls. Marti glanced at the clock. It was 7:30 a.m.

"Sorry, Neon," she muttered to herself, dialing his number. "No rest for the wicked."

The line rang eight times before Neon picked up. "Do you know what ungodly hour it is, Marti?"

Marti chuckled. "Morning, sunshine. I need a favor."

"Of course you do. It's the only reason you ever call." Neon grumbled, but there was no real heat in his voice.

"And you need cash to maintain all those liquid-cooled chips." Marti knew part of him relished the challenges she sent his way. The money was often secondary.

"Good point. Cash isn't a bad alarm clock. What's up?"

"I need contact information for Maria Rodriguez and Audrey Chen. Non-public, hard contact info. I need to reach them asap. The only things I have are employer names and LinkedIn profiles for each of them."

There was a pause on the other end of the line. "I could probably do that. You know it wouldn't exactly be legal, right?"

Marti sighed. "I know, Neon. But it's necessary. I promise I won't use it for anything shady."

He laughed. "I'm just kidding. It might be the least illegal thing I do today. Give me 20 minutes."

"Thanks, Neon. I owe you one."

"You are so far past one, Marti. I'll just add it to your tab," Neon said and hung up.

Marti stared at her phone for a moment before setting it down and turning back to her computer. Neon would come through. He always did. Now, she just had to prepare for the conversations to come.

As she sketched out her strategy and delved further into any background information she could gather online about Maria Rodriguez and Audrey Chen, a strategy for the boardroom confrontation began to form in her mind.

Chapter Thirty-Two

While she waited for Neon, Marti decided to take a break from her basement office and refill her coffee back in her apartment. She'd prefer a fresh Americano from Cafe Grand, but that felt like an unnecessary risk given what Miles had said about the man watching the building. She could get by on homebrew for a few days if necessary.

As she exited her office, she bumped into Ms. Jenkins, her elderly neighbor whom she had observed earlier tending her roses from her apartment window. Ms. Jenkins, clad in a floral print housedress and pink clogs, was busy sorting her laundry.

"Morning, Miss Marple," Ms. Jenkins greeted her with a wink. It was an old, shared joke that had long since passed its expiration date, but Marti chuckled politely. She saw herself more as a Luther than a Miss Marple, but she humored the older woman.

"Morning, Ms. Jenkins. You're up early," Marti remarked.

"I could say the same for you, dear," Ms. Jenkins replied. "Who has time to sleep with so little sand left in the hourglass? You'll learn that lesson eventually. I'll sort through the laundry before going back to my roses. Plus, a new episode of 'Endeavour' airs tonight, can't miss that. Must get my chores done. Business before pleasure."

"I don't need any more mysteries in my life," Marti said, shaking her head. She was about to say goodbye and head upstairs for the coffee, but paused and asked a question that had been on her mind since last night. "Ms. Jenkins, if you had the chance, would you want to live forever?"

Ms. Jenkins stopped sorting the laundry for a moment and looked her in the eye. "Forever is a mighty long time, Marple," she said. "I've lived a good life. I've seen things, done things ... loved and lost, laughed and cried. It's been quite the journey, but I believe one trip is enough."

"Even if you could be young again?"

"Especially then," Ms. Jenkins replied, resuming her laundry sorting. "You see, dear, the beauty of life lies in its fleeting nature. It's because we only have limited time that we learn to appreciate the moments we have. At least we should. No, I wouldn't trade the memories I have for another bite of the apple, even if I could be young again and do it with my real teeth. I'm sure at the very end, it may not feel like enough. Maybe I'll beg and fight for one more day, even one more minute, but I don't think I'd want forever. It would be fool's gold."

Marti nodded and placed a hand on the older woman's thin arm. "Thank you, Ms. Jenkins," she said. "I think I needed to hear that."

Ms. Jenkins smiled at her. "Any time, Marple. Now run along and get your coffee."

***

Marti refilled her mug and returned to her basement office. She checked her emails and found one from Neon. Two names and two phone numbers were listed. No reason to wait. She took a deep breath and dialed the number for Audrey Chen. It rolled quickly to voicemail. Not unexpected. After leaving a brief message for Audrey outlining why she was calling, Marti dialed the number for Maria Rodriguez. She expected another voicemail and was rehearsing her message, but to her surprise, the call was answered on the second ring.

"Hello?" The voice on the other end sounded slightly out of breath. There was some background noise, likely a treadmill or some other piece of exercise equipment.

"Maria Rodriguez?" Marti asked.

"Yes, who is this?" Maria's tone was cautious.

"Hi, Ms. Rodriguez. My name is Marti Wells. I'm a private investigator. I'm sorry for calling so early, but I'm working on something important and I believe you could help." Marti took a pause, gauging Maria's reaction.

"What is it about?" Maria asked, sounding more curious than annoyed. Marti took that as a good sign and plunged ahead.

"I'm working on a case involving Alex Calderone's daughter, Cassidy. She's recently discovered his paternity and is seeking recognition from the company but is running into ... problems. We've filed a suit in California, but there's a strict gag order. With the special board meeting coming up, and given your history with Alex and the company, I thought you might be interested in helping."

There was a moment of silence on the other end of the line. "What was your name again?"

"Marti Wells."

"How did you get this number?"

"I'm a private investigator." It was the only thing Marti could think to say. Let Maria Rodriguez draw her own conclusions.

"I'm going to call you back."

"Wait, don't—" But Rodriguez had already disconnected.

Marti leaned back in her chair and tried to figure out the next step. She needed these women's cooperation or at least assurance that she wouldn't be thrown out of the boardroom before she even started. She stared up at the gray ceiling. Chen was still a possibility but if Rodriguez blew the whistle on her, Marti knew the chances were very slim that Chen would even call her back, never mind agree to help. The board was too small. If word got to Rathbone that she was poking around the board members, he could easily shut down that avenue. She was digging through her notes to find the name of the third board member she'd identified as a potential ally when her phone rang.

"Hello?"

"Sorry, I had to check you out," Maria Rodriguez said. The background noise was gone now. "With Alex's death, there's been a lot of craziness."

"I understand," Marti replied.

"You don't sound crazy and my friend says you have a valid PI license in Jersey, so you sound mostly legit. Legit enough to at least give you five minutes."

"I'll take that for now and get right to it," Marti said, then continued, aware of the woman's implicit threat to hang up at any time. "I believe in the importance of corporate integrity and ethical responsibility. Cassidy's claim, if ignored, could damage the Calderone reputation. I also know how much you shared Alex's vision for a company that values people just as much as profits. This is an opportunity to uphold that vision. His daughter is just as much his legacy as the company. You can't ignore her."

Maria was silent for a moment. "Go on," she said finally.

Marti took a deep breath before she continued. "There's more. I didn't just take Cassidy at her word when she came to me. While doing my own research and due diligence, I've learned about a project within Calderone, named Project Lazarus, being spearheaded by Rathbone."

"Project Lazarus? I've never heard of it."

"I'm not surprised. I think Rathbone is keeping it very tightly under wraps. It's a radical and potentially dangerous approach for using advanced AI to extend human life by transferring human consciousness to a machine."

"What? No. That can't be right. The board would have heard about a project like that. He'd need approval, not just from us, but probably from outside regulators or advisory boards. It would require ..." she trailed off.

"Experimenting on humans."

"Yes."

"What if he was experimenting on himself?"

"On himself? Why would he do that?"

"Are you aware that Victor Rathbone is dying? That he's received a terminal cancer diagnosis?"

"No, I haven't heard anything about that."

"I believe it's true and I believe it might have pushed Rathbone to accelerate his plans and push both the technical and ethical limits. If he is successful, I fear ... well, I fear a lot of things, but I think most of them would deviate from the vision that Alex Calderone had for the company."

Maria was silent for a moment before she said, "I was not aware of any of this. I'll need to verify this, you understand, but you've given me a lot to think about, Ms. Wells."

"I'm glad you're willing to listen." Marti didn't want to scare the woman, but she wanted to impress upon her the potential danger and the need for caution. "If you plan on asking people within the company about any or all of this, please be very careful."

"I understand, believe me. You don't survive long on a board like Calderone without some instincts for self-preservation. I have people I trust."

"Good. Can we talk again soon?"

"Yes, I think we should," Maria agreed.

As she hung up the phone, Marti felt a glimmer of hope. This was just the start, but it was a step in the right direction.

***

Marti spent the rest of the morning digging into her other cases, tracking down leads and making calls. She relished the mundane tasks, the routine of it all. It allowed her to process the conversation she'd had with Maria and how she might approach the board meeting. Frank Reynolds had put her on the shift schedule for Astral Tower that night, it would give her a chance to be seen by the other guards and get a feel for the place. She was just about to head upstairs, her stomach rumbling in protest of her delayed lunch, for food and a nap when she heard a knock at her door.

She opened it to find Pedro, holding a thick envelope. "Delivery for you, Marti," he said, handing it over. "This thing is heavy."

"Thank you, Pedro," Marti said, balancing the heavy envelope in one hand and holding the door open with the other.

"Working on another big case, huh?" Pedro asked, eyeing the bulky package.

"Something like that," Marti replied with a half-smile. She sometimes shared stories and lower-profile case details with Pedro. He was often a surprising source of out-of-the-box leads, but in this case, the less Pedro knew, the better.

"Well, good luck with whatever it is," Pedro said, taking the hint and giving her a quick nod before heading back down the hall.

She wanted to ask him if he'd seen anyone hanging around the building but didn't want to unduly alarm him. If he saw someone, he would mention it.

Marti closed the door and turned her attention to the package. She tore open the envelope and pulled out a stack of corporate documents. These were the details on the Calderone board from the lawsuit discovery process that Angela had promised. She spread the papers out on her desk, her lunch forgotten. These papers held the information she needed to dig deeper into Calderone. The devil was always in the details.

Chapter Thirty-Three

Marti checked her reflection in the mirror and barely recognized herself. Her usually kinky hair lay straight around her shoulders, and a hint of mascara and lipstick added an unfamiliar polish to her face. She was eager to get out, being holed up in her building all day working had made her jittery. She needed to feel the city's energy again.

She buttoned up her security uniform, grimacing at the feel of the stiff, scratchy fabric against her skin. It was a far cry from her usual attire, but she had a role to play. She clipped her ID badge to her hip, the name Marcia Brown etched in bold letters.

Before leaving, she made a final check on Rita Mae. The cat seemed unbothered by Marti's transformation, her green eyes half-closed in a state of contented relaxation. "Hold down the fort, girl," Marti said, giving her a quick scratch behind her ear.

She made her way down the building's stairs, her boots echoing on the concrete steps. The maintenance key jingled in her pocket. The key was a perk of her deal with Pedro. It opened her office door, but also all the other service doors in the basement. She used it first to open the door that connected their building to the one next door, then walked the length of that building and exited through a nondescript door on the far side of the neighboring building. She didn't overuse this perk, but it came in handy from time to time. She emerged a block away on a different street, effectively avoiding any prying eyes that might be watching her building's front entrance.

It was a chilly night. It had rained at some point during the day and the city's lights reflected off the wet pavement. She breathed in the crisp air, savoring the sense of freedom. She blended into the evening rush, just another second-shift city dweller on her way to work. She was careful to keep her senses alert, scanning her surroundings for anything out of the ordinary, but she picked up no weird vibes as she made her way to the PATH station.

She took the transit train under the Hudson and rode up to 34th Street before she switched over to the NYC subway system and took the 1 train 20 blocks north to the edge of Midtown. She exited and walked two blocks west. The city was alive around her, but she felt invisible in her security guard uniform. She was Marcia Brown now, heading to her first shift at Astral Tower, the imposing glass monolith that was the East Coast home of Calderone Innovations.

Her nerves were humming with a mix of adrenaline and anticipation as she pushed through the revolving lobby door of the tall office building. She didn't expect any trouble, it was now after 8 p.m. and most of the building's occupants would be gone for the day, and she didn't plan to cause any either, but she would still be in the proverbial belly of the beast. Her plan for the night was simple: Familiarize herself with the building's layout, routines, and personnel.

***

She was taken aback when she arrived and saw Scott, the front desk man from Reynolds Security, waiting for her. His bulky frame was casually leaning against the reception desk, a familiar smile on his face.

"Frank doesn't trust me, huh?" she asked, arching an eyebrow at him.

Scott chuckled, his deep voice echoing in the empty lobby with that subtle twang. "He likes to keep an eye on things even from afar."

Marti crossed her arms, a playful smile tugging at the corners of her mouth. "Are you here to watch or help?"

Scott straightened up, his gaze steady on her. "I'm here to protect the business. What that means is up to me."

"Good to know."

Throughout her shift, Marti kept herself busy, making small talk with the other guards and taking the opportunity to walk the Calderone floors during rounds. Calderone used three floors. The 46th and 47th floors served as the operational hub, featuring a mix of cubicles, private offices, and meeting rooms for the company's administrative and managerial staff. The topmost 48th floor housed the executive suites and a large conference room, with a large mahogany table, high-tech A/V equipment, and a seamless single-pane floor-to-ceiling window offering an expansive view of Central Park and the rest of the city to the north.

Her key card worked without a hitch, and her presence elicited nothing more than the occasional nod or casual greeting and small-talk banter. The job likely was a high turnover position and a new face wasn't unusual. It was dull work, reminding her of her early days as a police officer when she was assigned to the more monotonous tasks. It was the kind of work that tested your patience and your ability to stay focused on the bigger picture.

As she walked the building's corridors, Marti made mental notes of its layout, memorizing the locations of emergency exits, stairwells, and the less frequented areas that could prove vital to her plan. Or, if things went sideways, potentially her survival.

***

A little after midnight, Marti descended into the basement. After navigating through the service corridors laced with pipes and duct work, she arrived at the maintenance staff office and break room. The break room was a rectangular room with a large wooden table and mismatched chairs in the center with a coffeemaker and a vending machine to the right and a bulletin board with workplace notices to the left. The room was currently empty, but she found the night manager, Robert Anderson, according to the plaque next to the door, alone in his small office next door. His salt-and-pepper hair was neatly combed, and a pair of glasses perched on the bridge of his nose. The office itself was cluttered, with stacks of paperwork covering the desk and shelves displaying various maintenance supplies.

Marti rapped lightly on the open door, catching Robert's attention. He looked up from his work, a slight frown creasing his forehead. Marti could read his face. An unexpected visitor likely meant unexpected work.

"Yes? Can I help you?" Robert asked, his voice tinged with a hint of weariness.

Marti's gaze drifted past Robert's shoulder, landing on a classic car calendar hanging on the wall. She recognized a familiar image.

"Hey, sorry to bother you," Marti began, leaning casually against the doorframe. "Couldn't help but notice that '67 Impala on your calendar. Beautiful car. My third husband was obsessed with muscle cars like that."

Robert's eyes softened, a flicker of nostalgia dancing within them. He adjusted his glasses and leaned back in his creaky chair.

"Oh? Small world, I guess. Not many of us left," he replied, a touch of warmth seeping into his voice. "Can't beat that classic American muscle. Did he ever own one?"

"No, Frank never got his hands on one, but he certainly dreamed about it," she responded. "He was quite the car enthusiast, always talking about restoring one. He was a mechanic by trade and we never pulled in enough dough to get one. But any time he got a chance to work on one, he'd talk about it for weeks. It was a favorite pastime."

Robert leaned forward, his eyes gleaming with curiosity. "I can understand his dream. Those kinds of cars have a way of captivating people."

Marti nodded. "Oh, absolutely. Frank would get lost in the details, describing the engines and the sleek curves of the body. It was as if he could see the whole history of the automobile industry unfold in front of him. He could go on for weeks, talking about it. It was infectious and annoying at the same time, you know?"

Robert chuckled, a sense of camaraderie building between them. "I know what you mean. My Darlene would say something very similar. What can I say? You're right. There's something about classic cars that just sparks that kind of passion in people. They become more than just vehicles; they become a part of who we are," he said.

"Exactly. You sound just like Frank. It's like they hold stories of their own or secrets of a bygone era. Anyway, sorry for rambling on about it. It's a topic that always makes me nostalgic," Marti replied, hoping she wasn't pouring it on too thick.

Robert waved off her apology. "No need to apologize. It's always nice to connect with someone who appreciates the same things. Now, what can I do for you?"

Marti straightened, shifting the conversation toward her true objective.

"Well, funny you should ask," she said. "My boss sent me down here. There's a bigwig meeting in three days, Thursday, board of directors or something up on forty-eight. And part of it is a surprise party for one of the guys. They want to bring up some people and a cake or something using the freight elevator. They don't want anyone in the lobby to see it. Is that going to be a problem?"

Robert frowned. His eyes roamed across the disorganized desk. "Hmm, normally we wouldn't allow that," he mused, his gaze settling on a stack of papers. "But I suppose we can make an exception. I know the people on 48 have some clout. This isn't going to land me on the news, is it? Bunch of strippers or drugs or something?"

"Oh, no; my boss didn't tell me anything like that."

"Okay then. Tell him we can't make it a regular occurrence and you'll have to keep it quick and discreet. I'll leave the doors to the delivery area and the freight elevator open. Just make sure everything runs smoothly."

"Great, thanks for understanding. I appreciate it. You can count on me to be efficient and inconspicuous," Marti assured him. He didn't know the half of it.

Robert made a note on his pad. "All right then," he acquiesced. "Just remember, it's a one-time exception. Keep it quiet."

"Of course."

As Marti walked back upstairs, she could only hope the board meeting was quiet and inconspicuous, but she had her doubts.

***

As she punched out at the end of her shift, a sense of satisfaction washed over her. It had been a long, tedious day, but she felt like she had some real momentum now. Every moment had been a step closer to the endgame. As her plan came together she could now visualize the players in the boardroom. She had always believed that preparation made its own luck, and she was determined to be as prepared as possible.

As Marti made her way to the exit, the ever-present Scott looked up from his perch at the desk. His shirt was still impeccably ironed, not a wrinkle in sight, and his smile was as bright as when she'd arrived. His chiseled features and perfectly combed hair gave him the appearance of a living Ken doll.

"Leaving so soon, Marcia?" he asked, the edges of his mouth curling upward.

"Shift's over, Scott. Some of us need our beauty sleep," she retorted, tugging at the stiff collar of her uniform.

He chuckled. "Well, you certainly don't look like you need it. I like the new hair by the way."

Marti felt her cheeks color despite herself. He had to be 20 years younger than her. "Flattery will get you everywhere, Scott. But not tonight. And Scott," she added, "don't forget to report back to Frank. Tell him I didn't break anything. Or steal anything."

She stepped out into the predawn hours of the New York City streets with the feel of Scott's eyes on her back. Or, some part of her anatomy.

***

At 4 a.m., the city was quiet, as quiet as the city ever got. Marti walked down the steps into the 50th Street subway station. The overnight eight-hour shift at the Calderone building had left her drowsy and out of sorts. She was too old to be staying up this late. Even with the prep nap that afternoon, this was pushing it. Usually vigilant, she felt the day's weight bearing down on her, subtly dulling her senses. She checked the digital status boards. Seven minutes until the next downtown-bound train.

The platform was bathed in the stark glow of fluorescent lights, casting long, shadowy figures that danced with the subtle movements of her fellow late-night/early-morning commuters. A young couple huddled close on a bench and whispered words she couldn't hear. Two women wearing maid uniforms were headed to work. A tall man wearing scrubs under a navy-blue fleece jacket stared at his phone. And an elderly man, possibly homeless, cloaked in an oversized raincoat and white sneakers, read a dog-eared paperback with an intensity that suggested it was more than just a book to him.

She walked the platform and then leaned against one of the iron pillars at the far end of the platform. The station was warm with the musky smell of diesel fumes, metal, and garbage. Her eyelids grew heavy. An uptown train roared in on the opposite side. A handful of people exited, a few changed places and boarded. The train pulled out and the station returned to a form of stasis. Two minutes until her train.

***

Her eyes slipped halfway closed, caught between wakefulness and sleep, her guard lowered in her fatigue. The pillar rocked and shuddered slightly as another uptown train, this one an express, charged through the station without stopping. She briefly jolted awake and looked around, but little had changed. The homeless man still read his book. The man in scrubs was gone. So was the late-night party couple. She watched a man, his head down, face obscured by the brim of a worn Yankees baseball cap, stride down the platform. His jacket was nondescript, an indistinct color that blended with the grimy tiles of the subway station, making him almost invisible to the casual observer.

She settled back against the pillar and flicked her eyes at the clock. One minute now until the train, then home and a reunion with her bed. She didn't register the danger until it was too late. The man with the Yankees cap had kept coming. She caught him in her peripheral vision. He was too close, moving too fast. She started to turn, but he was on her. He extended his arms and shoved her off the platform.

Marti's body hit the tracks hard, jolting her fully back into consciousness, but she was momentarily stunned, trying to piece together what had happened. She heard someone scream and was vaguely aware of people and faces looming above her, but then shock gave way to fear as the familiar rumble of an oncoming train resonated in her bones. The sound grew louder, the hot wind whipped up by its approach tugged at her clothes, and the harsh glare of the headlights grew larger and brighter as it approached the station from the tunnel.

There was no time to climb back onto the platform. Acting on pure instinct, she scrambled to her feet and ran. A corner of her mind gave silent thanks that nothing had broken or twisted in the fall. She almost tripped and went down on a railroad tie but stayed on her feet.

The front of the train was usually less crowded, and her habitual positioning at that end of the platform to wait just might save her life. The roar of the train was deafening, its blaring horn a terrifying reminder of the impending danger. The screech of emergency brakes pierced the air, but she knew the train couldn't stop in time.

The end of the station platform loomed ahead; the shadowy tunnel beyond was her only chance at survival. She pumped her arms and forced her aching legs to go faster. The train was so close she could feel its metallic breath on her neck. With one final, desperate leap, she threw herself toward the darkness.

***

The world fell eerily silent. She lay there for a moment, heart pounding in her chest before she slowly rolled over and looked up. The driver's eyes, wide with terror, met hers. Half of Marti's body was under the front of the train. Carefully, she pulled her legs out from under the massive machine, not daring to wonder if there had been enough clearance for her whole body. She was alive, and for now, that was all that mattered.

Chapter Thirty-Four

The clock on her wall read just past nine when Marti finally found herself back at her apartment—a cruel reminder of how long her day had stretched. The transit authorities had been kind enough to offer her a ride home, an ironic gesture considering how, at this time of day, the subway would have probably been faster. But she thought it might be a little while before she went back on the subway. She was shaken, rattled in a way that felt more internal than external. The skin on her hands was grazed and raw, and she could already feel the tender spots on her knees and elbows where new bruises would bloom by morning. But, all things considered, she had come out of the ordeal remarkably unscathed.

After her near miss, emergency services swarmed around her, checking her vitals and fussing over her minor injuries. Then came the questioning. She had given her statement to the transit police, feigning ignorance. There was no need to complicate things further. Despite the array of CCTV cameras littered across the station, she knew the odds of identifying her assailant were slim to none. The witness accounts had corroborated her statement. A man, frustratingly vague in description, wearing a hat and dark jacket, had blindsided her, pushed her onto the tracks, then walked up the stairs and out of the station.

It would be written off as a random one-off attack, a small blip in the city's safety record.

Back in the safety of her apartment, fatigue clung to her like a second skin. She was tense and fidgety, her nerves still sparking with the adrenaline of her close call. She lay on her bed, staring at the ceiling, every noise from the city streets below jarring her awake. The events of the day replayed in her mind, a cruel highlight reel of her brush with danger. She closed her eyes, but sleep remained a distant promise. With a sigh, she rolled out of bed and entered the bathroom.

The old clawfoot tub was usually a source of relaxation for Marti, an oasis of calm in her hectic life. But today, even as she filled it with warm water and the calming scent of lavender from her favorite Epsom salts, it felt oddly out of place under the bright morning sun.

She tried to coax herself into a semblance of normality, pouring herself a glass of her usual bath-time merlot, despite the time. She didn't need much persuading, the rich red liquid providing a familiar comfort. She also picked up a favorite golden-age cozy from her bookshelf to read, but even as she sank into the soothing water, letting the scent of lavender envelop her, her mind refused to quiet. A second glass of merlot went down as easily as the first and had the same token effect. She contemplated a third dose, but she didn't want to drown these feelings.

Climbing out of the tub, Marti dried off, her eyes wandering to her running shoes tucked away in the corner of her bedroom. Running usually cleared her head, the rhythmic pounding of her feet on the pavement was a meditation in itself. But she knew stepping out alone would be foolhardy, akin to poking a bear in the eye with a stick. She wasn't in the mood to invite more trouble. Not yet. Not unless it was on her terms.

But she also realized she didn't want to be alone in her apartment either. The walls appeared to be inching closer to her. She reached for her phone and dialed Gwen's number. Gwen answered, the background noise of her flower shop bustling with morning activity.

Marti quickly explained the early-morning events, her voice steady despite the lingering nerves. Gwen was silent for a moment and didn't ask any questions before speaking, "I'm on my way."

"Bring your running shoes," Marti added before ending the call.

***

Marti and Gwen leaned over the kitchen island, each nursing a bottle of water as they caught their breath from the run and the final sprint up the tenement's steps to her door. The tension that had been coiled in Marti's chest had eased up. Maybe it was the run, or maybe it was Gwen's reassuring presence.

Despite her petite build, she was a self-defense expert, a fact that Marti knew well from the classes she'd taken with her. Before she'd opened her flower shop, Gwen used to occasionally work close protection for celebrities who didn't want hulking bodyguards drawing attention. Gwen's small frame made her easy to overlook, but she was as deadly as a cornered viper, perhaps even more so than a superficially imposing man.

Throughout their run, Gwen had made sure to steer them along bustling, pedestrian-filled streets. Marti had felt safe under her friend's watchful eyes, her anxiety ebbing away with each step.

Once they'd stopped sweating and their breaths had steadied, Marti said, "Since I won the race, I'm going to take the first shower."

Gwen, looking at her critically, said, "You don't look like a winner. Maybe you should lie down, as well."

"I will," Marti promised.

After a hot shower, and tending to her scrapes, she could finally feel sleep tugging at her. As soon as her head hit the pillow, she was out. Until Oscar time.

***

Marti's downstairs neighbor, Oscar, was a retired mail carrier with a lifelong passion for the accordion. Oscar dedicated an hour each day, typically in the late afternoon, due to a building-wide consensus, to practicing his beloved instrument. Whether it was a polka or a melancholic ballad, Oscar's unique melodies seeped through the walls and floors of the apartment building each afternoon. Rain or shine. A few minutes after 4:30 p.m., the notes started to float up into Marti's apartment, rousing her from a deep, heavy sleep. Despite the oddity, there was a certain charm to it—a soundtrack that, in its way, made the building feel more like a home. She stretched and then winced at a few sharp barks of pain around her left hip and both knees before she gingerly rolled out of bed.

She took three more aspirin, washed down by the dregs of the second glass of red wine beside the tub, then wandered into the main room and found Gwen perched on the couch, with Rita Mae as copilot, working on her laptop. "Feel better?" Gwen asked, not taking her eyes off the screen.

"Yes," Marti replied, walking to the sink and filling a glass with tap water. She did feel better, more balanced, and centered after the few hours of undisturbed sleep.

"What's the plan?" Gwen asked as she looked up.

"Glad you asked," Marti replied. "I'm going to need your help."

***

The setting sun streamed through the windows of Marti's apartment and cast the worn wooden surface of the kitchen table in a golden light. The table was littered with documents and Marti's laptop. Marti's brows furrowed in concentration as she sifted through stacks of legal documents and company profiles, her fingers dancing across the keyboard now and then to jot down notes or look up related information.

After a couple of hours of detailed reading, her eyes now felt tired and she decided to take a break. The apartment was quiet and still. Rita Mae was stretched out in the sun on the windowsill. Gwen had gone back to the city to check on the flower shop and grab more supplies. Marti wasn't sure what she meant by supplies and didn't ask. She let Gwen do her thing. She picked up her phone and tapped Angela's contact number.

"Hey, Angela, it's Marti. I wanted to talk more about these documents you sent over, but first, how's Cassidy?"

"She's doing all right, I think," Angela responded, her voice guarded. "I talked to Savvy this morning. She kept it vague but said we can probably come get her in another day or two."

"That's great," Marti replied. Angela's tone was still cautious; she didn't know Savvy or have the history with her that Marti did. "If Savvy says a day or two, that's what it is." Marti was optimistic. "She'll get through it."

Angela murmured in agreement.

"Do you have a plan once she's clean?"

"I'll talk to her about it, but in the short-term, I rented a place up north. I thought we'd use that until the paternity suit and board decision are complete."

"How did you rent it?" Marti asked with a slight tinge of worry.

"I went through a subsidiary that the Rothchild company owns. They handle a lot of property. I suppose, if someone was determined, they might piece it together, but it would be like looking for a needle in a haystack."

Marti couldn't think of a different or better plan at the moment and let it go.

They moved on and delved into the details of the Calderone board and the other incorporation documents Angela had sent over.

"How are the board members appointed?" Marti asked.

"It varies a lot by company, but in Calderone's case, there are two ways to get on the board. First, a board member can nominate a candidate who then must be approved by the rest of the board. The second way is to be appointed by the CEO. The current corporate structure for Calderone allows this without any additional approval process."

"That seems like a lot of power for one person. Is that common?"

"I wouldn't say it's uncommon. Remember, Calderone, despite its size and influence, is still private. It's not unusual for board members to be appointed by the CEO, especially in smaller or privately held companies. The CEO often has significant influence in shaping the composition of the board to align with the company's strategic goals and vision."

"Another place where the untimely death of the CEO without a clear succession plan could wreak havoc," Marti said.

"Yes, the uncertainty could create some tension in the short-term."

It was a situation that Marti continued to wonder about. Was Calderone's death an accident or was it more complicated than that? Would Rathbone really orchestrate the death of his brother-in-law? Given how the death occurred in Asia, far, far away from any domestic authorities, they might never know. But Marti wondered if they might also be able to take advantage of the situation.

The conversation stretched for 20 more minutes, leaving Marti with a better understanding of the current business situation, and a stomach growling for attention.

"One last question," Marti asked. "How does the voting on the board work?"

"It's by a simple majority with the CEO being able to override any ties."

"So, six votes."

"Well, you need a quorum, which is seven present members, and then the majority vote. So it could be less, and likely would be right now with Alex's death and his seat open, and the open seat that hasn't been filled since Lancaster's retirement."

"That doesn't seem like much."

"You're right. It's pretty weak governance. If I had to guess, I think Alex wanted the company to be responsive. He didn't want things held up in committees or at the board level. He wanted to be able to respond and keep the company nimble. He wanted the appearance of governance without the strictures of it. With this setup, he could still wield significant control."

"Which is great, in theory, if Alex were still alive. But what happens when there's no captain to steer the ship?"

***

She was just thinking about a late dinner, a sure sign that she was feeling better both mentally and physically, when her phone rang. The number was familiar, but she couldn't place it.

"Marti Wells," she answered, keeping her tone professional.

"Ms. Wells, this is Audrey Chen. Maria Rodriguez suggested I give you a call."

Marti remembered. The second potential Calderone board member. "Yes, thank you for calling," she replied. "Did she tell you why?"

"No, Maria was very ... circumspect but insistent I should talk to you."

"Ms. Chen, what do you know about Project Lazarus?" Marti asked.

Chapter Thirty-Five

M arti had just put the phone down from her call with Audrey Chen when it buzzed again on the table.

"I'm at JJ's. Shawarma or falafel?" Gwen asked.

Jersey Joe's was a popular local takeout spot known for their loaded chicken shawarmas and garlic fries. Marti's stomach gave a Pavlovian response. She felt as if she could smell the fries.

"Shawarma and a large fry."

"Fries are not negotiable and go without saying. I'll grab the food and then make a quick sweep of the neighborhood." Gwen said, her tone suddenly serious.

"Okay, be careful," Marti replied.

"No worries, Marti. I've got this. See ya in twenty," Gwen assured her before hanging up.

***

In the silence, Marti started to feel the familiar prickle of anxiety creep up her spine. She tried to ignore it, focusing instead on the dimming light outside her windows. She took a deep breath, reassuring herself that she was safe. But the question of how the hitman had been able to follow her into the subway kept nagging at her. There were multiple options, she realized, and all were equally troubling.

When Gwen returned, they sat down with their shawarmas and fries, eating in silence at first.

"See anything?" Marti asked.

"No one on the street."

The aroma of the spices and the garlicky tang of the fries filled the small eating area. Marti brought up her concerns about the hitman tracking her between mouthfuls.

"There are either multiple people watching all the places related to the case, or they were on you all night, side door escape or not."

"That would be expensive and a big team," Marti said.

"Maybe, but the one thing we know is Rathbone has money and he's motivated."

"True. Angela and Cassidy think they had some sort of surveillance net on Cassidy at one point."

"The other option is ..." Gwen's voice trailed off as they both thought about the more troubling possibility.

"They've got some sort of electronic surveillance on me," Marti finished. "I think I need to call Neon."

"Good idea," Gwen agreed. "Get him to sweep the apartment and your office. We need to figure out what we're dealing with here."

With a nod, Marti picked up her phone and dialed Neon's number. The moment Neon answered, Marti could tell he was awake, sharp. His voice was alert, devoid of the usual sleep-induced slur she was accustomed to. "Thanks for calling at a normal hour for once," he quipped, earning a wry smile from Marti.

"You're welcome." She hesitated before diving into her request. She had never asked him for something like this before. "Neon, can you sweep my place for bugs? Is that something you do?"

There was a pause on the other end of the line.

"Have you ever met a decent hacker who's not paranoid?" he shot back, a hint of humor in his voice. "Sure, I can do it. I sweep my place once a week. My gear isn't high-end, so if you're worried about the CIA or NSA, I probably won't catch anything. But if it's lesser stuff, online spy store stuff, I should be able to handle it. When do you need me?"

"Can you come over now?" Marti asked. They rarely met in person; their relationship was mostly maintained in the digital realm. In the flesh, Neon was a different person—less brash, less confident.

There was another pause, longer this time. "Uh ..." he began, uncertainty creeping into his voice. Marti interrupted him before he could finish his thought.

"I'll save you some fries from Jersey Joe's," she bargained. "Plus, an in-person bonus on top of your usual fee."

There was a sigh on the other end of the line, followed by a resigned, "All right. I'll see you in half an hour." She could almost hear him steeling himself for talking face-to-face with another human.

***

There was a knock at the door and Marti opened it to see a young man standing there. His hair was a vibrant green, like fresh spring grass, and he had a pair of piercing, pale-blue eyes that almost seemed to glow against his light skin. His clothes were casual, a black hoodie over a band tee, and worn, faded jeans, scuffed white Chucks on his feet.

"Hi," he said, those blue eyes sliding off hers to the floor. Any of the bravado from their phone and email conversations was also long gone. This was a man much more comfortable with machines.

"Hi, Neon. Thanks for coming," Marti said and stepped back to let him inside.

He was clutching a backpack and, as he stepped into the apartment, he swung it off his shoulder and onto the coffee table. The backpack opened to reveal a collection of unmarked electronic devices. He glanced at Gwen but didn't say anything. He turned back to his pack and picked up two of the devices, turned them on, and started moving around the room.

As he worked, he mumbled to himself, adjusting the settings on the devices, his gaze focused and intent. His movements were careful and methodical, covering every inch of space. Now and then, he would stop, take a few steps back, and look around, like an artist surveying his canvas. He disappeared into the bedroom.

Fifteen minutes later, he reemerged and nodded to himself. "All clean," he declared, looking around the apartment. "Nice tub, by the way."

"Let's do the office."

Marti led him downstairs to the laundry room where he repeated the procedure. It took less time, but his expression was more serious when he finished.

"Got any change for the machines?" he asked, pointing to the washer and dryer in the corner of the room.

Marti looked at him, confused. "What? Change? For the dryer?"

He nodded, "Really."

She sighed and went into her office, pulling out a roll of quarters from her desk drawer. He took them and fed two of the machines and turned them on before going into the office. She followed and he turned to her. "You've got a camera with a mic outside. The office itself is clean, but there's a setup in the laundry room. Audio and visual."

Marti felt a chill run down her spine. "Where?"

"Opposite wall from your door," he replied. "You want me to disable it?"

Marti thought for a moment and forced herself not to look in that direction. "No," she said finally. "Not yet, at least. It could be useful."

With that, they left the office. She walked Neon up a floor to the front stoop, where he hitched his backpack on his shoulders and unlocked an old single-gear bike from a lamppost. He gave her a nod, a brief smile touching his lips, and then he was off, pedaling down the street and out of sight.

Chapter Thirty-Six

The shrill ringing of her cell phone yanked Marti from the depths of sleep. With a groan, she reached out, her hand flailing in the dark. The phone toppled off the bedside table, clattering to the floor and continuing its incessant ringing. Marti groaned again, pushing back the heavy quilt, leaning over the side of the bed to retrieve it.

Her fingers found the cool, smooth surface of the phone and she squinted at the screen, the bright light piercing the darkness. The clock on the phone read 5:15 a.m., an unholy hour for anyone to be calling. Maybe it was Neon getting revenge. But no. She rubbed her eyes, the numbers blurring and then coming into focus again. The caller ID displayed initials she'd added just yesterday: AC. Audrey Chen.

"Hello?" Her voice was rough, sleep-tinged, and confused. "Audrey?"

"Marti," a voice responded. But it wasn't Audrey's. It was deeper, harsher, accented, and decidedly not female. It was vaguely familiar, but her brain was still stuck in the fog of sleep, refusing to cooperate and identify it.

"Hello?" she tried again, her confusion mounting.

"Wells, is that you?"

The voice clicked into place. "Klein?" She felt a shot of adrenaline zing through her, dragging her fully awake. She sat up straight in bed, her heart pounding in her chest. "What's going on?"

"I thought you might be able to tell me," Klein responded, his voice serious.

"Why are you calling from Audrey Chen's phone?" Marti asked, her mind racing.

A pause, then, "How do you know Chen? Wait, let's not do this over the phone. Can you get over to the Regency on 68th?"

"Yes," she answered automatically. "Why?"

Klein's next words were like a punch to the gut. "Audrey Chen is dead. And you are the last person she called."

***

Marti swung her legs out of bed, her bare feet hitting the cold wooden floor. She quickly dressed in the dark, pulling on the first clothes she could find. She didn't want to wake Gwen, who was sleeping on the couch in the other room. At least, she thought Gwen was sleeping.

When she stepped into the living room, she found the couch empty, the blankets neatly folded, looking untouched. Gwen was standing by the window, a takeout cup of coffee in hand. Marti's eyebrows furrowed in confusion. "Did you sleep at all?" she asked.

"I just got in when your phone rang," Gwen answered.

"In from where?" Marti asked, her mind still trying to catch up with Klein's sudden wake-up call and now Gwen's nocturnal activities.

"I went to check out the supper club and see if Herschel was around," Gwen said casually, maybe a little too casually.

"Was he?"

"Yes."

Gwen's one-word answer hung in the air. Marti wasn't sure if she wanted to know more. Gwen had a dark side and she was fiercely protective of her friends. She could handle herself, that much was sure, but Marti couldn't help but worry.

"And?"

Gwen only shrugged. "The man likes to drink. I escorted him home."

"Stalked him."

"Escorted from a distance."

The silence stretched between them until Gwen broke it. "Who was on the phone?"

Marti snapped back to the present, the urgency of the situation crashing back over her. "That was Klein, the NYPD homicide detective. Audrey Chen is dead." Gwen's only response was a slight twitch of her mouth. "He wants me to come down to the scene at the Regency."

"I'm coming with you," Gwen said. She held up a hand, forestalling any protests. "No arguments. I'll drive."

And with that, they were out the door, into the cool predawn darkness. Gwen's truck was parked a block down, its silhouette looming in the dim light. The city was still sleeping, its slumber undisturbed by the news of Chen's death. Marti paused by the passenger door. A bread truck rumbled past. The sun would rise in a few minutes. A few minutes after that Ms. Jenkins would be out with her pruning shears. Audrey Chen was dead. Marti wasn't. Life was already moving on. Marti climbed in. Gwen dropped the truck into gear and headed across the river.

***

Twenty minutes later, Marti stepped out of the truck.

"I'll find someplace to wait. I'll be close. Call me if you need me," Gwen said and pulled away.

Marti paused for a moment on the sidewalk, taking in the grandeur of the Regency. The iconic New York luxury hotel, with its majestic limestone facade, loomed at the edge of Central Park. The hotel was famous for its opulence and exclusivity, housing the rich and powerful, celebrities and royalty. Today, in the early morning, its entrance was bathed in the harsh light of police cruisers, their flashing red-and-blue lights bouncing off the polished brass fixtures and casting an eerie pallor on the scene.

The usual doormen in their green-and-gold brocaded uniforms were conspicuously absent. In their place stood a uniformed officer, looking grim and out of place in front of the hotel's ornate revolving door. "Klein told me to come down," she stated. The officer barely glanced at her, jotting her name on a clipboard and then speaking into his shoulder mic.

"Far side of the lobby. Just follow the commotion," he instructed, stepping aside and letting her pass.

Marti walked through the revolving door into the lobby. The Regency's interior was as extravagant as its exterior. Polished marble floors reflected the ornate crystal chandeliers that hung from the vaulted ceilings. Rich, dark mahogany paneling lined the walls, and the air smelled faintly of fresh flowers from the arrangement on the concierge desk.

She followed an intricate oriental carpet toward the inner atrium. But that morning, the usual calm of the lobby was shattered. In the center of the inner atrium, normally filled with lush greenery and the sound of soft ambient music, was a crime scene. Police officers, paramedics, hotel staff, and a few bleary-eyed guests in bathrobes were scattered around, watching as the medical team worked around a covered body on the floor.

She passed a knot of suited and nametagged employees behind the front desk. She could pick out the manager by how hard he was wringing his hands. Death was an inconvenience for guests, and he'd greatly appreciate it if the police would wrap up their work before the breakfast service started.

Detective Klein spotted Marti and waved her over. His face was grim.

"What happened?" Marti asked, her eyes drifting to the covered body. "Someone throw her over?"

Klein eyed her. "Why would you ask that?"

"What do you mean?"

"Everyone else who's shown up has assumed she was a jumper."

"Weird place to choose to jump," Marti replied.

"Hard to know the mind of anyone who chooses to go that way," Klein remarked. Marti was sure he'd seen his share of jumpers during his career and he was likely right, very few made sense. "But in this case," he continued, "you're right. We're pretty sure someone threw her over."

"When?"

"A little after 2:15 this morning."

"I know why I think someone threw her over," she raised a hand, "and I promise to tell you, but why do you think that? Weird or not, she still could have jumped. Late at night. Maybe a few drinks. She's alone. Maybe she was already leaning in that direction, depressed, she walks out of her room and it's an impulsive thing. She just ... does it."

"You see a lot of jumpers? I know you were a cop for three seconds back in the day."

"A couple, nowhere near the number you've probably logged."

"I'd be happy if I never see another. Do you know what I've noticed about suicides? They almost always land flat and protect their face somehow. They might have jumped, they might want to die, but they don't want to be completely erased." He nodded in Chen's direction. "She landed headfirst. Looks like she tried to dive through the floor."

Marti thought about it. "You think she was unconscious when she went over."

"It's not definitive. Your scenario could still work, but we've got fibers on the rail and the techs found wood chips in the back of her head, what's left of it; someone gave her a whack. They're doing renovations in the ballroom two floors below Chen's. There's two-by-fours there."

They both looked up. The interior of the atrium opened up to the fifth, or maybe sixth, floor. The balustrades of each level were lined with potted plants, providing a cascading effect of greenery. In the morning gloom, they cast long, ominous shadows onto the marble floor below. Marti wasn't sure how high it was, but it was certainly high enough to kill.

"Pretty cool customer if your theory is right. Walks in. Finds a weapon. Tosses her over inside. This isn't like throwing her out a window. Anyone could have chanced on him."

Klein was nodding. "Cool as ice. Probably not his first rodeo."

A question occurred to Marti. "How does the killer get her to open the door?"

Klein shrugged. "I can think of a few ways. Maybe she wasn't alone. Maybe somehow she brought the killer back with her."

"When did she check in?"

"Today."

"She picked up someone that quickly?"

"It wasn't her first trip. The hotel says she was a semi-regular guest. She might have had someone when she came to town."

"Who then happened to decide to kill her this time? Doesn't sound too plausible."

"Maybe it wasn't planned. Maybe it was an accident and they panicked."

"A little better but still thin, and it negates your theory that the killer went down two floors to get a weapon."

Klein was nonplussed. "Just a theory. I'm amenable to other ideas. Maybe someone posing as hotel security?"

"At that time of night? What could they possibly want? If I were Chen, I wouldn't open the door to Security in the middle of the night. Not without more."

"If I've learned one thing in all my long years, it's that you never get all the answers, just the outcomes. She opened the door for one reason or another and it cost her."

"Any movies?"

"No cameras on guest floors outside the elevator bays. We have her coming up alone a little after 11 p.m. A few other people come up after her, but only two go in the same direction as her room and the hotel staff has verified them as registered guests. We already talked to both. They're not crossed off, but we consider them unlikely."

"Any other ways up?"

"Yup, fire stairs at either end of the hallway. No cameras there. Cameras in the lobby partially cover the doors, but there are blind spots. If you know about the cameras, you could potentially slip past unnoticed."

They fell silent for a moment, each thinking it through, then Klein said, "Your turn, Wells. I've shown you mine, now you show me yours. Why are you the last person Audry Chen called?"

Marti blew out a breath. She didn't think she could keep this under wraps any longer, and she wasn't sure she wanted to anyway.

Chen was dead.

She'd almost been run over by a subway train.

Cassidy had been shot.

She looked around. "Is there someplace to talk around here that doesn't include a body?"

Chapter Thirty-Seven

Marti and Klein left and exited through the revolving door back onto the street. The sun on her face and the taxis driving past felt wrong after the depressing scene inside the lobby. Marti used the short walk to refocus. Klein led them to the Liberty Diner, a coffee shop located around the corner from the Regency on a quiet stretch of avenue between a small bookstore called The Whispering Page and a trendy fashion boutique featuring racks of clothes that Marti thought might cover one of her legs.

Retro decor, cozy booths, and the soft hum of conversation greeted them as they stepped inside. The friendly waitstaff, dressed in vintage bowling T-shirts, moved between tables, tending to the small but eclectic mix of early-rising patrons.

The scent of freshly brewed coffee filled the air as they settled into a booth. Klein wasted no time and ordered a stack of pancakes and bacon. Marti ordered coffee and a blueberry muffin.

While they waited for their food, Marti recounted the details of her case thus far. She divulged everything she knew, except for Cassidy's drug rehab, recognizing the delicate nature of that information. She didn't see how that might be relevant to Klein's case. She didn't hold back as she had before when he'd visited her apartment. Lives had been lost and lives were still at stake. Marti's own had been perilously close to the edge. Her story about the subway shover received a raised eyebrow from Klein but no immediate comment.

"I talked to Chen and another board member. Maria Rodriguez. I can give you her contact details. Maybe you should check on her."

"That's a good idea," Klein said. "How did you leave it with Chen yesterday?"

"I told her the things I'd learned about Project Lazarus and what I suspected Rathbone might have planned. She said she would check it out and get me proof if she could."

"And she hit a trip wire of some sort, a warning system. And decided she was too close. There's no laptop in her room. We did find a piece of a phone, the battery cover in her hand, but not the phone itself. Maybe she was trying to hide it or was holding it when the killer got to her."

"You're assuming this is related to Calderone and Project Lazarus."

Klein raised an eyebrow. "I'll admit I don't believe in coincidences, but I do believe in the preponderance of evidence, even circumstantial. It would be too weird if all of what you just told me was swirling around her and she happened to get killed for another reason. People's lives, on balance, just aren't that interesting."

"She could still be a jumper."

"Maybe. I like that better than random coincidence."

"You're the expert."

"I feel like you remember that when it's convenient for you."

"Maybe." Marti smiled slightly and then waved a hand to dismiss the potential argument. "I don't think any leak about Chen came from my end." She explained about Neon. "I spoke with her one time, from my apartment." Klein nodded. But then another thought occurred to

Marti. She hadn't spoken to Chen from her office, but she had left a message. Was that enough to kill her? Marti didn't know and probably never would.

The waitress dropped off their food and topped up the coffee. Klein spread butter and syrup over the warm pancakes and began to cut them up. If he was surprised or angry or confused, he didn't show it. He appeared to be wholly devoted to his plate.

Marti picked at her muffin and thought of one more question.

"And how did you end up involved in the Chen case?" she inquired.

Klein paused mid-bite, his fork hovering in the air for a moment before he set it down.

"I didn't choose to be a part of it," Klein replied, a hint of frustration creeping into his voice. "After the shooting and kidnapping attempt earlier in the week, I put a flag on your name and contact information in the system. It was a precaution, given the circumstances. I had very few leads, so it was more of a desperation move on my part, but I could tell you were … not telling me everything." An eyebrow accompanied that statement. "It was my way of keeping my foot in the door. And when Detective Overmairer, who officially caught Chen last night, ran the information from Chen's phone through the system, your name popped up alongside mine. Overmairer called me, and I called you."

Marti's eyebrows furrowed as she processed the intricate web of connections that had brought them together again. She didn't mention the warning about the hitman.

"Could I potentially be arrested for all of this? Is Overmairer looking at me?" Marti asked.

Klein's gaze met hers. "If I were Overmairer, you'd be on my list. Maybe not high, but someone I'd need to talk to. I'll give him this background, but you'll have to come in and make a statement."

"Of course. That's not a problem." Marti sighed, realizing the potential weight of her predicament. "I'm sorry, Klein. I should have told you more at the start. I didn't foresee it escalating to this extent. I believed it would end in court or at the board meeting."

Klein nodded in agreement but to his credit refrained from any 'I told you so' jibes. He stabbed the last few remaining pieces of his breakfast before he pushed the plate away and said, "I don't think the ending to this will be quite so genteel as a court ruling."

"Me either."

Marti and Klein departed Liberty Diner, the conversation still lingering in Marti's mind as they made their way back to the hotel entrance. Marti couldn't help but notice the absence of the police presence.

"I'm surprised the police have already cleared out," Marti commented, a touch of disbelief in her voice.

Klein smirked, a knowing look in his eyes. "Well, you see, the mayor's cousin happens to be a part owner of this place. You know how power works."

Marti nodded, understanding the dynamics at play. Power could smooth the edges and make things disappear. She thought Rathbone might be counting on just that. "The wheels turn faster for some."

"I'm sure the techs are still inside working, power can only push so far, but we gotta play the game just like everyone else."

Klein bid her farewell and headed back inside the hotel. Marti noticed with the police absence, the doormen had returned to their stations at the entrance. Marti retrieved her phone and scrolled through her gallery until she found the photo she wanted. With a few taps, she zoomed in and centered the image to ensure the face was visible.

She stepped closer to the entrance. The doorman offered her a polite smile, trained to maintain a pleasant demeanor. However, the apprehension in his eyes betrayed his wariness, perhaps suspecting her to be a member of the press. The Regency Hotel was notorious for its aversion to any media attention, never mind a murder. But he'd also just watched her arrive with a detective. She could use that.

"Were you on duty yesterday? Last night, specifically?" Marti asked.

The doorman nodded, his eyes flickering with a mix of curiosity and caution but he didn't ask for ID. "Yes, ma'am." Marti winced at the ma'am. She looked the guy over. She was what? Maybe 10 years older? Twelve max. She'd give him a pass. She probably wasn't looking her best either. She forced herself to smile and focus on the man's words. "I'm covering double shifts. Two of the guys are on vacation. I worked four to midnight here, then I was on-call and available inside for any guest requests."

"Great," Marti responded, a glimmer of hope flickering within her. She believed she deserved a stroke of luck at this point. "Take a look at this," she held out the phone, "did you see this guy around the hotel?"

The doorman took his time, studying the image intently before finally handing it back. "No, he wasn't here." Marti felt her glimmer of hope fall and shatter on the pavement at her feet. She was about to thank the man for his time when he continued. "Not last night but I've seen him before," he finished, nodding in recognition.

"At the hotel?"

"Yes," he said, nodding more confidently now. "He's been here before."

"Thanks," Marti said, pocketing her phone.

***

Marti settled back into the truck's passenger seat, her mind still on her conversations with Klein and the doorman. She realized Gwen had asked her a question.

"What?"

"How did Klein react?"

Marti let out a weary sigh. The all-nighter was catching up to her. "He wasn't happy, to say the least, but he kept his feelings mostly in check. In the end, he promised to help in any way he could. The problem is, Audrey Chen's death isn't technically his case, the paternity court case is all the way out in California, and we have no real evidence on the attempted kidnapping that we can share."

"Klein didn't get any video or witnesses off the street?"

"No, he's at a dead end. He's not going to get to Herschel or his crew for that. I did get one other thing this morning. The doorman at the hotel told me Herschel had been spotted at the hotel in the past. He couldn't say it was last night, but he recognized him."

"That's interesting," Gwen said.

"But not definitive. Nothing in this case feels very definitive so I'm not sure what Klein can do to help, but good to know he's there if we need him. Rathbone and his team are skilled at covering their tracks. It's unlikely we'll find any direct evidence tying him to any of this. It's just noise. Call it what you want. A distraction. A warning. It's all designed to keep us busy and keep us away from Calderone and Rathbone until it's too late."

Gwen's hands tightened around the steering wheel. "So, what's our move now?"

Marti leaned back and stared out at the city streets. "We need to gather more information and hopefully more allies before the board meeting tomorrow. I think our best shot is to force them into making a mistake that undermines their position."

"Have Rathbone take himself out."

"Right. It sounds like the cancer might do that for us eventually, but we don't have the luxury of time. We can't let him lock up the means and opportunity to make his AI plan a reality even after his death."

***

Gwen's truck cruised south along the West Side Highway, the Hudson glittering darkly to Marti's right. Marti's thoughts turned over the conversation with Klein, remembering his comment about the phone piece being found in Chen's hand. Gwen exited on Canal and wrapped around to the entrance of the Holland Tunnel that would take them back to Jersey City. As they exited 14th Street and made the right onto Grove, Marti pulled out her phone.

After a few rings, Neon's distinctive voice crackled through the line. "Hey, Marti, I see you're back to your old ways. Don't ideas ever occur to you during my normal business hours?"

"Sorry, Neon, but your normal business hours are not all that normal for others." After the morning she'd had, she wasn't much in the mood for their usual banter. "I need your expertise. I'm going to send you a mobile number. Can you poke around and see if there were any texts or emails sent from the number last night?"

He must have picked up on her tone. "Consider it done. Send me the number, and I'll see what I can find."

"Listen, I'm not sure if it's a personal or corporate number but someone else might also be interested. Be careful."

"That's ominous."

"Good; that was the point."

Chapter Thirty-Eight

M arti, back in the comfort of her apartment, checked on Rita Mae, who gave a lazy twitch of her tail in response to Marti's concern, then picked up her phone and dialed Maria Rodriguez's number. She was sure Klein would pass on the information she'd shared and check on Maria, but she wasn't sure how quickly Overmairer or the other detectives might follow up on it. She wanted to hear the woman's voice for herself.

As soon as Maria answered, Marti knew the police, or perhaps the corporate rumor mill, had already reached her. Her voice was a mix of anger and unease.

"What the hell is going on, Marti? Is it true? Did they really kill Audrey?" Maria asked.

"I'm afraid so," Marti answered. "I'm sorry."

"What the hell happened? I just spoke to her yesterday."

"So did I. She reached out last night and I told her the same things I told you. She said she was also in the dark about Rathbone's plans, but mentioned she was going to dig a little deeper into Project Lazarus and let me know. Then, late last night, early this morning really, the police called to inform me about Audrey's death. Mine was the last number called from her phone."

Maria's voice wavered with a mixture of emotions. "I didn't know Audrey well. We really only spoke at the board meetings, but we did serve together for several years." She cleared her throat. "We were friendly. I just ... can't believe it. Rathbone ... is he really behind all this? It just seems insane. I mean, he's always been intense and a little eccentric, but that could describe a lot of people in the tech industry, but killing people? It's beyond comprehension," Maria said.

"I understand and I don't have hard proof, not yet, but all the circumstantial evidence points at him and now he knows more people are looking. I don't know if he has your name or not. You need to be extra cautious, Maria. Are you safe?" Marti asked.

"For now, I think so. I'm not flying in until tomorrow and I've already told my assistant to switch hotels and make the reservation under her name," Maria replied.

"Good. Be very careful. We can't underestimate Rathbone or his motives. So you're still planning to attend the upcoming board meeting?" Marti inquired.

Maria's voice hardened with resolve. "Damn right, I am. I want to look that man in the eye and see if there's even a trace of humanity left in him," Maria declared.

"Did you hear from Audrey at all yesterday after you spoke? Do you know if she managed to uncover anything else about Project Lazarus or Rathbone's plans?" Marti questioned.

Maria sighed. "No, Audrey had more contacts within Calderone. She was going to try to reach out and gather more information before we talked again."

"And you don't know who she was going to talk to?"

"No. I'm sorry."

"Don't be sorry. It probably saved your life. We're treading on dangerous ground here. Rathbone might be brilliant and eccentric but he's also clearly ruthless, and we can't afford to underestimate him. Stay safe," Marti advised before they ended the call.

As she stared out the window and watched a plane approaching Newark Liberty to the south, Marti couldn't shake the unsettling feeling that lingered in her gut. The danger continued to escalate and the time continued to shrink to expose the truth. Was it worth it to keep pushing? Would it be better to walk away and keep everyone involved safe? Rathbone would be dead soon if the rumors of the cancer were true. Maybe his vision would die with him? But if it didn't? She thought back to her conversations with Lancaster and Miles. There was tremendous good that might come out of such a huge technological advance. But there was also tremendous exploitation and evil that might also emerge. Should it be up to just one man or one company to decide that fate? She weighed the arguments back and forth and reached an inescapable conclusion.

She wanted to be an optimist but humanity had a very bloody track record.

***

Marti spent the next three days prepping and putting as much of her plan if you could call it that, it felt more like sticks and feathers and rocks held together with duct tape, in place for the board meeting confrontation with Rathbone.

Gwen continued to have her back and stay at Marti's apartment, but after the attempt in the subway and the Chen murder, it felt like everything was building toward the meeting. Neither she nor Gwen ever spotted anyone hanging around the apartment building. They went on the occasional run to fight off cabin fever, but Marti spent much of her time in her apartment on the phone or reviewing documents. She didn't go to her basement office. Let whoever was on the other end of that camera waste time reviewing the footage.

The day before the board meeting she called Savvy. She needed to check on Cassidy and her recovery. "Savvy, it's Marti. How is Cassidy doing? I wanted to see if I could swing by and pick her up," Marti said. Cassidy was the linchpin. If she wasn't capable of standing up to Rathbone and the board, there was no amount of propping up or hand waving that Marti could do that would change the situation.

"Hey, Smartie. Good to hear your voice. Physically, Cassidy is improving. The bullet wound is healing nicely, and she should regain full range of motion eventually. We've been gradually weaning her off the painkillers, so now she's mostly relying on Extra Strength Tylenol. I'm being cautious with stronger medication, considering her history. She understands that too, and she's not complaining," Savvy explained. "But it's not been easy, either."

Marti nodded on the other end of the line, relieved to hear about Cassidy's physical progress. She understood the delicate balance they needed to maintain.

"And mentally?" Marti asked.

"Mentally, she's doing better. Cassidy is tough, and she's only going to get tougher. You know I've seen a lot of people like her. She's showing some grit. You know I like to see that. It won't be an easy road, but I believe she'll get there," Savvy said.

"Good," Marti replied. She trusted Savvy's opinion implicitly. "She's going to need every ounce of it."

***

Gwen's truck rumbled through the streets of Jersey City, crossing over into the bustling streets of Lower Manhattan. The early-morning traffic weaved around them as they made their way toward the heart of the city. Their first stop was Gwen's flower shop. Gwen parked the truck and turned to Marti.

"All right, I'll just be a minute. Need to check on the shop," Gwen said. "Make sure they're not robbing me blind." But she said it with a smile.

Marti watched as Gwen disappeared through the shop's entrance, leaving her alone in the truck. Her gaze wandered, taking in the vibrant tapestry of city life. Pedestrians hurried along the sidewalks, lost in their own worlds, their footsteps a rhythmic soundtrack to the bustling streets. The aroma of butter and sizzling bacon grease wafted from a cafe across the street, mingling with the crisp morning air. Marti's eyes were drawn to the charming brownstone buildings lining the street, their stoops adorned with flower pots and colorful flags, a characteristic sight in the Village. It was a neighborhood with a distinct charm, where the bustling energy of the city coexisted with a sense of community and history.

Five minutes later, Gwen emerged from the flower shop, a satisfied smile on her face. She climbed back into the truck, ready for the next leg of their journey.

"Everything's looking good," Gwen confirmed as she started the engine.

The truck maneuvered through the city streets, the familiar stop-and-go rhythm of New York traffic accompanying them. They eventually arrived at the imposing Rothchild building, a venerable structure with a rich historical legacy that commanded attention with its ornate stone facade and intricate carvings depicting scenes from a bygone era.

Marti turned to Gwen. "I'll go inside and meet with Angela. You stay in the truck, keep an eye out," Marti instructed. She knew they hadn't been followed, Gwen would have noticed, but they weren't far from the subway station where Marti had been attacked and she could feel the paranoia seeping in like an oil slick.

"Be careful out there, Marti," Gwen said.

"Always," Marti said with perhaps more confidence than she really felt.

***

Marti sat on the edge of Angela's office desk, her fingers tapping nervously against the surface. Marti had just finished telling the woman about Project Lazarus and Chen's death. The weight of the pending board meeting and the uncertain outcome of the paternity case Cassidy had brought also hung heavily in the air. She looked at Angela, her eyes filled with anticipation.

"So, how did it go? Did you talk to the lawyers about our idea? Did you use the documents?" Marti asked.

Angela leaned back in her chair. She had circles under her eyes, and her hair lacked its characteristic shine. She glanced at her watch and sighed. The last few weeks were taking their toll on everyone. "Yes, I did. We had a call with the lawyers this morning. They seemed intrigued by your proposition."

"And? What did they say? Is it something we can use?"

Angela took a moment to gather her thoughts before responding. "They think it's a long shot, Marti. Challenging the paternity through unconventional means like this is risky. The burden of proof will be on us and we have to convince the judge that our theory holds weight."

Marti's shoulders slumped slightly, but she maintained her resolve. "The burden of proof was already on us. It's the time that I'm most worried about. There is no time to drag this out. That plays into Rathbone's hands. If there's a chance, I think we have to take it."

Angela nodded in agreement. "I understand. Trust me, I do. The lawyers have prepared a strong argument, but ultimately, it's up to the judge. There's a meeting in chambers with the judge this afternoon at three. We should know by the end of the day."

"Okay," Marti said. "I hate when there's nothing left to do but wait. The board meeting is an immovable object, and we'll either have the tools to get around it or not."

Angela reached out and placed a comforting hand on Marti's shoulder. "We've come this far, Marti, mostly because of you. I promise we won't give up now. We'll do everything we can to support Cassidy and uncover the truth."

"I know." Marti stood and moved to the door. "Let's go see how she's doing."

***

Savvy met Marti and Angela at the roll-top entrance to The Iron Sirens' clubhouse; the scents of leather, motor oil, and chrome filled the air. As they stepped inside, Marti realized she was nervous. Without Cassidy, they had no hope of stopping Rathbone. They needed her. Inside, it was dim. The club was more of an evening place, not mid-afternoon. Cassidy was taking glasses out of a rack and placing them on a shelf above the bar that ran across the back of the main room. She used her right arm, the other was tucked into a blue medical sling that kept it immobile against her body.

Marti watched from a distance and couldn't help but notice a subtle change in the young woman. Though her physical appearance hadn't drastically transformed, it had only been a week, there were subtle cues that said something had changed. She moved with more self-confidence and when Marti got closer, she could see a clarity in her eyes that hadn't been there in their previous meetings.

Cassidy finished putting away the barware and approached all three of them, her strides more purposeful, her shoulders squared. The once fragile and vulnerable girl seemed to have shed her previous self, like a cicada shell.

Marti exchanged a knowing look with Angela, silently acknowledging the positive transformation in the woman. Maybe it wouldn't last. Maybe she'd return to her old destructive habits, but it was a start. Marti would take that much.

"Hey, Cassidy," Marti greeted her, a warm smile spreading across her face. "You're looking good. How are you feeling?"

Cassidy met Marti's gaze, her expression determined yet calm. "I feel different. I've tried rehab before before but ... I was just going through the motions. I guess I really didn't want it. Savvy and the Sirens have helped me find my strength again. I won't let anyone intimidate me or push me around anymore. I'm ready to face Rathbone head-on."

Marti liked the fire and brimstone but felt a need to temper it. "I'm very happy you're feeling better, but let's not get overconfident. We'll talk about the next steps soon. One day at a time, right?"

Angela nodded in agreement. "We believe in you, Cassidy."

Cassidy smiled. "Thanks." She turned to Savvy and gave the woman a one-armed hug. "And thank you and all the Sirens."

"You're a Siren now, too. You're welcome back any time. Work the steps. Just because you're walking out of here doesn't mean you're cured."

"I know."

As they left the clubhouse, Savvy pulled Marti aside. "Be careful with her. She talks a good game but she's still young."

"And stupid, I know."

"Any trouble or stress could make her backslide."

"We'll take care of her," Marti assured her old friend; she hoped to God that she was telling the truth.

Chapter Thirty-Nine

Marti felt the weight of anticipation settle in her chest as she dressed in the borrowed security guard uniform. She noticed a slight tremble in her fingers as she buttoned up the crisp, white dress shirt. The gravity of the situation weighed heavily on her mind—there was a good chance she would make it up to the boardroom, but the odds of walking back out were far less certain. Rathbone had already demonstrated he was ruthless in pursuit of his goals. Would several potential witnesses deter him or embolden him? She wasn't sure.

She pushed the thoughts aside and finished dressing. She gave herself one last look in the mirror, adjusted her uniform slightly, and checked that the coat covered the gun in the holster at the small of her back. She didn't love that carry position. It was awkward and difficult to access quickly but she felt she had no better option.

She took the ID badge off the dresser and clipped it to her belt. Marcia Brown was ready. Was Marti? She took a deep breath. Worrying wouldn't help her now. Gwen was waiting, Angela and Cassidy were waiting, Maria Rodriguez was waiting, and even Victor Rathbone was waiting. It was time to go.

As she moved down the hallway toward the door, there came an unexpected knock. Marti paused, her senses on high alert. "Yes?" she called out. She wasn't expecting anyone.

"It's Pedro. I have a package for you," the familiar voice called from the other side.

Marti opened the door, finding the handyman standing there, slightly sweaty and disheveled. "Pedro? What delivery?" she asked, a hint of confusion in her voice.

"I'm sorry, Marti. I left it downstairs by your office this morning and just noticed that it was still there," Pedro explained, his tone apologetic. "I have to look at Ms. Jenkins' refrigerator, so I thought I'd bring it up."

"That's all right, Pedro. I haven't been downstairs today. I've been busy and mostly working up here," Marti replied, accepting the package from him. "Thank you for bringing it up."

Pedro nodded, giving her a tired smile. "No problem. Have a good night."

"You, too," she said, closing the door behind her. Marti carried the package into the kitchen. It felt thick, filled with what seemed like a stack of papers similar to the delivery of legal documents she'd received earlier from Angela. There were no markings on the package except for her address. Curiosity piqued, she reached for a steak knife from the block and carefully slit open the package.

As she pulled out the sheath of papers, a frown formed on her face, but gradually, as her eyes scanned through the documents, it transformed into a smile. She grabbed her backpack from the closet and shoved the papers inside. The pieces were falling into place, and she was determined to use every tool at her disposal to take down Rathbone. She knew she might need every one of them.

***

Marti and Cassidy were two blocks north of the Calderone skyscraper. Through an earpiece, Marti maintained contact with Gwen, who was driving a rental sedan in a grid around the building. Her voice crackled with urgency as she relayed Rathbone's arrival in a private car.

"He's here. Going inside now. Looks like he has four private security guards staying with him for close protection," Gwen said.

"Roger that," Marti said and checked her watch. It was 6:45 p.m. The board meeting was scheduled for seven. She took out her phone and called the general number for the building.

"345 Madison Avenue. How can I help you?"

She recognized the accented voice that picked up. She was counting on it.

"Hi, this is Marcia. I might be a few minutes late," she said. She wasn't sure who else might be listening.

"All right, Marcia. Not a problem. We have plenty of people on duty here. More than enough. Take your time. Drop your things at the employee entrance in the back when you arrive," Scott said and hung up.

"Who was that?" Cassidy asked.

"A friend," Marti said. "I think. An ally for tonight, at least. He works for the company that runs security for the building." She indicated her uniform. "But it appears that Rathbone has also brought his own security. I'm sure they all have our pictures and orders to stop us from getting upstairs."

"So what are we going to do?"

"A goal without a plan is just a wish."

***

Marti led Cassidy down the street toward the rear service entrance, her grip tightening on the key card. She offered a silent prayer to Robert, the night manager, hoping that he had come through for a fellow Impala enthusiast.

Approaching the outer door, Marti swiped her key card and, with a flicker of relief, it granted them access. Now, they were faced with the inner door, one that was reserved for maintenance personnel. Marti held her card up to the reader and her heart sank as the key card failed to unlock it.

Just as disappointment started to settle in, Marti's eyes caught sight of a small wedge jammed at the bottom of the door. No key card necessary. No record of their entrance. She whispered a silent word of thanks to Robert. She quickly pulled the door open and motioned for Cassidy to follow.

They moved through the service corridor, navigating the maze of pipes and ductwork. The air was heavy with the scent of dust and hot metal. Marti's mind raced, her senses heightened, as they moved deeper into the building. If Rathbone's men found them now, there was nowhere to run, but they made it to the service elevator without seeing anyone. Marti pressed the call button and with a rumbling ding, the doors slid open, revealing the dimly lit and scratched-up interior of the elevator. Marti and Cassidy stepped inside, then after a brief shared glance and a nod, Marti pressed the button for the 48th floor. The elevator jolted into motion.

Marti's heartbeat quickened as the elevator climbed higher. They'd made it to the belly of the beast, but the hard part was yet to come. She knew they had to remain undetected until they were inside the boardroom itself.

The elevator doors finally opened on the 48th floor, revealing a large storage closet with shelves filled with office supplies, extra furniture, custodial supplies, telecom and networking equipment. But no guards. She went to the door and peeked out. Empty cubicles and glassed-in offices. She could hear activity but nothing close. The boardroom and regular elevator lobby were on the opposite side of the floor.

"Here we go," Marti whispered. "Stay close."

Marti led Cassidy deeper into the heart of the building. Her mind recalled the details of the floor plan. This was where her previous shift would pay off. She knew they couldn't afford any missteps.

***

Marti and Cassidy moved with deliberate caution along the deserted corridors of the office floor, their footsteps muffled just enough by the thin carpeting. Every sound, every creak of the floor, held the potential to alert Rathbone's security detail. They couldn't afford to make a mistake now.

During her rounds, she'd noticed that the conference room had three doors. One at each end that opened onto the main lobby but also a third on the opposite wall.

Just ahead now was the entrance to an executive suite. Perhaps, Alex Calderone had used it when he was alive and visiting the East Coast. Or, perhaps it was just part of the floor plan and never used. At least until Marti stumbled on it. It was now their ticket to gaining access to the conference room without raising any alarms. The suite's entrance location offered an advantage, effectively a back door to the meeting—an opportunity to bypass the more commonly used entrances near the lobby, where Rathbone's additional security would likely be stationed.

As they neared the empty administrative assistant's desk outside the suite, Marti glanced at Cassidy. The young woman nodded, her eyes reflecting a mix of determination and trust. Marti paused in front of the closed door, her hand lingering on the doorknob. With a steady grip, she turned the handle, her heart pounding in her chest. She had to hope that Rathbone continued to underestimate her.

The door swung open smoothly, revealing the quiet and empty expanse of the executive suite. Marti and Cassidy slipped inside and Marti let out a breath she didn't know she'd been holding. Two small security lights cast long shadows on the elegantly appointed furnishings, from the polished mahogany desk to the plush leather chair arranged neatly behind it. The room exuded an air of refined but empty opulence. There were no personal artifacts of any kind. No clutter or misplaced paper. No smell beyond the acidic tang of cleaning fluid. It was as sterile as a photo from an office supply catalog.

Marti strode across the room until she reached the door that led to the conference room on the far side. She could hear the murmur of voices from within. It was ten after seven and the meeting had started. The conference room lay just beyond this threshold. She stared at the line of light escaping under the bottom of the door. One more door, one more step, and they would be in the middle of it all. Marti pulled out her phone and sent two quick texts, then steeled herself and grabbed the door handle.

Chapter Forty

The room turned as one and looked at them. No one said anything. There were seven people seated around the large table. Marti recognized Maria Rodriguez to the left and Dr. Anil Sharma next to her. Marti locked eyes with Rodriguez and the woman gave an almost imperceptible nod. She recognized each of the remaining four board members from her previous research. The only person she didn't recognize was an older woman sitting slightly away from the table with a laptop on her lap. Perhaps an assistant charged with taking the official meeting minutes.

Finally, her eyes came to rest on Rathbone at the head of the table. Marti didn't know if that was a power move or his usual seat. She suspected the former. If you keep acting like the boss, eventually people start assuming you really are the boss, board approval or not. Fake it until you make it, in other words.

He was not a physically imposing man, but Marti could feel his formidable charisma and control of the room. His once thick, dark hair she'd seen in magazine profiles had thinned and turned powdery-gray, framing a weathered face marked by deep lines and a prominent jawline. Despite his body failing him, his eyes still held a sharpness and intensity that conveyed his shrewdness and many hours spent locking horns in conference rooms just like this one. Unlike Marti.

He broke the silence and spoke first. "Ms. Wells and Ms. Bergman, I presume." Pointedly using Cassidy's mother's maiden name instead of Calderone. If he was surprised by their sudden appearance, he didn't show it. "Please, have a seat."

"Victor, what's going on? Who are these people?" He glanced down at a sheet of paper on the table in front of him. "I don't see them on the agenda."

The man, Marti knew his name was Charles Harrington, a corporate lawyer who specialized in mergers and acquisitions, was older, late 60s, and through genetics or an amazing toupee, still maintained a full head of thick, silver hair. Given his old-money background and long tenure on the board, Marti had thought he would not be overly sympathetic to Cassidy's paternity claim or stopping Rathbone's AI plans. In her experience, rich, white men liked nothing more than to maintain the status quo.

"Indeed they are not on the agenda, but I think we can afford a few minutes to hear them out before moving on to more official business." He turned to the woman with the laptop in the corner. "Liz, no need to keep notes or record this portion." The woman nodded and closed the laptop, then reached over to a side table and pressed a button on a starfish-shaped device.

This was unexpected but if Rathbone was counting on her to wither or meltdown in the glare of the board's attention, she was equally determined to prove him wrong. She was ready and prepared. If she was right, this was the man who had decided she should be pushed in front of a subway car. She was going to give it to him with both barrels. She moved to the opposite end of the table with Cassidy in her wake.

She put her backpack on the chair but didn't sit. She felt better standing. "Ladies and gentlemen, this woman," she indicated Cassidy standing next to her, "is not Cassidy Bergman. She is Cassidy Calderone, Alex Calderone's daughter. And your new CEO."

She paused as the board members burst out in simultaneous responses to that deliberately provocative statement. Everyone except Rathbone and Rodriguez. Go big or go home, she figured. She didn't know how long she'd get to make her case. Might as well come out with a haymaker. She locked eyes with Rathbone across the length of the long table. He gave her a small smile and then raised a hand. After a moment, the room fell silent again.

"Alleged daughter. As you can imagine, Alex Calderone and his wealth, and the circumstances of his death, have made him a target of many," he glanced around the room and then directly at Cassidy, "many attempts at fraud and exhortation. Like the other potential cons, we are actively fighting this in court."

"You knew about this?" Harrington asked.

"Yes, the company is aware and is taking the appropriate steps. Just as we have in past cases."

"Past cases were brought to the board's attention."

"There are more pressing matters that deserve the board's attention than frivolous and farfetched claims."

"And who made that decision?"

"I did," Rathbone replied, staring Harrington down until he looked away. Another power play, another point for Rathbone, but Marti was encouraged by the ripples of dissent. These were not people accustomed to having decisions taken away from them or being placed in the background. Marti was about to resume speaking when another board member, Dev Patel, an M&A specialist, spoke up.

"She has his eyes." It came out sounding tentative, like a question.

"What?" Rathbone said.

"Maybe it's not so farfetched or frivolous, Victor. Look at the woman. It's like looking at Alex. She has his eyes."

"Nonsense. Okay, I apologize to you all. Perhaps I should have made you more aware of her claim, but don't let the surprise of it cloud your judgment. Don't let this woman plunder a great man's legacy."

"You'd rather have that opportunity for yourself, right?" Marti jabbed.

"What? Of course not. If anything, I'm only acting as a steward, a stand-in, right now until we can all decide the best path to move Calderone Innovations forward."

His tone aimed for righteous indignation at such an accusation, but it rang hollow to Marti's ears. She wasn't sure if the other members heard it too; she suspected some might have and she moved to capitalize on it. She reached into her bag and tossed two packets of paper on the table. There hadn't been time to make copies but she thought one would be enough. The board could learn to share in this case.

"Here are two things that I believe will help clarify matters. First, Mr. Rathbone is correct, Calderone is contesting Cassidy's paternity claim in the California court and she welcomes that scrutiny, but she is concerned that Calderone's motivations, or perhaps Mr. Rathbone's, given the board's apparent lack of awareness, are less about protecting the legacy of her father and more about ensuring Mr. Rathbone's current objectives."

Rathbone cut in. "My objectives are Calderone's objectives."

That was met with a beat of silence and he realized he'd misstepped.

"What I meant was that my objectives are part of Calderone's long-term strategy."

Another beat of silence.

This time Marti cut in and seized back control of the conversation. "We'll get back to your objectives and how they might or might not align with Calderone's long-term strategy in a moment, but first I'd like to draw this group's attention to the documents on the table. Mr. Harrington, I believe you are a lawyer and can help the others understand the implications of the set of documents on the left." Harrington reached forward and drew the set of papers closer. Marti continued, "Today, the judge in the case granted Cassidy an ex parte order. For those not familiar, and Mr. Harrington can attest, an ex parte order can be made without the presence or input of the opposing party. They are most often used in emergencies like child custody disputes or personal safety. But there is another use: For the preservation of assets in cases of potential fraud or misappropriation."

"Which don't apply in this circumstance," Rathbone retorted, but his confidence and control seemed shaken. He was smart and intelligent but not a lawyer by trade.

He looked toward Harrington who was flipping through the pages and didn't respond, but Dr. Sharma did. "Ex parte orders are, by definition, temporary. How long is this effective?"

"That's correct. This order is good for 25 days until a full hearing and judgment can be held. It freezes all of Calderone's assets from further appropriation and recognizes, based on current scientific standards and previous testing, Cassidy as Alex's legal heir. You'll find the test results in the second set of papers. Ms. Patel was correct. She does have Alex's eyes and the science proves it."

"What? That can all be faked. She's bluffing. Charles, that can't be right?" Rathbone stood and grasped at the papers. Harrington had finished reading and placed a hand on top of the stack.

"If she's bluffing, it's very convincing and one phone call, it's still business hours in California, would be enough to prove or disprove the legal part. It would be a stupid bluff, and Ms. Wells doesn't strike me as a stupid woman, but much of this order relies on one thing, something we can also prove or disprove quite easily.

"Victor, what is Project Lazarus?"

Chapter Forty-One

Marti watched the calculations flash across Rathbone's face before he spoke, but she was still a little surprised when he spoke. He had decided to go all in and make his pitch to the board. Marti had to admire the approach, it's what she might have done in his place, but she also worried about his reaction if it didn't go his way.

"Project Lazarus is the future of Calderone."

"This is you speaking for us again?" Harrington said.

"No, this is me speaking for me, but I hope you'll hear me out." Harrington waved a hand and then sat back in his chair. Rathbone took that as consent to continue. "Thank you. Project Lazarus is a groundbreaking project that will revolutionize human existence.

"The essence of Project Lazarus lies in the convergence of advanced neurology, computational neuroscience, and cutting-edge artificial intelligence," Victor began. He had everyone's undivided attention. "It is what Calderone has been working toward for more than 25 years. Through the process of neural mapping, we aim to create a digital replica of an individual's neural network, capturing the intricate connections and patterns that define their consciousness."

As Rathbone spoke, his voice resonated with conviction, filling the room. Marti was impressed. He was clear and concise despite the very technical material. He likely would have made a good CEO if not for the splinter of true believer she could see in his eyes as he made his pitch. It was a manic quality that reminded her of photos she'd seen of people in the throes of euphoria, blissfully disconnected from reality. Marti knew at that moment that Rathbone believed in his work completely and would do anything to see it to fruition.

"Using proprietary technology, we will deploy a fleet of nanobots capable of tracing the neural architecture of the human brain at an unprecedented level of detail. These tiny robotic agents will navigate the neural pathways, scanning and capturing the brain's activity, synaptic strengths, and molecular configurations that constitute an individual's unique consciousness."

Victor paused, allowing the significance of his words to sink in before pressing on. "Once the neural mapping is complete, we will employ quantum computing algorithms to process and emulate the complex computational aspects of the human brain. These powerful quantum processors will serve as the foundation for the artificial substrate, providing the computational power necessary to sustain the transferred consciousness.

"With the digital replica of the individual's neural network residing within the artificial substrate, their consciousness will be seamlessly transferred, allowing for a continuation of their cognitive experiences and memories," Victor explained. "The artificial substrate will be designed to mimic the intricate dynamics of the human brain, enabling the transferred consciousness to interact with the digital environment and perceive a sense of continuity."

Marti looked around the room. Harrington looked shellshocked. The board members were in varying states of disbelief, shock, or acceptance. It was difficult to tell. Harrington cleared his throat and spoke first. "Victor, the idea of transferring consciousness is fascinating, but are we sure it's ethically and morally sound? It seems like you want to toy with the essence of life itself."

Victor nodded, understanding the concern. "I assure you we are not playing; we have assembled a team of experts who will be strictly adhering to ethical guidelines throughout the project."

"Who sets these guidelines? Have you already done experiments on people? How far along is this project?" Dr. Sharma said. "I'm shocked the board has not heard of this before now."

"We recognize the gravity of what we're attempting, and the well-being and dignity of the individuals involved will be of utmost importance," Victor replied, not exactly answering Sharma's question.

Marti took that as a yes, however. Maybe it was just experiments on Rathbone himself, but maybe not. The gleam in his eye told her he would push the envelope as far as he could. Before anyone could follow up on Sharma's question and Victor's response, Maria Rodriguez chimed in. "What about the metaphysical implications? Do you truly believe you can replicate a person's consciousness, including their thoughts, emotions, and subjective experiences in a machine?"

"Replicating subjective experiences is indeed a formidable task, and it may be impossible to fully re-create every nuance of a person's consciousness. However, that is not our goal. Not at the start. Our goal instead is to preserve the core aspects of an individual's identity and memories, providing them with a continuation of their cognitive experiences and a semblance of continuity."

"You're talking about immortality," Rodriguez said.

"Yes, in some ways."

Another board member, Marti recognized him as Tim Ryan, asked, "Victor, this project must represent a significant financial investment. Can we see those numbers? And how confident are you that it will yield practical results within a reasonable timeframe?"

Victor's expression turned resolute. "Project Lazarus is a high-risk, high-reward endeavor. While it's true that we can't predict all the challenges we may encounter, our team has made significant strides in neural mapping and quantum computing. We are confident that, with the resources and talent at our disposal, we can make meaningful progress in a relatively short period."

"Did Alex know about this?" Maria asked.

"Yes," Rathbone replied but unlike his other answers, he didn't elaborate further.

"And he was okay with creating an elite group of individuals who could afford this procedure, effectively granting them immortality? That's not the Alex I knew. How do we address the ethical implications of creating such a disparity in society?" Rodriguez kept pushing.

Rathbone acknowledged the gravity of the issue. "We understand the importance of making the benefits of this technology accessible to a broader demographic. As the project progresses, we will be exploring avenues for responsible distribution and ensuring that the benefits are not confined to a select few. This is not just about serving the elite. The project has the potential to revolutionize medical science and unlock the doors to a new era of human potential."

To Marti's ears that sounded freshly printed from a press release and distinctly divergent from reality. She could see Maria saw through the answer, too. "I'm not sure I want to unlock that door," she said. "Not yet and not without a lot more discussion of the potential impacts."

"And that is the key question," Marti interjected. "You are the board and you have the power to stop this project." She locked eyes with Victor, but he just smiled back. She wasn't sure if it was real or manufactured confidence. Maybe it didn't matter.

"Yes," he said, leaning forward in anticipation, "let's put the motion to a vote. Liz, perhaps we should go back on the record for this so there are no misunderstandings later. Should Project Lazarus continue in its current state?"

Marti held up a hand. "Sorry, Victor. Before a vote, I think we should clarify the board composition." This was the crux of their plan. For all of Rathbone's technical genius, Marti was counting on the fact that he hadn't read the incorporation documents for Calderone in any detail.

For the first time, Rathbone looked confused. "I don't think that's necessary. Everyone present constitutes a quorum of the current board and they are now vetted on the project details."

"True," Marti said. "Everyone present save me and Liz are voting members. I'm glad we all agree. As a reminder, the ex parte order," Marti indicated the documents still in front of Harrington, "that grants Cassidy temporary control of the Calderone estate which also grants her power as CEO and board president."

"Wait. What? No, that's not correct," Victor said, looking concerned, maybe sensing the balance of power in the room shifting.

"Charles?"

Harrington looked uncomfortable, but the truth was in black and white in the legal documents in front of him and his long tenure at the bar made those difficult to ignore. "I'm afraid that is correct, Victor."

"Good," Marti said. "Then I believe Cassidy has a few points of order before a vote is taken."

Marti stepped back. She could see a line of perspiration at Cassidy's hairline and a slight tremor in her fingers as she placed a hand flat on the conference room table, but when she spoke, her voice was clear and unwavering.

"First, I'd like to appoint two new board members to fill the two vacant seats."

"No, no, no. She can't just pick board members," Victor said. Marti watched his eyes flick to the doors and she wondered if he would call his goons in, but he seemed to realize it was too late to have Marti and Cassidy removed. The boulder was rolling downhill and he was squarely in its path.

"Charles?" Cassidy said.

"She's right," the lawyer responded. "Alex had that power and now as his ... daughter and CEO, she does too. At least temporarily."

"Angela?" Cassidy said, and the same door they had entered through opened again and Angela entered with Dr. Richard Lancaster and Dr. Benjamin Ackerley. One last favor from Scott and Frank Reynolds had gotten the trio inside and upstairs.

Marti enjoyed the gobsmacked look on Rathbone's face when his old business partner walked through the door. Revenge would be served very cold in this case. It was also her cue to exit. She would let Angela, far more well versed in boardroom meetings than she, handle the final details with Cassidy. With Cassidy's vote, plus Maria and the two new board members, the vote would go their way and Project Lazarus would be stopped in its tracks.

She glanced at Rathbone slumped in his chair as she went through the main door. She realized that while the man looked defeated, he didn't look done. Not completely. And that gave her pause as she stood in the vestibule and waited for the elevator. He looked like he'd lost the battle but still planned on fighting the war. Marti thought briefly about Hiroo Onoda, the Japanese soldier from World War II, who hid out in the jungles and continued waging a battle that was long over. It was a favorite story of her father's. He would trot it out on many different occasions. Hiroo Onoda became an oft-used shorthand expression for dedication and courage, but also for stubbornness and delusion. She pushed past the thought and stepped into the waiting elevator. Rathbone could keep fighting just like Onoda but it wouldn't make any difference. His fate was sealed both personally and professionally.

***

She caught Scott's eye at the desk as she exited. She scanned the rest of the lobby, but it appeared that things had returned to normal. She didn't spot any extra goons hanging around.

"You can tell Frank he can sleep easy again. I'm all done and we're square. I'll mail him back Marcia's key card and uniform."

Scott smiled. "I'll pass that along and, don't repeat this, but I have to tell you, I think the old man enjoyed being shin-deep in your shit these past few weeks. He had a little extra pep in his step."

"He always did have a thing for bad girls," Marti replied and rapped her fist on the desk before turning on her heel and heading for the door before she risked another of Scott's southern smiles. She was feeling happy and didn't want to be held responsible for what she might do.

Chapter Forty-Two

Marti stood on the street, her heart still racing from the adrenaline-fueled meeting. There were still details to work out and plenty of paperwork for everyone involved, but her part, the part that Angela and Cassidy had hired her to do, was over. She retrieved her phone from her pocket and dialed Gwen's number. The phone rang and, after a few seconds, Gwen's voice echoed through the line.

"Everything okay? Where are you?" Gwen's voice sounded tight and concerned. She wouldn't relax until Marti was back across the river.

"I'm good. Everything went as planned. Cassidy and Angela are still inside, but it's all a formality now. I'm done. I'm out front," Marti replied. "I need you to pick me up."

Gwen's voice sounded calmer, but still tense. "Walk one block north and one block east. I'm circling. I'll be there as soon as I can."

Marti nodded, even though Gwen couldn't see her. "Okay, I'll see you in a minute," she said before disconnecting. She took a deep breath, inhaling the crisp night air and the smell of cool concrete and exhaust fumes distinct to city life, and started walking.

The deserted streets of Midtown Manhattan stretched out before her, devoid of most signs of life with business hours long over. The center of Manhattan was always the quietest after sundown. Taxis and Ubers zipped by, their headlights illuminating the empty sidewalks.

The absence of food carts, tourists, and bustling activity created an eerie atmosphere.

As she stepped off the curb to cross Fifth Avenue, Marti noticed headlights approaching from the west, growing brighter with each passing second. She paused and tried to make out the car model but couldn't recall Gwen's rental. The car's engine revved louder. It was moving quickly, too quickly, bouncing over the manhole covers and potholes. Marti realized it wasn't going to stop. The driver either didn't see her or expect her to be in the crosswalk or ...

Her phone vibrated in her pocket, but she couldn't risk taking it out. Panic surged through her as her mind caught up to the imminent danger she was in. Marti's survival instincts kicked in and she broke into a sprint.

She cleared the crosswalk and ran down the short side street, eschewing the longer avenue, and continued up the sidewalk. The empty street offered no refuge except for a collection of plastic garbage cans, which would do little to impede the speeding car.

There was the screech of tires as the car made the turn, the sound of the engine grew louder behind her, and she knew she had to find some shelter or get off the street to survive. There was no time to reach for the gun at back. It would likely make no difference against the onrushing car. She ran on. Her lungs burned. Bright spots danced in her vision. She tasted blood in the back of her throat. She kept going. She sprinted harder, pushing herself until her legs went numb, begging her body to hold on until the end of the block. She stumbled, her legs finally too oxygen-deprived to keep her upright, but desperation drove her on a few more feet until she collapsed around the corner. It might only give her a few seconds reprieve but she'd made it. It felt like a victory.

She managed one gasping breath on her hands and knees before the headlights found her again. The car was coming like a shark. Dodging around the corner wouldn't save her. She needed to keep moving. She clawed at the bricks of the building in front of her, determined not to go out on her hands and knees, but she couldn't find a grip and collapsed back down.

She could hear the car approaching. She needed to stand up and keep going but she was spent. She thought of her gun again. She reached back for it but couldn't get it with her shaking hands. She started to crawl toward the glass doorway of a closed jewelry store when a second car, coming from the opposite direction, screeched to a halt right in front of her. Marti managed to raise her head. A figure emerged from the vehicle, their features obscured by the blinding headlights, but it was not Gwen.

She couldn't hear over the rushing of the blood in her ears and the shadowy figure had to say it again. "Get in!"

Without questioning it, Marti used her last bit of strength to scramble to her feet, throw open the passenger car door, and dive inside. The car's engine roared, and they sped away just as gunshots rang out, piercing the night air.

As the car raced through the empty streets, Marti remained slumped against the door, her body spent. But her mind raced ahead trying to untangle the last two minutes.

"You okay?" Miles asked.

"I thought it was over," Marti replied, her breath slowly returning to normal. "How did you find me?" she asked.

"I told you I've kept tabs on you. I knew the board meeting was tonight and I know Rathbone plays for keeps."

"I can't figure out if this was in retaliation for the board meeting or if it was always the plan."

"I don't think Rathbone has any intention of stopping or abiding by any of those decisions. I think the board meeting was a charade. He'll let it play out. Make it appear he's been outmaneuvered and then do what he wants. He has limited time and he's past civilities."

Marti rubbed at a raw spot where her fall had skinned up her elbow. "I think you're right. He's going full Hiroo Onoda."

"Who?"

***

The sedan's tires screeched around corners, as Miles drove south, maneuvering expertly through the city streets and keeping an eye on the mirrors.

"Anything?" Marti asked.

"No."

Marti glanced out the window, the illuminated cityscape blurring past in a whirl of lights and shadows. Five minutes later, Rothchild drove the car down a ramp into an underground parking garage below a glass high-rise somewhere in Battery Park City.

They took an elevator to a penthouse on an upper floor. When the door opened, she had an uninterrupted view that extended across the river to the distant horizon, the lights twinkling like stars against the darkening sky. If she craned her neck just the right way, she could almost see her apartment across the Hudson. But this was not her view. It was too clear. Too perfect. It was so striking and unique that it momentarily left her feeling disoriented, as if she had stepped into a different world altogether.

She turned away and sat in an exceptionally soft armchair. She finally felt herself relax, her back and neck loosening as she sank into the buttery leather. She looked around the apartment. Furnishing the living area were other plush and luxurious pieces that quietly exuded comfort and sophistication. The interior of the penthouse was an elegant fusion of high-end design and modern aesthetics. Polished marble floors with intricate patterns sprawled across the open-plan living area, guiding the eye toward the focal point of the space—a magnificent painted gray wall where a massive piece of swirling, colorful modern art was showcased, reminiscent of the iconic style of Jackson Pollock. She realized with a start that it probably was a Jackson Pollock.

Her phone vibrated in her pocket. She pulled it out and saw she'd missed countless calls. She hit redial and Gwen answered, relief in her voice. "Where are you? Who was that in the car?"

"You saw all of that?"

"Yes, I was behind the car trying to take you out, but too far back. I tried calling. But it was over before I got close enough to help."

She glanced across the room where Miles sat watching her. "It was a friend, of sorts."

"Nice timing."

"Indeed. I didn't know he was out there," she said, keeping her eyes on him. He didn't look away. "We have some mutual interests in this and some shared history."

"You're still with him," Gwen asked picking up on Marti's circumspect conversation.

"That's right."

"But you're okay?"

"Yes. I'm fine."

"Okay. I followed whoever was following you, but I'm sure you probably already guessed the answer."

"Herschel?"

"Got it in one."

"But probably working for Rathbone."

"Yes, I think he's still calling the shots. Or at least paying the bills. Herschel's loyalties strike me as being defined by the dollar."

"I thought we'd reached the end of this."

"Me, too."

"What's the plan now?"

Marti had been thinking the same thing. "I'll tell you when you get here."

She asked Miles for the address and then texted it to Gwen. "We're going to have some company." He just nodded and then stood and disappeared into another part of the apartment. While she waited, she called Angela and was relieved when the woman answered. Marti could hear various voices in the background.

"Still at it?" Marti asked.

"Yes, at least another hour but no surprises so far, just working through the details."

"Has Rathbone been there the whole time?"

"We took a break for 10 minutes, but otherwise he's been here and largely silent."

"Okay." Marti didn't want to spook either Angela or Cassidy, but she needed to make sure they were safe. Rathbone might not be so bold as to murder or kidnap the two women in the office, but she didn't want to take any chances. "I'm going to send a friendly up to make sure everything stays nice and quiet right up until the end. His name is Scott."

Chapter Forty-Three

They spread out across the open living room. Gwen and Marti were seated on a loveseat. Cassidy and Angela were in matching chairs to the left. Miles stood and leaned against the wall. His expression was neutral. If he felt uncomfortable with the meeting in his apartment, he didn't show it. Marti glanced around and realized this might not even be his place. There was nothing to distinguish it as his. No photos or mementos or personal items strewn around. It was clean and sterile and largely inscrutable. Much like the man himself.

As Angela and Cassidy were the last to arrive, Marti filled them in quickly on what had happened after she'd left the Calderone building.

"He tried to kill you? Why?" Cassidy said. She looked wrung out whether it was from the meeting or fighting for her sobriety, Marti didn't know, but she had dark circles under her eyes that no makeup could cover. She looked like she could sleep for a week. Marti was sure she didn't look much better herself.

Marti gave a half shrug. "I don't know. Take your pick. Maybe we scared him. Maybe I pushed him too far at the meeting. He's been operating at a level where he's rarely, if ever, told no. Maybe it finally made him see his mortality. Maybe it was always the plan. He needed a target and I was convenient."

"Needed?"

"In my experience when a strong emotion like anger, resentment, or even love, hits a person, they tend to react in one of two ways. It can make them turn inward and self-destruct or it can make them lash out."

Cassidy took that in and sat back in the chair.

"Are you still in danger?" Angela asked.

"I think you all are," Gwen responded.

"I agree," Marti said.

"What can we do?" Angela said.

Marti turned to Miles. "Can you get a message to the Bellini brothers?"

"Yes."

"Good. Use my name and set up a meeting with them and Rathbone for tomorrow afternoon."

He gave her a cold smile. "Where?"

She turned to Gwen. "Are you still able to get reservations at The Red Lantern?"

"It's been a while but, I think so, yeah. Ming would take my call."

"Okay, tomorrow at 3 p.m. at The Red Lantern."

"Where's that?" Cassidy asked.

"They'll know," Marti said and glanced at Miles. He nodded.

"But I still want to know. Where is it? We're going to be there, too." She looked at Angela who nodded. Marti thought she might have been able to convince one of them alone to stay away, but together they would buttress each other.

"I don't think that's necessary," Marti responded. "These are bad people, Cassidy. We'll be sitting down with the devil. More than one."

Cassidy sat forward again. "We have to be at that meeting."

Almost any other time, Marti might threaten to drop the case and walk away, but that wasn't an option here. She was in as deep as her client and in just as much danger.

Angela looked at Marti as if reading her mind. "I don't want her there either, but she's tougher than she looks. I think she needs to be there."

These were her clients but it still felt wrong. After the satisfaction she felt walking out of the boardroom earlier, now this whole case might go sideways right at the end, but, Marti thought, if you're not up for the challenge, don't get in the ring.

"Gwen?"

"Yeah?"

"Why don't you take these two back to your place and then bring them with you to The Red Lantern tomorrow."

Gwen gave a half nod.

"Thank you," Cassidy said.

Marti wanted to tell her to keep her thanks or at least wait and see how much gratitude she felt after the meeting.

***

Miles led her down a hallway to a guest bedroom. They had all decided that returning to her apartment before the meeting was an unnecessary risk. Miles insisted she stay at the penthouse. She agreed but held up a hand. Miles paused and waited. She pulled out her phone and called Mrs. Potts, her next-door neighbor, who had a key to Marti's apartment and asked her to bring Rita Mae over for the night. Marti was pretty sure Rita Mae liked Mrs. Potts more than her anyway. She closed the phone. Miles smile said he didn't completely understand caring for another living thing, but then he put his mask back on and waved an arm and she stepped inside. The room was softly lit with a large window that would allow plenty of natural light in during the day. Soft, sheer curtains hung in front of the window, affording privacy and a touch of elegance to the room.

A queen-sized bed with a white duvet and an array of pillows occupied the center of the room. The bed frame and headboard were dark wood. The walls were painted in more soothing and neutral tones. On one side of the bed, there was a matching dark nightstand with a small lamp that emitted a soft, warm glow. The nightstand held a vase of fresh flowers beside the light.

"Bathroom is through there," Miles said, indicating an adjoining door to the left. "There are robes and towels on the shelf in the bathroom. And toiletries in the drawers by the sink. Help yourself." And then he was gone. Marti closed the door and stared at the lock for a long time, trust was a dangerous emotion in Marti's line of work. Eventually, she turned and went into the bathroom.

The bathroom was big and elegant with a glassed-in double-head shower and whirlpool tub, but right now she'd give anything for her old tub back in her apartment. She did have to admit, however, that it did feel good to get out of the scratchy fabric of the Reynolds Security uniform. She placed her phone and gun on the vanity and then examined her elbow which now sported a ragged hole to match the pavement rash on her arm. Somehow it was her only souvenir from the frantic late-night encounter. Her only physical one. She thought she might still dream of a racing engine and creeping headlights. She hung the uniform and the rest of her clothes on a towel rack and then took a long hot shower. She used a toothbrush from the drawer and then wrapped herself in a long terrycloth robe and climbed into bed.

She was asleep almost instantly. If she dreamed of the car barreling down on her, she didn't remember it. She was thankful for that as she woke up to dappled sunlight through the curtains. She lay in bed for a moment. The apartment was hushed in silence, total silence, which she realized felt weird when she was in the city. But, she thought, she wasn't actually in the city right now. She was floating high above it.

She might not survive the events of the day, but lazing in bed wasn't an option either. She got up and walked down the hallway to the living room. Quiet and empty. She walked into the next room and found a modern kitchen, more marble and stainless steel. A tray of pastries and fresh fruit along with carafes of juice and coffee sat on the counter. She poured herself a cup of coffee and noticed the note propped up against the fruit bowl.

Everything is set. Looking forward to lunch. See you at three—M

Devils and angels and everyone in-between were ready to play their parts.

***

Marti returned to her apartment. With the meeting agreed upon and set, she saw little motivation for Herschel or anyone else to try to get the drop on her now. Why waste the time? They knew exactly where she'd be this afternoon. She didn't completely throw caution to the wind. She had Manuel, her Uber driver, do a few laps around the neighborhood before she agreed to get out. She told him she was watching out for an abusive ex and would give him an extra tip. He just nodded and followed her directions, and Marti was left to wonder which part motivated him more. Helping her or the promised tip. Probably the money, but she was tired and feeling cynical.

Eventually, she made it inside; no one accosted her on the sidewalk, and she was met with the sound of Pedro's hammering somewhere a floor or two above. She climbed the stairs to her apartment and was greeted inside the door by a flying, angry furball attacking her ankles.

"Okay, lady. Hold on."

She dropped her keys and phone on the table in the hall and managed not to trip over Rita Mae on the way to the kitchen. She filled the cat's two bowls, adding a little extra to make up for the lack of dinner the night before. She wasn't sure if Rita Mae completely forgave her, but she didn't turn her nose up at the food, either. She left the cat to it and went to the bedroom to change into clean clothes.

When she returned to the kitchen, Rita Mae was in her spot on the back of the sofa and Marti's phone was ringing. Marti picked it up expecting Gwen or Angela, but it was her sister, Emily.

They'd been close as kids but once their mom passed, when they were both in their early 20s, the connective tissue was gone and they drifted apart. Marti was more like their father. Emily was the opposite. She was a stay-at-home mom and real estate agent in Ridgewood, which was only about 30 miles from Jersey City but always took more than an hour to get to. They saw each other only a few times a year.

"Hi, Em, what's up?"

"Pendergast just called again. Dad had another incident."

If there was one person Marti liked less than Victor Rathbone, even after he tried to have her killed, it was Bob Pendergast, the head administrator at Maplegate Senior Care Center. On one level, Marti knew he was just doing his job but the way he went about it, cold and officious, made her want to throttle the man and push back on anything he said.

"What happened?"

"Dad didn't come out for movie night and Eleanor went looking for him. He was in his room but he didn't recognize her and became violent."

"Violent?"

"He pushed her."

"That doesn't sound too violent." Marti knew she was avoiding the real subject.

"Marti, Eleanor is almost 83 years old. She fell and miraculously only had bruises and no broken bones. His mood swings and confusion are getting worse. They want to move him to the memory unit."

"No," Marti said. She'd seen that floor when they toured the facility and never wanted to see it again. She'd lost her mother to breast cancer at 48, younger than she was now, and she sometimes worried about that fact, but losing her mind terrified her far more.

"We might not have a choice. The only reason they aren't doing it already is that Elle told the nurses she tripped, but she pulled me aside and told me the real story."

"And you believe her?"

"C'mon, Marti. She's covering for him because she cares for him and wants her friend around. She was scared."

Marti blew out a breath. She felt her shoulders bunch up. "And what did Pendergast want?"

"He didn't know I'd stopped by and talked to Elle. He was just following his beloved protocols." Emily herself loved her rules and regulations, but even Bob had managed to get under her skin. "But it's clear that a decision is coming. I just wanted to let you know." There was a pause. Marti thought about the upcoming meeting and her chances of living to see another morning. Why had her sister called now? Was it a bit of kismet? Marti felt a sudden torrent of words bubbling up in her throat. Words that had been stuck for years. But she couldn't get them out in time.

"You should go see him," Emily said before she hung up.

Chapter Forty-Four

"Hello, Ms. Ming," Marti said to the owner and host of The Red Lantern.

"A pleasure to see you again, Ms. Wells," she replied with a thin smile. There was no pretense of warmth. Marti had been in The Red Lantern a few times in her career. None had been what Li Ming would consider legitimate means. Marti also knew Ming did not approve of the way this meeting had come about. She was a dangerous woman in her own right, but she was also pragmatic and chose the path of least resistance in consenting to the request.

"I didn't know The Red Lantern could be rented out for private events." Marti nodded back toward the sign that hung in the door's window.

"We make exceptions based on certain clientele."

Marti knew it wasn't her status that afforded them this privilege. She thought it more likely that the Bellini brothers, or Miles, or perhaps the unexpected combination of the pair of them and Gwen on the same reservation prompted Ming's decision.

The Red Lantern was a completely legitimate and very good restaurant, but over the years had also cultivated a reputation as a safe and neutral spot for certain criminal elements to discuss business and hash out deals without the fear of an intermezzo course that featured guns.

"Your party is right this way," Ming continued and led Marti to a long table set for nine.

Angela and Cassidy were already seated and Marti sat on their side of the table next to Cassidy. The young woman still looked hollowed out, like a tank slowly refilling, but she looked better than when they'd parted the previous night.

"Do you have a plan for this meeting?" Cassidy asked as Marti settled into her chair.

The rest of the dining room was empty and, like the city's silence she woke up to in Miles's guest room that morning, it was eerie.

"Yes. Do you? Is that why you wanted to be here?"

"I plan to tell the truth," Cassidy replied.

"And shame the devil."

Marti admired the woman's principles, but she wondered if she was too naive. How much power would the truth have against Rathbone's intentions or the Bellinis' corruption?

"What?"

Before Marti could explain the expression, Ming appeared with four more guests. Victor Rathbone, Robert Herschel with his buzz cut and chest tattoo peeking out of his collar, and, finally, the Bellini brothers. Both brothers were showing the years and toil it took to stay at the top of tristate organized crime but each still cut a formidable figure.

Sal, the elder of the brothers, stood at around six-feet tall, with a stocky build and wide shoulders that lent a commanding presence. His once jet-black hair was now gray and he kept it slicked back, revealing a prominent widow's peak. He wore a tailored black suit and dark red tie.

Vinnie was slightly shorter than his older brother but no less imposing. He maintained a muscular build despite his age. His once sharp features had softened with time, and he sported a well-groomed salt-and-pepper beard that added an unexpected air of sophistication to his appearance. He was dressed in a more casual manner than his brother, opting for a Polo shirt and trousers, topped off with a crucifix on a gold chain around his neck.

Herschel pulled a chair out for Sal before sitting himself. Sal took a moment with his napkin and then looked across the table with bright-blue eyes. "Ms. Wells, I've been hearing your name a lot lately." There wasn't a question there and Marti didn't respond. "You and your friend," he nodded at Angela, "can get up and walk out and you'll be fine. You have my word."

"Thank you for the offer, but we're inclined to stay."

Marti saw the surprise flash across his face. She didn't think he was used to being turned down. He seemed honestly surprised.

"There's no reason for you to be here," Rathbone said. "This is a Calderone matter." He stared at Cassidy. "A family affair."

"I'm the one who called this meeting and it's about more than Cassidy. It's about you, your plans, and your alliance with these men," Marti said.

"You are nothing," Rathbone replied. His face began to color, and Marti had a glimpse of what it might be like to work for this man and have to tell him no. He was a spoiled child. And Marti knew that the type of technology he was seeking should never be in the hands of someone like that. "You can't stop me. You can't stop us. You are a bug that's going to get squashed on the windshield of progress. I don't know if it's pride or stupidity but just get up and go for God's sake. This is the last chance I'll give you."

No one moved and Rathbone appeared to be working himself up to say more before Sal cut in. "Shall we get down to business then?"

"In a moment, there are still two empty seats."

"Who ..."

Ming led Miles and Gwen to the table. Marti had to admit that Miles did have a flair for the dramatic. His timing could not have been better. And neither could she have scripted the reaction of Sal, Vinnie, and Herschel. Marti wasn't sure how much they all knew about the two of them, but she was sure that if she'd heard rumors of the pair's exploits over the years, then the three men across from her had probably heard far more.

This was an unusual situation for Marti. Typically, her work was done in the shadows. Most of the time her targets never knew she was there. On the rare occasions where that wasn't the case, she usually felt confident enough that she could hold her own, either through brains or brawn. That was not the case today. She was far down the pecking order in the most dangerous category with those sitting around the table.

"I believe some of you at the table might know Mr. Rothchild and Ms. Torres."

Gwen took the empty seat next to Marti and Miles took the remaining chair at the foot of the table.

"Who?" Rathbone said.

Sal Bellini leaned over and said something to Rathbone.

"So what?" The elder Bellini frowned but Rathbone continued. "Sal here tells me you two are dangerous and have some level of power in the city. Let me tell you, none of you know what true power is. This city is just a speck on the map. I can have it wiped out. I have friends with real power and they all owe me favors. I call and they pick up the phone. I ask and you no longer exist."

Marti watched almost in fascination as Rathbone's fervor built and increasing amounts of spittle flew from his mouth and sprayed the surrounding area, including the Bellini brothers. Marti began to fear, not for herself, but for Rathbone, whose face began to resemble the color of an aged Cabernet. If his blood pressure didn't do him in, Marti thought someone sitting at the table might step in and snap his neck to stop the sneering diatribe he'd unleashed.

Marti tried to think of some way to inject and stop him when Cassidy stood and shouted, "Shut up!"

It had the desired effect as Victor stopped midsentence and his mouth hung open.

"We all know about your money, power, and influence, and no one, at least on this side of the table, cares about any of it. I may never have met my father, but I share his blood and I share his name and I care about his legacy and I don't believe he would support anything that you are doing. The secrets and lies have to stop."

Rathbone was still breathing hard and Marti could see his fists grip the white tablecloth in front of him. There was a sheen of sweat across his brow.

"You might know all about advanced technology that I'll never understand," Cassidy continued, "but I'm not a Luddite. I was an only child. I grew up tethered to a screen. I know very well how to use them and I know the power of them. I know you used your influence to squash our first attempt to get this story in the newspaper. That was our fault. That was a timid and scared approach. It was a slow approach to appear legitimate through an old and respected media outlet. I didn't make the same mistake this time."

"What are you talking about?"

"Before I came to this meeting, I released my DNA results and relationship to Alex Calderone on various social media platforms.

Plus, all the documents and research on Project Lazarus. It's no longer your little secret. It no longer belongs to you."

"No."

"Yes." She picked up her phone. "You should be trending now."

Checkmate. It hadn't happened in the boardroom, but it did now. Marti watched Victor Rathbone's spirit break. His face lost all his color as he backed away from the table and fled the room.

The Bellinis had more dignity. If the specter of Miles and Gwen was not enough to deter the brothers, Marti thought that Cassidy's actions would soon make Victor Rathbone radioactive. She doubted the brothers would be stepping in to do the man any favors. They stood up, dropping their napkins on the table, and nodded once before following Rathbone out the door.

Herschel almost got it right. He stood, smiling, before backing away, but as he turned to leave he made a gun with his hand and pointed it in our direction. That was a mistake.

Chapter Forty-Five

C assidy was right. The released documents quickly went viral and were scooped up by major and minor media outlets around the globe. Beyond putting a stop to Rathbone's goal, her posts also caused a groundswell of support for more regimented oversight and safeguards on the use and development of artificial intelligence. It remained to be seen if that support translated into actual action, but that went far beyond Marti's expertise. She was happy that Cassidy was safe and Rathbone's plans were now exposed.

By the time the ex parte orders expired and a full hearing was held, the court-ordered independent DNA results had been completed and showed without a doubt that Cassidy was Alex Calderone's daughter and rightful heir. Rathbone's last-ditch efforts to appeal were quickly squashed.

After initial attempts to justify Project Lazarus in the wake of the documents release were met more with hostility and skepticism than acceptance, Rathbone resigned and disappeared from the public eye. Occasionally, over the next year, Marti would search for his name online but without any results. She hoped he found some peace in his remaining days. She doubted he would be able to get anywhere close to his ambitions without the money and influence of Calderone backing him. Angela, now CEO of Calderone, had assured her that she kept feelers out and hadn't heard a thing. Most days, this was enough for Marti, but some days she wondered …

She didn't know it at the time, but after he stood up and left The Red Lantern, Marti wouldn't see Miles again for almost three years. And when her favorite psychopath did reenter her life, he brought more trouble and a river of blood. Some of it her own.

Chapter Forty-Six

M arti sat at her cluttered desk, engrossed in the mundane tasks of running her private investigation business. She'd left the door open and the rhythmic hum of the dryers filled the room as she shuffled through paperwork and filed away case files. Pedro's knock on the doorframe broke her concentration.

"Hey, Marti," Pedro greeted with a warm smile, handing her the day's mail. "Here you go."

"Thanks, Pedro," Marti replied, returning the smile. She took the stack of envelopes, her eyes scanning them. Most were the usual assortment of bills, advertisements, and junk mail. But one caught her attention—a cream-colored envelope with her name written in swirling cursive script. It stood out among the rest, practically emanating an aura of mystery.

Setting the other mail aside, Marti carefully examined the envelope. There was no stamp or return address, just her name, further adding to its enigmatic nature. She did like small mysteries. With a sense of curiosity tinged with caution, she reached for a slim letter opener and slid it along the top.

Inside was a matching cream-colored card bearing the words: My condolences, elegantly printed on the front. She opened the card, revealing an empty interior save for a folded piece of newspaper tucked inside.

Marti's pulse quickened as she unfolded the newspaper clipping, her eyes scanning the words that detailed a grisly discovery of a body found near the Quabbin Reservoir in Massachusetts. The body was missing its head, arms, and feet. A section of skin missing near the neck added an unsettling twist, leaving authorities puzzled and speculating about possible gang involvement or cannibalism. Marti folded the newspaper clipping and placed it back in the envelope.

As Pedro's footsteps faded down the hallway, Marti remained in her office. She looked at the blank whiteboard. She wiped off the notes last week. The Calderone case might have concluded, but the haunting echoes lingered.

It wasn't the kind of justice she wanted for her old partner and the truth would likely never be told, but it was a certain kind of justice and maybe it would bring Marti a certain kind of peace.

About the Author

Mike Donohue is the author of the Max Strong and Marti Wells thriller series. He lives with his wife, two daughters, and Dashiell Hammett outside Boston. Dash is the family dog.

Mike doesn't think reading during meals is particularly rude. Quite the opposite.

You can find him online at mikedonohebooks.com.

9 781736 829783